PRAISE FOR
THE BERLIN EXCHANGE

"*The Berlin Exchange*, by the veteran spy-story author Joseph Kanon, expertly describes what happens when a disillusioned former agent tries to come in from the cold. . . . Kanon vividly evokes the suspicion, hypocrisy, and relentless grayness of life in the East. . . . The plot shifts into high gear and turns into a complex, high-stakes operation in which Martin, thrillingly, is pulling all the strings. He's one step ahead of his enemies, and three steps ahead of us."

—Sarah Lyall, *The New York Times Book Review*

"In Joseph Kanon's skillful telling, Keller's elaborate scheme for escaping with his family to the West is heart-poundingly suspenseful."

—*The Washington Post*

"From the opening paragraph of *The Berlin Exchange*, with its matter-of-fact immediacy, you feel you're in safe hands. . . . It's superbly accomplished, from the Swiss watch plot and crisp dialogue to an atmosphere so well realized it feels as if it is written in black-and-white film. . . . Bold disguises, car chases, and handbrake-turn twists wind inexorably to a climax at the border that shows that Kanon can do not just the talk, but also the tensest of spotlit walks. Expect this to exchange the page for the screen, but before then let yourself enjoy a modern master at work."

—*The Times* (UK)

"Joseph Kanon is, for my money, the best spy writer working today, an author of rare gifts as a stylist, plotter, and creator of characters. He is also the greatest writer ever of historical espionage fiction. . . . He is absolutely worth his place in the pantheon of the greats."

—Tim Shipman, *Spybrary*

"Thoroughly absorbing, a thoughtful and subtle evocation of a place and era, with occasional invigorating bursts of violence . . . When [Kanon's] at his best, you get the rare sense of a writer whose style, plot, and characters have been perfectly aligned to convey his vision of the world."

—*The Sunday Telegraph* (UK)

"A novel that gives paranoia a new name, Kanon's latest in a brilliant collection—including *Leaving Berlin* (2014) and *Istanbul Passage* (2012)—may be his most tightly rendered. The suspense builds quietly, almost stealthily, before tightening its grip. Another super-sophisticated spy thriller from a ranking master."

—*Kirkus Reviews* (starred review)

"Kanon balances a convincing portrayal of spycraft with fleshed-out characters, while vividly depicting the impact of secret lives on the loved ones of those engaged in espionage."

—*Publishers Weekly*

"A master stylist of concise yet eloquent writing, Kanon re-creates the corrupt atmosphere of East Berlin in 1963, to riveting effect. . . . Kanon's books are a gold mine for lovers of espionage. Here he tackles the morality of the humanitarian exchange of political prisoners, a program that filled East Germany's coffers. . . . Kanon baits the hook with an early murder and adds seduction and betrayal to bring about the grim conclusion. Fans of Alan Furst and John le Carré will include Kanon as the third member of a Cold War troika."

—*Library Journal*

THE
BERLIN
EXCHANGE

A NOVEL

JOSEPH KANON

SCRIBNER

NEW YORK   LONDON   TORONTO   SYDNEY   NEW DELHI

Scribner
An Imprint of Simon & Schuster, Inc.
1230 Avenue of the Americas
New York, NY 10020

First Scribner trade paperback edition March 2023

SCRIBNER and design are registered trademarks of The Gale Group, Inc.,
used under license by Simon & Schuster, Inc., the publisher of this work.

For information about special discounts for bulk purchases,
please contact Simon & Schuster Special Sales at 1-866-506-1949
or business@simonandschuster.com.

The Simon & Schuster Speakers Bureau can bring authors to your live event.
For more information or to book an event, contact the Simon & Schuster Speakers Bureau
at 1-866-248-3049 or visit our website at www.simonspeakers.com.

Manufactured in the United States of America

1   3   5   7   9   10   8   6   4   2

Library of Congress Cataloging-in-Publication Data

Names: Kanon, Joseph, author.
Title: The Berlin exchange : a novel / Joseph Kanon.
Description: First Scribner hardcover edition. | New York : Scribner, 2022.
Identifiers: LCCN 2021020387 (print) | LCCN 2021020388 (ebook) |
ISBN 9781982158651 (hardcover) | ISBN 9781982158675 (ebook)
Subjects: GSAFD: Spy stories. | Suspense fiction.
Classification: LCC PS3561.A476 B47 2022 (print) | LCC PS3561.A476 (ebook) |
DDC 813/.54—dc23
LC record available at https://lccn.loc.gov/2021020387
LC ebook record available at https://lccn.loc.gov/2021020388

ISBN 978-1-9821-5865-1
ISBN 978-1-9821-5866-8 (pbk)
ISBN 978-1-9821-5867-5 (ebook)

For Penny and Dick Alford

GREATER BERLIN 1963

SOVIET ZONE

FRENCH SECTOR

BERLIN WALL

Area of detail

BRITISH SECTOR

SOVIET SECTOR

AMERICAN SECTOR

0 Miles 5 10

0 Kilometers 10

MOABIT

SOVIET ZONE

Spree

CHARLOTTENBURG

TIERGA

Landwehr Canal

Lützowplatz

KURFÜRSTENDAMM

WILMERSDORF

SCHÖNEBERG

BERLIN 1963

KUFSTEINER STRASSE

RIAS

FRIEDENAU

to Potsdam
approx. 16 mi./26 km.

to Oranienburg,
approx. 22 mi./35 km.

PRENZLAUER BERG

BERLIN WALL

RYKESTRASSE

DANZIGERSTRASSE

WEDDING

VOLKSPARK
FRIEDRICHSHAIN

STRASSE

Charité Complex

LUISENSTRASSE

SCHIFFBAUERDAMM

Berliner Ensemble

Alexanderplatz

Interhotel Berolina

KARL-MARX-ALLEE

MITTE

FRIEDRICHSTRASSE

Reichstag

UNTER DEN LINDEN

enburg Gate

Soviet
Embassy

Hotel Adlon

Gendarmenmarkt

Weberwiese

FRIEDRICHSHAIN

BERLIN WALL

Checkpoint
Charlie

Spree River

KREUZBERG

Landwehr Canal

0 Miles   1

0 Kilometers   1

to Köpenick and Adlershof
approx. 7 mi./11 km.

Tempelhof
Airport

TEMPELHOF

© 2021 Jeffrey L. Ward

CHAPTER 1

Berlin, 1963

The exchange, it was decided, would take place at the Invalidenstrasse checkpoint. The press kept an eye on Glienicke Bridge now, hoping for another Powers-Abel swap, and the international crossing at Checkpoint Charlie would be crowded, cars streaming out of the American sector on day visas. Invalidenstrasse had the virtue of being discreet, out of the way, designated for the few West Germans heading east. And it was in the British sector. This was officially a British exchange, Martin for an MI6 operative the East Germans had held for years and two English students caught helping friends over the wall. Small fry. For someone who'd made headlines. Well, years ago. How many of the young guards up ahead would even know who he was? All they'd see would be the prisoner skin, the unmistakable pallor of someone who'd been inside. There was a different light in prison, even in the exercise yard, the sun itself filtered, behind bars.

"We get out here," McGregor said, his escort since Heathrow, guiding him through customs at Tegel and across the British sector, staying close, as if he were afraid Martin would pick his moment and bolt. Where?

"We walk?"

"Just to the other side of the bridge," McGregor said, nodding to the checkpoint barrier up ahead. They had stopped on the western side of one of those canals that trickled out of the Spree. "The car needs to turn around here."

Martin got out, feeling the cold through his coat. There it was, the wall he'd seen in a thousand pictures, more brutal somehow in real life, a gray slab running along the water, broken here by a gap the width of a car. Some men were getting out of a black sedan on the other side.

"Right on time," McGregor said, checking his watch. "Germans."

A few minutes and he'd be free. Which wasn't how Digby, the junior warden who'd handled his release, had seen it. "You ask me, it's changing one prison for another. Different walls, that's all." But how could he know, someone who went home at night? "They're trying to get out over there, not in. You'll be getting parole soon. You'd have a choice. And who'd choose–?"

"I have a son there. A wife."

Digby looked at him, surprised. "A wife. Who never visits. Not as long as I've been here."

"Ex-wife."

Digby took this in, then side-stepped. "Now, Moscow, that would be different. I mean, that's who you did it for. The spying. A hero's welcome there, wouldn't it be?"

Martin smiled a little. "Except they haven't asked for me. The East Germans have."

"And that's the wife asking, is that it?"

Martin ignored this. "I didn't do it for the Russians."

"No. Who, then?"

"I thought I was doing it for everybody."

Digby looked away, uncomfortable. "But that's not the way it worked out."

"No."

Digby handed over his personal papers, the American passport on top. "I still say, hold on to this. Ticket home. You never know."

Home. Where they'd executed the Rosenbergs. Getting caught in Britain had saved his life. Under British law, only high treason, working for the enemy in wartime, was a capital crime. They gave him the maximum sentence, fourteen years, but he was alive.

"They'll miss you at the library. You've done a nice job there."

"It passes the time."

"Well, that's what it's all about, isn't it?" Digby turned to go, then hesitated. "I wish you luck. I've enjoyed our chats."

Martin looked up, not expecting this. What had they talked about?

"You keep your cards close to your vest, though. A wife. First I've heard of it."

"Before your time."

"Still. You don't give up much."

"Less for you to pass along." To whom, Martin wondered. MI5? The head warden? Was anyone still interested?

"You think that?" Digby said, pretending to be offended. "Not very nice. But I suppose you have to think like that. In your line of work."

"My line of work."

"On second thought, maybe you'll fit right in. With the Krauts. They say everybody's got an ear out over there."

The men on the other side had now formed a line, like a team taking positions, their clothes so similar they might have been uniforms: gray baggy raincoats, mufflers, rimless German glasses. Except the last one, smart in a belted camel-hair topcoat and thick black-framed glasses, the fashion look a surreal touch in the morning gloom. But what wasn't surreal in Berlin? Even on the drive in from Tegel he had been disoriented, once familiar streets now unrecognizable. There were still pockets of bomb damage, after all these years. Stretches of wasteland next to new apartment buildings. An empty space where Lehrter Station had been, the whole ornate pile gone, vanished.

At least the Charité hospital complex was still there, across the canal, its nineteenth-century red brick evidently strong enough to survive the wolf's blast, like the clever little pig's house. Or just lucky, the bombs falling somewhere else. Hospital wards and classrooms shoehorned into Wilhelmine mansions, Luisenstrasse with its medical supply shops and textbook sellers, the streets running off it lined with old apartment buildings where students rented spare rooms or pooled their money to share a place of their own. And gave parties. How he had met Sabine. A casual invitation from Georg, a break from Göttingen, carrying his overnight bag from Friedrichstrasse Station, the rush of hot smoky air and music when he opened Georg's door, music the Nazis disapproved of, just playing it an act of rebellion. A beer thrust into his hand before he could even put his bag down. And then, a sudden opening through the crowd, her eyes looking up at the same time. She'd been sitting on a couch, legs curled beneath her, an ashtray in her lap, a cigarette in one hand, the other at her elbow, as if she were holding herself down, about to float away with the smoke. She stared at him, a snapshot second, head half-turned, like someone who'd been tapped on the shoulder. Yes? Then Georg came over to greet him and he lost sight of her again behind the crowd. That had been the beginning. A party at the Charité. Just across the bridge.

"Now what?"

"They start. Then we start. *High Noon*."

4

"Without the guns."

"Now," McGregor said, beginning to walk. "Not too fast. We want to be there at the same time. When you get to the barrier, they'll raise it and you keep going. The others will pass you coming out. So nobody's first. Nobody pulls anything."

"That ever happen?" A chess piece yanked off the board.

"No, they're just like that. By the book."

Over the water now, the wall ahead. Behind it a heavy turn-of-the-century building big enough to have been a government ministry, its façade unscarred by bombs. Massive doors and pediments, built to last. The confident years.

The man in the camel-hair coat stopped, as McGregor had, the three in raincoats coming on by themselves. Three for one. The road barrier was raised and Martin walked through the checkpoint, the others passing on his left, nobody hurrying, wary, as if they were expecting something to go wrong at the last minute. And then they were in the West and Martin was in East Berlin, free.

He stopped for a minute, breathing in the damp air. He was through. Nobody was going to pull him back, lock him up again. He'd paid and now it was over.

A smile from the man in camel hair, hand outstretched.

"So. Welcome to the better Germany. As we like to say. I'm Kurt Thiele. You had an easy trip?"

"Sabine's husband."

"Yes," he said, still smiling. "She's anxious to see you. After so many years. And of course Peter."

"You arranged this," Martin said, waving his hand to take in the whole border crossing.

"It's what I do," he said easily. "These exchanges with the West. It's a kind of specialty. I used to work with Vogel, the lawyer. You've heard of him?"

"No, sorry."

"He arranged the Abel swap. And many others. Now too many. So there's business for me," he said, breezy, a car salesman. But she'd married him. Made him Peter's father. Did Peter call him that?

"Then I have you to thank."

"No, no. Sabine. The British would say no and she would say, ask again. Offer them more. I think she feels—you know, you're so many years in prison. Only you." So he knew. But of course he would. "But the British still said no. I think because the Americans didn't like it."

"And then you changed their minds."

"Well, the Americans. It's a long time and maybe they don't care so much anymore. And I made the point that your parole would come soon. After that, they don't have you to trade, so why not make a deal now? Get something for you."

"Like those dangerous characters," Martin said, cocking his head back toward the raincoats.

"Yes, Boothby. Just in time for his pension. The students." He waved his hand in dismissal. "So also some political prisoners for the West Germans. They'll be exchanged tonight at Herleshausen. And the West Germans will be very grateful to their British friends. So everyone gets something." The salesman smile again. What was he talking about? Political prisoners. Martin just a piece of contraband. But what did it matter? He was here.

"Sabine didn't come?"

"No. This business, it's better if it's done quietly. But you will come tonight. For dinner." He hesitated. "You know, I maybe should be a little bit jealous. The first husband."

"A long time ago."

"Still. The first love," he said.

Martin looked over to the Charité complex, then back at him. "A long time," he said again. "I'm grateful for everything you've done."

A faint nod. "Peter. He's always known you were his father. We made sure of that. So he's curious. He thinks you're a socialist hero."

"Hardly."

"The man who gave us the bomb. That's what they used to say in *Neues Deutschland*. You know you'll have to give them an interview. It's not so usual these days, coming east."

"Why all the secrecy, then? If it's going to be news."

"No secrecy," Kurt said. "It's better people don't know how these things are arranged. The details. That's all. It's enough to know you are here. Well, there's the car. I'll drop you at the hotel."

"The hotel?" Not with Sabine and Peter, his family. But they were Kurt's family now.

"The Berolina. Only the best for a distinguished guest," Kurt said, a wink in his voice. "We'll find you an apartment later. When your plans are settled."

"That's very generous. I didn't expect—"

"Apartments are assigned," Kurt said, explaining. "I'll get you a priority on the list, but until then, the Berolina. A guest of the state." He lowered his voice, suddenly practical. "You still have an English bank account, yes? Hard currency. Very valuable here when you transfer the funds. Well, come."

An ambulance was pulling into Invalidenstrasse, life going on. The raincoats had disappeared into their pickup car. Martin looked at the bridge, empty now, the road barrier still up, waiting for them to leave, the final exit of the play.

"Of course you will also have a pension from the state," Kurt was saying. "You will be comfortable."

"But I'd still want to teach, do something. Be useful."

"A good socialist," Kurt said, another wink. He nodded. "You will be. Don't worry about *Neues Deutschland*. I'll help you—what to say. One interview only. Be careful," he said, suddenly pulling at Martin's sleeve. "They don't slow down." Backing them away from the path of the ambulance, then doing a double-take. "But it's the wrong way. *Alt!*" A shout to the guards, who were stepping back to let the ambulance pass, then springing forward again to stop it at the wall opening.

"*Alt!*"

A sudden roar, the ambulance shooting ahead, crashing past the checkpoint, no barrier, a moment they must have been watching for. Just a second from the bridge. A gun sticking out the passenger window, pointing. Martin froze, the old instinct, a leopard about to leap out of the tree, then ducked, pushing Kurt to the ground with him, the bullet passing over their heads, the whole quiet morning erupting with sound, gears grinding, another shot, closer, his face against the pavement now, trying to sink into it, out of range. He glanced up at the guards, rifles out, but looking at each other, not sure what to do. Another bullet from the ambulance, hitting the waiting car. A shout from the Western side of the bridge. Now the guards at the wall crouched down, aiming at the ambulance as it came toward them, a burst of tat-tat explosions that finally made it career into the wall, out of control. Scraping metal until it stopped.

"Fools," Kurt said, his breath ragged.

The guards rushed over to the ambulance, yanking open the door, guns on the driver, slumped forward over the wheel.

"Out!" Motioning with the gun.

The driver stayed slumped over, but a young man opened the passenger door, hands up. "Don't shoot." He looked at the driver, distraught. "You killed him. Murderers."

The guard moved the driver's head back, putting his fingers on the neck, checking for a pulse.

"He's alive. Still bleeding," he said, pulling his fingers away, queasy.

"How many in the back?" Kurt said, getting up and brushing his coat, the movements jerky, shaking. He held out his hand to help Martin to his feet.

The passenger shook his head. "Nobody else. He's going to die."

"I can't help that," Kurt said, suddenly in charge, the guards as young as the passenger. Then, coming back to himself, "Call the hospital. This one's useless now." Waving his hand at the ambulance. "Did you steal it?"

The passenger shook his head. "It's ours. I mean we work on it. For the Charité."

"Even worse. State property. Stealing state property. For this foolishness. What were you thinking?"

"I didn't mean to hit him," the guard said. "We're not supposed to use guns. During an exchange."

"No one's blaming you," Kurt said.

"It went through the windshield," the guard said, tracing the trajectory. "Off the hood."

"He'll die," the passenger said, hands still up in the air. He looked at the empty bridge, his eyes watering. For a moment Martin thought he would run, chance it, but his eyes now were on the guard's gun, the years ahead.

"I'm sorry for this," Kurt said to Martin.

Martin nodded, holding his hands steady, the gunfire still in his head, like radio static.

The driver moved, his body pitching sideward, about to slide out of the seat. The guard stuck the rifle against his shoulder, prop-ping him, then looked over to see the Western guards rushing over the bridge, following the noise.

"Stay back!" the guard shouted. "It's finished."

The Western guards, also young, hesitated, trained not to cross the border line.

"He's bleeding to death," the passenger yelled, a plea.

"Then he can bleed here. In his own country," Kurt said. "Take him away," he said to the guard holding a gun on the passenger. Then, to the other, "You have a field phone? Call the hospital." He looked to the bridge, raising his voice. "Go back."

The Western guards took a minute, hands on their guns, then backed away, boys standing down from a fight.

"You see what it's like," Kurt said to Martin. "They see things on television. The paradise in the West. And then look." Taking in the crashed ambulance, the slumped driver. "Flight from the Republic is a serious crime."

"What'll happen to him?"

"Prison." He watched the passenger being led away. "So, another chip."

"Chip?"

"The West Germans will want him. There is no East Germany to them. Only German citizens, all of us. So by this logic, we're putting their citizens in jail. They have a responsibility to get them out."

"How?" Martin said, watching the guard on the phone.

"Trade someone, like you." He paused. "Or buy them out," he said, almost a grin.

"Buy them?"

"All this business, a spy for a spy. It's valuable, yes, of course we must do it, but what we really need is hard currency."

"Not old spies."

"Don't misunderstand. It's an honor to do this for you. But as a practical matter—"

"You can't sell people. That's—"

Kurt jumped in. "Yes, I know, how would it look? To the good West Germans. Hypocrites. But here are two more." He nodded to the young men. "What do we do with them? More expenses."

An ambulance was coming around the corner, followed by a car of border police.

"Let's go," Kurt said, leaving the guards to deal with whatever reports were going to be made. "It's another matter, the exchange. Nothing to do with this. We don't want them confused. Come." Protecting himself.

They got into the back of the black sedan, saying nothing for a minute, still shaken.

"Not a very pleasant welcome," Kurt said as their driver pulled out. "I hope you won't think this is typical. Very rare. Before the wall, it was a problem. The state trains someone, years of free education, and then one day he takes the S-Bahn to the West and all the skills are lost. Years of investment gone. You heard them. Their ambulance. Skilled medical workers."

They were speeding past the Charité grounds, nurses and students filling the street. Sabine hadn't been a medical student, just a friend of Georg's brother, a girl at a party.

"I'm too much a coward," she'd said. "All the blood. I don't have the stomach for that. It doesn't bother you?"

"I'm not in medicine. Physics."

"Oh, physics. I don't even know what it means. Something they teach at the Kaiser Wilhelm Institute, I think. I met someone from there once. He said it was how the world works. Yes?" Her eyes moving all over his face, studying him, already familiar.

"He meant the underlying principles of—"

"I know what he meant," she said, a quick smile. "You're at the Kaiser Wilhelm too?"

"Göttingen. I'm just here for the weekend."

"So you don't know Berlin?"

"A little."

"Well, I don't know any Americans. You're the first." Looking at him, the eyes again.

"What do you think? So far."

"You're a serious person," she said, glancing at the rest of the room, her voice throaty with smoke. "That's what I think. So far."

"Serious. Is that good?"

"For me, yes." She drew on her cigarette. "Are you political?"

Almost a laugh, caught in time. Then, when she kept staring, "We don't have politics. Not like here."

"Everybody has politics."

"What about you?"

"Don't you know it's dangerous to ask a German that?"

"Unless you're a Nazi, you mean."

"We're all Nazis now. If you ask that."

He looked at her. "Not you."

"How can you know?"

"You're here, for one thing. In this crowd."

"That doesn't mean anything."

He shrugged. "I trust my instincts."

"Ouf," she said, dismissing this. "Instincts."

"You trusted yours, didn't you? When you started talking to me?"

She smiled, then looked away. "No, that was flirting. A difference." The word running through him, a jolt, the eyes sexual now. She turned back. "But you're right. I'm not a Nazi. The opposite."

"What, a Communist?" he said, not serious, party talk.

"Not officially. But up here, yes." She touched her head. "I used to think I was anyway." Something people didn't say out loud, the boldness of it another jolt.

"But not now?"

"Now? If I were a Communist in Germany now, I'd be dead."

But of course she had been, even then, something he would have known if he'd been listening, too busy hearing the rush of blood in his ears, the throaty voice. At the beginning, when he believed everything she said.

And then, abruptly, "Do you want to leave?"

"Leave?" he said, surprised. "I'm staying here."

"Georg won't mind." Another smile, conspiratorial. "He'll be impressed." She touched his arm. "I just have to get my coat." Moving away, everything decided. Around him people were talking and smoking, unaware that anything was happening.

The car turned right on Chausseestrasse.

"You're all right?" Kurt said.

Martin nodded.

"He's right, you know. The guard. They have orders not to shoot, during an exchange. Such a tense moment. You can imagine what would happen if— They must have known about it, those two. The time of the exchange. How?" He leaned over. "That's where Brecht used to live," he said, pointing. "Another one who joined us in the East. And was very happy here." Still apologizing for what had happened at the checkpoint.

Martin looked out the window, then up, following the line of the buildings. The contrast with the West had become a magazine cliché—the shiny cars reflecting the lights of the Kurfürstendamm, the gray shabby streets of the East—and it was true that the buildings were dingier on this side, neglected, but it was still the same city, the same architecture. They passed Torstrasse. She'd lived near here, an old tenement building in Albrechtstrasse, because it was close to the theaters and she wanted to be an actress, was an actress, except it was all foolishness in the theater, nothing serious, you had to scrape by with walk-on bits out at the UFA studios. When you could get them. And the building was all right, your own bathroom, not a shared toilet down the hall.

He remembered that the stair lights had a timer. You had to hurry if you lived at the top, and that was how they'd first kissed, the light clicking off, pushed against the wall, slightly out of breath from the climb, opening his mouth to her. The taste of cigarettes and the smell of her perfume, the same brand for years and he'd never known which, just the smell of her. They pressed against each other on the stairs, and then she clutched his coat and pulled him up with her, and when they were inside, the back of the door was like the stairway again, pushing against it, but now they were taking their clothes off as they kissed, moving toward the bed. No drinks, no conversation, working up to something. They were already there, so excited he thought it would happen too soon, and then in, panting now, not caring who heard. And when they came, her eyes were on him again, taking him in, seeing him.

After, they lay still for a few minutes, and then he rolled off, slightly embarrassed, afraid he'd given himself away, who he really was. She reached over and took out a cigarette, something he imagined she would do every time, the way he'd first seen her, smoking.

"Would you like to know my name?" she said, drawing in smoke, amused. "You never asked."

He smiled. "I guess I didn't," he said, only half there, lazy with sex.

"Well, I didn't ask either. I wanted to see first. If we fit."

"What?"

"If we fit. You know, like this," she said, waving her hand between them.

He sat up halfway, propped on his elbow. In the light coming in from the street he saw the gleam on her skin, the dark patch farther down, and then the red tip of her cigarette. He ran his hand over her, a physical contact to make sure she was really there.

"Why?"

She hesitated for a moment, drawing on her cigarette. "You want to know? All right. We should never lie to each other, don't you agree?"

He nodded, not sure where this was going.

"So we'll know what's true, between us. The others? That's something else. But between us, the truth."

He hitched himself up a little higher. "Which is?"

"You're an American. I thought, he can get me out of Germany."

"Out?"

"What's going to happen here? A war. Things will get worse and worse. And now it's not so easy to go. But an American. And then you looked at me like that."

"Like what?"

"The way you want someone to look at you. Like a hunger. And I thought—if we're telling the truth—maybe with him. But I had to know first. If we fit. You see, I don't lie to you. I wouldn't say this if we didn't fit."

He was quiet for a second. "But we do."

"Yes," she said, crushing out the cigarette and looking at him. "It's a good fit. And once that's right, you always have it."

And they did, again that night and for years after. They always had the sex. Even after things changed, after they became different people, they had the sex. One of their secrets. Sometimes, in prison, he wondered if he had done it for sex, had been that much of a fool. But it hadn't felt that way at the time. Something the Party needed, the world, if it was to have peace. Serious reasons.

He hadn't done it for her, the spying. But he wouldn't have done it alone.

Now he was riding down Friedrichstrasse with her husband. How did they fit? he wondered. Don't. Past the station, turning onto Unter den Linden, the imperial route. But the street looked more run-down than the ones by the Charité, the old Schinkel buildings sooty and damaged, what they must have looked like right after the war. Down toward the Gendarmenmarkt you could still see heaps of rubble that no one had bothered to cart away.

"The *Schloss* is gone," Martin said, seeing the empty space where the palace had been. Across from it, the Dom was streaked with black char.

"Yes, a long time now. It was dangerous, not worth saving."

"A shame, though."

"Well, perhaps. But a bad symbol. There was so much to do after the war. And no money. What do you do? Save the past, patch it up? Or build the future. A socialist society—we had to look ahead. Wait till you see what they've done in Alexanderplatz."

The station looked the same, but everything else, the maze of small streets that had fed off it with their pickpockets and lottery sellers and whores, the usual station riffraff, had been razed, paved over, and turned into a shapeless open plaza surrounded by glass high-rises, a cheap version of West Berlin.

"You see there? They're building a radio tower. The tallest in the world. Much higher than the Funkturm." A point of pride, winning some invisible race. "For television too. You know that Peter is on the television?"

"No." Or anything else about him. What he smelled like as an infant. The look of him in Sabine's arms. How it felt, seeing him. Then not seeing him.

"Yes. *Die Familie Schmidt*. A program on the DFF. He plays the son. At first, a small part. Sabine arranged it. You know, she has friends in the theater. Now television. The work is there. So why not use Peter? A little extra money. And you know, she's drawn to that life. So maybe it's for her a little too. And then what happens? People like him. The funny one. But a good boy. So more lines. Now he's well-known. One of the *Publikumslieblinge*."

Martin looked at him, unfamiliar with the expression. "Public darlings?"

"Yes, audience favorites. Not necessarily the star part, but people look forward to seeing you."

Martin sat back. East German television. What could that possibly be like? Something else he didn't know.

"How long has he been doing this?"

"Two years. Of course, the way he's growing now, he may grow out of the part soon." The proud father.

"Why don't they just let him get older, if he's such a favorite?"

"No, he needs to be a child. That's the point, you understand. A family show. Peter does something he shouldn't, some mischief, and then his father teaches him a lesson. How a good socialist behaves. It wouldn't work if he were older."

Is that what you do? Martin wondered. Teach good socialist lessons?

"And does he enjoy it? Acting?"

"Well, but he's not a professional. Sabine coaches him, but the reason it's good is that he's so natural, a real boy. That's my theory anyway. Of course he likes having the car, things like that."

"The car?"

"To drive him to the studios. In Adlershof."

Martin glanced out the window. Another glass high-rise, dreary in gray Berlin, designed for sun. The socialist experiment, with car and driver.

"It's a good experience for him," Kurt was saying.

An audience darling. He imagined holding the car door for him, his chauffeur, some absurd turnabout. But what had he thought they'd be doing? Playing catch? Going to ball games?

"You don't approve?"

"No, I was just thinking—how much I don't know. How much I've missed."

"Well, but you're here. You'll get to know each other better. Ah, look. Karl-Marx-Allee. Now you'll see what we have done in the East. You remember when it was Frankfurter Allee? After the war, the bombing, there was absolutely nothing. They made a mountain in Volkspark Friedrichshain with the rubble. Now look."

Now look. A broad divided avenue lined with apartment blocks as far as one could see, not the cheap glass of Alexanderplatz, but solid stone, Soviet wedding cake style, modern and curiously lace curtain at the same time, what you saw in pictures of Moscow.

"Different architects," Kurt was saying. "You can imagine the competition, to be a part of this. Your design. Yet a harmonious effect."

One giant building after the other, their long façades broken by numbered entryways and hundreds of windows, not like the dim *Hinterhofs* of old Berlin, one courtyard behind another. A traffic circle with a fountain.

"Who lives here?" Martin said.

"Everybody. Workers. Of course, in the beginning, a privilege. Hot water, central heating, these things were luxuries in those days. But now everywhere. We live not far from here. In Weberwiese. You'll see later."

"Not Party leaders?" Martin said, still looking.

"Out in Pankow. They prefer villas. All close together. Maybe to keep an eye on each other." He arched his eyebrows, making a joke. "And maybe a little old-fashioned. This is—modern for them. So, here we are. Interhotel Berolina. Nothing but the best."

The hotel was brand-new, located on its own plaza behind the Kino International, a theater with a swooshing curve to its roof, as if it had been streamlined during the trip from Miami. The hotel also had a tropical look, its front faced with blue glazed tiles, like a beach resort. Inside, the lobby furniture was Scandinavian modern, dotted with plants in pots. Anywhere.

There were no forms to fill out at the desk, everything having been arranged by Kurt and the manager.

"Your key, Herr Keller," the manager said. "Welcome to Berlin. There is no other luggage?" Looking at the overnight bag, all he'd been allowed in prison.

"No."

"We must fix you up with some new clothes," Kurt said. "Bodo Jahn, I think, no?" A question to the manager, who nodded. "A tailor," Kurt explained. "Out in Biesdorf. Very good workmanship." He ran a hand down the side of his suit. "Always busy, but he'll fit you in if I ask. But today you'll want to rest." Locked in another room. "I'll have the car come for you at seven, all right?"

Martin nodded. Agree to anything. Alone soon.

"Well, Kurt." A voice behind them. "It's lucky to run into you." A stocky man in a bulky shapeless overcoat, glancing at Martin, expecting to be introduced.

"Hans," Kurt said, suddenly hearty. "What are you doing here? During working hours." He looked at his watch. "Not some assignation, I hope. The hotel has a reputation to protect."

Martin looked at the man more closely. Short and balding, with ferret-like eyes, an unlikely candidate for an affair. But who knew? He took the joke, or maybe just the intimacy, as a kind of compliment, smiling and nodding.

"No, I thought you might be here. And here you are. So, a good guess, no? You always bring your visitors here," he said, looking at Martin, waiting.

"And family friends. Martin, Hans Rieger. *Neues Deutschland.*"

Martin raised his eyes but said nothing, waiting to take his cue from Kurt.

"You came to see me?" Kurt said.

"For details. About the incident this morning."

"Incident?"

"At Invalidenstrasse. Wall jumpers. In an ambulance. I think something new, using an ambulance. I don't remember anyone before—"

"And did they make it?" Kurt said.

Martin looked at him.

"No. One dead. Just now."

"Dead?" Martin said.

"Your news travels fast," Kurt said.

"A tip."

"A friend at the hospital?" Really asking.

"Everywhere. You know the news business."

"*Neues Deutschland?*" Kurt said, an exaggerated skepticism, playing.

"Yes, I know. The SED Congress, the trade delegation. But that's not all we are. A man shot dead in Invalidenstrasse? People want to know."

"But will the SED want them to know? Nobody dies at the wall these days. You still have your old habits, Hans." He turned to Martin. "Hans is a refugee from the West. He used to work for

Springer, so he's a bloodhound with a crime story. Except there is no crime in the Republic."

"So you saw nothing?" Hans said. "I thought maybe— It's your favorite crossing, no? Back and forth he goes," he said to Martin. "The only one these days."

"I have business in the West. In the interests of the East."

"But not this morning? It's easily checked." Looking up at him.

Kurt stared back, deciding something. "There was an exchange, yes," he said flatly. "The incident must have been after."

"Well, as I said, it's easily checked."

Kurt shrugged. "They will never print this story. So why—?"

"I know. You're right—old habits. What else would I do?" He looked again at Martin. "The exchange was for you?"

"Let me introduce you. Martin Keller."

Hans peered at Martin, rifling through some mental file drawer. "The spy?" How he'd be known now. Hans turned to Kurt. "You might have told me. I suppose he's already promised to Gerhard? Some favor you owe him."

"It's not in my gift, Hans. They want Gerhard to do the interview. I'll make it up to you."

"Oh yes? How? Maybe that interview with your son you keep promising."

Kurt held up his hand. "And if it were up to me, you'd have it. But you know the DFF, they control everything. Every move."

"You could talk to them. You're his father."

Kurt glanced at Martin, uneasy.

"I can ask again, yes. But you know what they're like." He paused. "What do you want to know? About this morning?"

Hans looked at him, surprised, an unexpected olive branch. "You saw it?"

Kurt nodded. "Well, if you call it seeing. A flash and then it's over. You understand I had to protect Martin, get him out of there, so I wasn't noticing much. What, in particular?"

"Nothing in particular. Just—what happened. Why didn't it work?"

"Why didn't it work?"

"The escape. The barrier was raised, the ambulance is close, nobody suspecting until the last minute. A minute is all they needed. So why?"

"Why? You'll have to ask them why."

"Only one now."

"All right, him, then."

"If I can get to him."

"Why," Kurt repeated, shrugging. "Maybe bad luck. Maybe kids who didn't know what they were doing. It's often the case. So." An end to it, about to move away. "I'm sorry about Gerhard. Next time."

Hans made a faint smile. "Your next spy." He looked at Martin. "You're the physicist, no? So here's another. My interview today." He tilted his head up, someone at the hotel. "A returnee. What do you ask a physicist? That a reader understands?"

"Returnee," Kurt said. "I thought the Russians sent the last one back years ago."

"Not Schell."

"Stefan Schell?" Martin said.

Hans looked over at him. "You know him?"

A look from Kurt that Martin couldn't interpret.

"Everybody knows him," Martin said, evading. "The first reactor."

"Everybody but me."

Another look from Kurt.

"In the field, I mean. Maybe not the general public."

"He's staying here?" Kurt said. "Not in Karlshorst?"

"To give the interview. Then Dresden. So what do I ask?"

"Ask him why he decided to return," Martin said. "After so many years."

"The Russians, I think, make that decision."

"Ah," Martin said, just a sound, an end, nowhere to go.

"You'll think of something," Kurt said, beginning to move. "You always do."

"One more thing?" Hans said.

Kurt stopped.

"At Invalidenstrasse. The barrier was up. For the exchange."

Not a question, but Kurt nodded.

"The right moment for them. If you have to crash through a barrier—even an ambulance—it would slow you down."

"So?"

"So how did they know? To be there?"

"You can see from Luisenstrasse. They must have been watching."

"Maybe."

"You have a suspicious nature, Hans."

"It hasn't occurred to you, this question?"

"Not until you mentioned it," Kurt said easily.

Martin looked from one to the other. Some dance between them.

"It would be a shame, in this work you do, if someone—"

"That's why I handle things myself."

Hans smiled. "Somebody you can trust. Well, maybe you're right, watching from Luisenstrasse. Amateurs."

"They'd have to be. If they thought they could drive through the wall." Kurt raised his eyes to the ceiling. "Good luck with the science quiz. Martin," he said, moving them off to the elevators.

"You don't have to come up."

"No, just a word." A glance to the lobby. "There he goes. I was afraid— But that was good, everybody in the field. He doesn't have to know you're a friend of Schell's."

"A hundred years ago."

Kurt nodded. "You were at Göttingen together. Old comrades."

Martin looked at him. "You know that?"

"It's not a secret, is it? Of course I know. In this work you have to know everything about your clients."

"But you don't want Hans to know."

Kurt looked up a second. "We want to be careful."

"Careful."

"You heard his questions? For a story they won't print. Why ask? He has two jobs."

"And *Neues Deutschland*'s only one of them."

"Just like Springer was. They always wanted to have someone inside at Springer. And he wanted the money. So, two paychecks."

"But then he got caught."

"That's why he's here," Kurt said, looking at him.

"And you?" Martin said, not thinking, blurting it out. "How many jobs do you work?"

Kurt took a step back, surprised. "You want to know, am I Stasi?" he said bluntly. "I can't be. The go-between? Both sides have to trust you. It's a tightrope sometimes. If I need to work with the Stasi, I work with them. How else, with political prisoners? But I can't be one of them. So they're suspicious. It's their nature. But they need me. They don't negotiate. Someone else has to negotiate. Someone the West will trust too. So, one job only."

"Hans doesn't think so."

"Hans is looking for an opportunity. To be noticed. But I don't give him one." He looked up at Martin again. "One job." He put his hand on Martin's arm. "Well, later, then. That was very good, not knowing Schell. So quick. You never lose the training."

"Not much training. I was just in the right place at the right time."

"The perfect asset. But you have to have the instinct too." He looked away. "Imagine that dummkopf Rieger. Not knowing who he is, his own interview."

"Can I call him? Schell. I mean, if he's just down the hall—"

"When the time is right."

"When the time is right," Martin said, an echo, picking at the words.

"You will have to trust me. Can you do that?"

Martin said nothing.

"Good. So, first come to dinner. See Peter. You want to see your old friend Schell? Of course. See anybody you like. Well, maybe not Ulbricht. Nobody sees him. Except Frau Ulbricht." He smiled, an easy joke, patching things over. "But there's a right time." He moved his hand to Martin's chest, a faint pat. "Let me arrange things."

———

The room faced the back, away from Karl-Marx-Allee, but was high enough to have a view over a neighboring roof. Not a cell. He'd left the door unlocked, opening it once to prove he could. Then opened the window, not minding the damp air, taking it in with deep breaths. No one outside the door, no bells to call him to the dining hall, no lights-out. His own room, open to the air.

On the desk the management had left a bottle of Hungarian

Tokay, wrapped in colored plastic, with a welcome card from the German Academy of Sciences, a VIP gesture. Then why this clutching in his stomach? Brought in quietly through the back door, not even a hello to Schell, Kurt arranging things. Not Sabine. This dinner, awkward even before it happened, wouldn't have been her idea. Kurt wanted to watch, the careful greeting, the forced small talk, forced just because he was there watching, his family now. Peter a good socialist boy. But why shouldn't he be? Isn't it what they all had wanted once? Still, this dread. Trust me.

He put the overnight bag on the bed and started unpacking. Not much more than a change and a Dopp kit. My tailor will fit you in. He hung his jacket on the curtain rod in the shower to steam out the wrinkles later. Peter's first look at him. Sabine's. What would she see? He stopped in front of the mirror, hands on the washbasin. Someone else looking back. The same high forehead, what Sabine said she'd noticed first "to hold all the brains," but the hair all gray now, and thinning. Prison skin, haggard, not puffy or slack, but worn, like his eyes, the sheen gone, set deeper than before, as if they were receding, tired of seeing. Ten years of his life and all of them visible here, in the creases. And she? A matron in a broad skirt? A fleshy line along the chin? No, she'd be the same, the only way he could imagine her. The same eyes, the same secret place at the back of her neck. And for a second, he wanted the impossible, to be as they had been, young, shiny, just the two of them. Except it had never been just them. There had been the secrets, the handlers, the close calls, Sabine knowing what to do, cool and excited at the same time, getting away with it.

He went back over to the window. No sun, but no rain either, the cloudy Berlin sky. He could go out, he realized, just open the door and go. A walk if he felt like it. He expected to be stopped in the lobby, but the man at the door merely nodded, a working man's version of a tipped hat. He crossed the plaza, then paused in front of the Kino. He wanted to walk and walk. Why not go all the way to Frankfurter Tor, see the whole street? There was a snap in the air. *Berliner Luft*, just like the song. He felt his face begin to move, an involuntary smile. Because he was walking.

This time he took in the ground-floor shops of the apartment blocks—a bookstore, a salon, even, improbably, a travel agency. Where could anybody go? State resorts on the Baltic, dormitory hotels. There were no posters in any of the windows, no sales signs. Or customers, the sidewalks mostly empty—an old man with a string bag, a mother pushing a pram. A showcase with an air of disappointment about it now, some promise not kept. He could imagine the architectural schematics, with trees and sidewalk cafés and open-shirted workers and their wives in sundresses bustling into the stores, everybody glowing with pride in the new buildings. You could still feel some of this ambition, just in the scale of the street, but the people in the drawings had gone. No one now but him and a lone window shopper over by the *Buchhandlung*.

He slowed. At the window but not really looking. A man in a hat and another shapeless overcoat, his body half-turned. If the street had been busy, Martin never would have noticed him, but now he felt a prickling at the back of his neck. Someone trying to be inconspicuous, betrayed by the empty street. Would he follow? Martin walked past the bookstore, the man in the hat still at the window. Another shop, entrance steps, Martin still in his sight line, but getting farther away. The man turned and started down the sidewalk. Heading east too, behind Martin, no crowds to swallow him up. So exposed Martin could hear his footsteps. At the corner Martin stopped for a pedestrian light and glanced back. The man was lighting a cigarette, the only excuse he could think of to stop, not catch up. For a second Martin was tempted to turn around and face him, almost a tease. But it wasn't a game, being followed here. It was a reminder, like bars on a window, that your life wasn't your own. What had Digby said? They've all got an ear out over there. Clumsy, too close behind in the empty street, but maybe the point was being obvious, so that both of them knew.

The light turned green but instead of crossing Martin turned back to the *Allee* and the stairs for the underground passage, built to avoid street traffic that wasn't there. The sound of his shoes on the stairs, then the man's steps. He forced himself not to look over his shoulder. Maybe the man was just going to the U-bahn station below. But when they passed the entrance, the sound of the steps was still there, persistent. The north side of the *Allee* now, looking toward the radio tower going up in Alexanderplatz. How long had he been out? All he'd wanted to do was take a walk. Now he felt his chest tighten, apprehensive, as if a hand were going to fall on his shoulder. Come with us.

He stopped, whirling around to face the man in the hat, startling him. The man halted, his body still pitched forward, and looked at Martin for a second. Not the way this was supposed to happen. Neither of them said anything, staring, and Martin wondered what showed in his face, the anger he could feel running through him, or a more hidden despair. This is what it was going to be like. He'd known, even at Invalidenstrasse, taking the first steps. His life now. And then the man, as if he had heard him, moved his mouth in a small smile and nodded. He started walking again, past Martin, everything understood. When he reached the Kino, he waited, as if he wanted to make sure Martin got home safely.

CHAPTER 2

The car was there at seven sharp. Weberwiese wasn't far, just a few blocks down Karl-Marx-Allee, somewhere Martin could easily have walked, the car more a statement than a convenience. Their building was behind the one fronting the *Allee*, an art deco tower facing its own small park, more attractive than the Soviet block on the street. He clutched the Hungarian Tokay, its plastic wrapping crackling like nerves. What would he say to him? I'm sorry I missed your childhood? What would he say to her?

But it was Kurt who opened the door and took his coat.

"Wine," he said as Martin handed it over. "Thank you. It's very generous. You didn't have to—"

"From the Academy of Sciences."

"Ah, yes, the welcome gift. They want you to give a lecture. In Dresden."

Over his shoulder Martin could see figures in the living room. What did they look like? But Kurt hadn't moved.

"A lecture? My physics is ten years out of date."

"But your memories are invaluable. Your old friend Klaus Fuchs is there, you know. At Rossendorf. The nuclear research center."

"We only met once or twice."

"He remembers you," Kurt said, cheerful. "And Sabine. I think he had a little crush on her."

"We weren't supposed to know each other. At the time, I had no idea—"

"No, of course not. Separate couriers, even. No links. No chain. That way you couldn't give each other away. If anything happened. And it didn't." Familiar with it.

"Not then, no." More movement in the other room.

"Well. Come. Sabine?" Raising his voice, almost a shout to the other room. "He's here."

At first all he saw was her eyes, locked on his, the way they did, everything around them stopped. Then she was coming toward him, her arm out, tentative. The same. No, older, her hair dyed, bottle blonde now, pulled back, but the body still wiry, tense, the girl on the couch.

"Sabine," he said quietly, not trusting his voice.

"Well, Martin," she said, there now, in front of him, eyes soft. The first awkward moment. A quick look to Kurt.

For a second Martin thought she was going to hug him, the arm stretched out to draw him in, but she stopped at his arm, gripping it, somewhere between a handshake and an embrace.

"To see you again," she said.

"A long time." Talking with their eyes.

"You're gray," she said, looking at his hair. "All gray."

"But not you," he said, smiling a little.

She touched the back of her head, self-conscious. "No. It's a vanity. I know."

"Sabine always looks smart," Kurt said.

"Yes," Martin said. "Look at you."

She had dressed for the evening, a navy-blue cocktail dress with a scalloped neck, pearls, heels. Half heels, he noticed, Kurt's height.

"A natural beauty," Kurt said, determined to be a third voice. "With some help." A husband's fond joke. "Peter."

Sabine stepped aside. "Yes, Peter. Come."

He had been standing there, waiting, his face solemn, not sure what was expected.

"And this is Peter," Martin said, an inane thing to say, his heart skipping. There could be no question: Martin's lean face, Sabine's direct look. Still waiting for his growth spurt, his head at Martin's chest. Hair combed back, dressed in a jacket for the occasion, Martin at age eleven, meeting one of his parents' friends. He stepped forward and shook Martin's hand, polite, on his best behavior, stopping Martin from crouching down, taking him in his arms, embarrassing everybody.

"What do I call you?" Peter said. "Kurt wasn't sure." Kurt, not *Vati*.

A flustered look from Sabine.

"Call me Martin. Would that be all right?"

Peter nodded.

"Well, or Father," Kurt said. "It's a lucky boy to have two, no? And look what Martin brought," he said, holding up the wine. "Shall we open it and have a toast?"

"*Mutti* got champagne. At the special shop," Peter said.

A second. "Well, let's by all means have champagne, then," Kurt said. "A celebration. Come in, Martin, come in."

The apartment wasn't large—a dining area, not a separate room—but comfortable. Pale wooden bookshelves with a television in one of them, a low-slung couch, the back draped with a bright Navajo blanket they'd bought in Santa Fe years ago. Everything modern, no

German clutter of knickknacks. The reading chair was black leather with a metal floor lamp, the coffee table glass. On the entry wall, a framed poster for *Die Familie Schmidt*, sized for a station platform.

"It's you," he said to Peter, glancing at the face in the bottom corner, a boy full of innocent mischief.

"It's from last year," Peter said.

"Kurt told me it was very popular. Do you enjoy it? The work, I mean."

"It's all right. Sometimes it's boring, the rehearsals. The boy who plays my brother—"

"He's jealous," Kurt said, popping the champagne cork. "Peter, here's apple juice for you." He poured out the glasses and passed them. "So, a toast."

"Welcome to Germany," Peter said, raising his glass. "Is this—?" He cut himself off.

"Yes?" Martin said, nodding. "It's all right. I know you have a lot of questions. What were you going to ask?"

"If it was your first time in Berlin, and then I remembered, no, it couldn't be because you met *Mutti* here. You were a student." The family story.

"That's right. At Göttingen. But it was very different then, Germany. Not like this." He made a gesture to take in the room, the city beyond. "Everything so new. So it's my first time in this Germany."

"And then you took her to America. But I wasn't born there. Later, in England. Why did you go to England?"

"Peter," Sabine said.

"It's all right. Well, they offered me a job there, and America then—it wasn't so pleasant, the political climate. Hearings and loyalty oaths and all the rest of it. Witch hunts. England was a little more European, so—" And the Service wanted it, access to almost everything at Harwell, Britain's Los Alamos.

"I always thought it was because it was easier to be a spy there. In America, it was a remote place, people would notice everything, but in England—"

"Peter," Sabine said.

"It was easier," Martin said. A train into London, a park bench in St. James's, a pub near Leicester Square, an envelope passed, everyone around them in the great city too busy to see. "But that's not why we moved. It was a better job."

"Was it dangerous, being a spy?"

Kurt and Sabine both started to say something, but Martin put up his hand, looking at Peter, who wanted to know.

"You mean, with guns and men chasing you and things like that? No. The danger was getting caught. And I was. So." The moral of the story, Peter ignoring it.

"But it took them years. You were a good spy. Nobody suspected, not even *Mutti*."

Martin glanced over at Sabine. The story she'd wanted him to believe, too late to change now. Peter had invested in the myth, his clever father.

"No, not even your mother," he said, aware of Kurt watching him. "But I did get caught. And went to jail. So I don't recommend it as a profession." Trying to be light. "Anyway, the world is different now."

"But we're still threatened by the West," Peter said. "That hasn't changed. You performed a great service." A phrase he'd got somewhere.

"Such talk," Kurt said. "Who talks politics with champagne?"

"Anyway, it's finished," Martin said. "All that business. It's done."

"I thought once you worked for them, you're always one of them. I read that. So maybe you're still—" What he wanted him to be. Peter's eyes widened. "And that's why you've come."

"No. I came to see you." He paused. "I wanted to know what you looked like," he said, his voice softer.

Peter raised his eyes, not buying it.

"You never saw pictures?"

"No," Sabine said. "They didn't allow it."

Martin looked at her. Who didn't? More mythmaking.

"No visitors either?"

"A few. English friends."

"Maybe spies too. To get you to talk."

Martin smiled. "I'd already talked."

"But you didn't tell them everything."

"Not everything, no," he said, a quick glance to Sabine.

"They always keep something back, spies. They're good at that."

"Where do you get these ideas?" Kurt said. "Those books you read. Boy detectives. He always has his head in a book."

Martin leaned toward Peter. "I was the same way."

"I know. *Mutti* told me you were a great reader. That's where I get it."

"It's like music, they say," Kurt said. "You can pass it down."

"How did you do it?" Peter said, not letting it go. "Did you photograph papers? With a little camera?" Something he'd seen in a movie.

"No. I memorized things. Sometimes I made a copy. A drawing, a proof. But mostly it was up here." He tapped his head. "And then I would meet somebody. That's all."

"Where?"

"Well, at Los Alamos nobody was allowed in, so you had to go out. To Santa Fe, somewhere away from the Project. Your mother had a doctor there, so that was the excuse."

"So you would meet somebody and then talk to him? Tell him secrets?"

"Yes. You see, no guns, nothing dangerous. I just talked." And betrayed.

"Then how did they catch you?"

"Someone gave me away. Told them about me. But that came later, in England. Not Los Alamos. There was no evidence there. Not enough to extradite me. So they let the British bring charges. That's why I went to prison there."

"What's extradite?"

"To send someone back, to stand trial. Of course, now it would be different. They'd have evidence. From people they caught later. Some of the people I met."

"And that's why you can't go back there? Why you came here?"

"No. I came to see you. Watch *Die Familie Schmidt*," he said, smiling.

"Well, now it's dinner with *Die Familie Thiele*," Sabine said, getting up and putting out her cigarette. "Come."

They moved to the dining area.

"You're here," Kurt said, pulling out a chair for Martin. "And, Peter, no more spy questions. Something nicer, for dinner."

"You know I've been to the West," Peter said, out of nowhere. "Before the wall, we used to go there. To shop sometimes for clothes. KaDeWe, all the big stores. So I know what it's like."

"Now we can get clothes at the Exquisit shop here," Kurt said. "Just as good quality."

"But you need West marks, hard currency," Sabine said, bringing in a casserole dish. "It's sauerbraten." This to Martin, an old favorite, but her voice clipped, on edge.

"Well, you have West marks," Kurt said.

"And what did you think?" Martin said to Peter. "Of the West."

"I liked the cars," he said, a child about a train set. "They're very good cars. We don't have them here. But we have a just society, so we have something better."

"Oh, that show," Sabine said. "You're being Erich again. That's how he talks."

"Well, but if it's true—" Kurt said.

"Is it easy for you, memorizing lines?" Martin said.

"You mean like you? So maybe that's passed down too in the family. What a spy can do," Peter said, impish, playing with it.

"This is your family," Kurt said. "No spies."

"Not in the Schmidts either," Peter said, still enjoying himself. "So now I have three fathers, if you count Dieter on the show. It's a lot for one person."

Martin smiled, the target of this, because he saw, what he hadn't expected, that Peter was trying to please him. Maybe the natural instinct of all actors, wanting the light. And tonight, at least, it was his, Sabine fading into the background, clearing plates, Kurt content to let him shine for the guest. Idle conversation, what a boy would talk about, but then something of the larger world, a glimpse of the adult he was becoming, the mix of ages professional children have.

"The worst thing is when Matty went to the West. My mother on the show. They put her on television there. So we had to write her out of the script and it was already done for that week. All night to write a new one and then we had to learn it in one day."

"What happened to the character?"

"A visit to her sister and then, on the way back, an accident."

"She dies?"

"How else? Another actress couldn't play her. Everybody knew Matty. So she had to die," he said easily. "Of course it was a chance for the family to come together. Maybe next season Dieter meets someone else and I have a new mother."

"Well, this mother thinks it's time for you to say good night so you can finish your homework," Sabine said, standing up.

"A little longer?" Peter said, a child again. "He came to see me."

"To see all of us," Kurt said.

"I'll see you again. I live here now."

"Where?"

"I don't know yet. Right now at the Berolina."

"Ho, nice." Worldly again. "And not far. Would you like to come to Adlershof, see the show, how we do it? It's interesting."

"Very much." A future promise.

"The car comes at six thirty. Could you be ready by then?"

"Tomorrow?" Kurt said. "No, it's not possible so soon. You need a pass, for visitors. It's not so easy–"

"*Mutti* could come. There's no problem if he's with her."

Martin glanced over at Sabine. "Would you mind? I'd like to."

"Mind? No," she said, fluttering a little. "I could do it. I have the time. That is, if you think–" This to Kurt, asking permission.

"Good," Peter said, settling it. "So six thirty at the Berolina. We'll pick you up."

"If you think–" Sabine said again, but Kurt waved his hand, giving in.

"Leave some time in the afternoon, though," he said to Martin. "We need to go over your schedule."

"My schedule?"

"Meetings at the Academy. Various matters."

"Like a call sheet," Peter said. "Makeup. Wardrobe. First scene. You get used to it." Two pros.

"Yes, fine," Martin said to Kurt, but he was looking at Sabine, seeing her for the first time on her own, not someone on the periphery of Peter's light. Still tense, lighting another cigarette, but glancing back, pleased, a meeting arranged, a chance to talk. With Peter in the car. But afterward there'd be somewhere. He turned away, not wanting Kurt to see the look between them, the way they used to talk.

"I'll be right back," Peter said. "I have something for you."

A boy's quick movements, back in a second with a shiny photograph in his hand.

"My picture," he said. "Now you'll have one."

A publicity still, Erich Schmidt, bright-eyed, eager, his face like young Martin's again.

Martin took it from him, holding it, a crack running through him, opening him up, so that he felt his insides might spill out. The way Peter looked now. But he'd also been three and five and eight, all of those moments gone, a lifetime Martin hadn't seen, photograph after photograph kept from him. He glanced over at Sabine. No letters. No photographs. Peter someone he had to imagine.

"Thank you," he said, trying to keep his voice steady.

Peter just nodded, self-conscious now, Martin's reaction somehow more than he had expected, the air heavier.

They had coffee and brandies in the living room, another piece of theater, what ordinary people did after dinner. Making conversation, careful, everything they might have talked about left unsaid, too soon. Sabine had curled up on the couch, the way she always did, legs tucked beneath her, ashtray on her lap. Kurt was swirling the brandy in his glass, leaning back in the leather chair.

"He's a wonderful boy," Martin said.

"He has an excellent mother," Kurt said, a smile to Sabine. "It's always the mother, how a child turns out."

Martin thought of his own, dead six months after the trial, of a heart attack and shame. She hadn't resigned from her bridge club, just stopped going, wrapping herself in the quiet of her big suburban house, no phone calls, the only sounds other people's lawn mowers down the street.

"It doesn't seem to have gone to his head, being on television."

"Well, but they tease him about it at school," Sabine said. "They call him Erich. His character. And he's not really like that. I tell him, just ignore them. But you know how it's hard at that age. I think sometimes he should leave the show."

"He can't do that," Kurt said. "Leave? He's the favorite. That would be the end for them."

"So what? What do I care, if it's not good for him?"

"You see," Kurt said, "it's as I say. A good mother. The lioness with her cubs."

"Let someone else learn the good socialist lesson," she said, an unexpected edge. She nodded toward Kurt. "He likes the privileges."

"And you don't? That dress? This apartment?"

"We had the apartment before he started with the show."

"Which was your idea. She forgets that sometimes. It was her idea. A chance to be an actor—why not? But now—"

"That's not acting, that show. It's—" She stopped. "Something else." She looked down at the ashtray.

"Well, he enjoys it. And we can't—"

"I know. We can't say no to them."

Kurt looked up, about to speak, but said nothing.

"You said he was growing out of the part anyway," Martin said, defusing it. "So it'll solve itself."

"But not yet," Kurt said. "A few seasons, maybe. Meanwhile it's valuable to the DDR to have such a show. You know they watch it in the West. That's very rare. They don't recognize us, but they watch the show. A little teasing at school—that happens to everyone. He never said anything to me."

"He wouldn't."

"Well, it's not serious. Maybe good for him. You have to learn to deal with all types."

"Yes."

"Sometimes, you know," he said to Martin, "his head is up there." Pointing a finger. "In the clouds. It's good for the work, it's easy for him to pretend. Make believe. He was always like that. And now he gets paid for it."

"And what happens when you pretend too much?" Sabine said. "Always in a story. Tonight, for instance. Now he's going to be in an adventure story with you. Spies together."

"That won't last long. He's curious, that's all. I'm something new. But then I won't be. He'll get bored."

"You think so? He wants to get to know you. Keller and Keller, international spies."

"It won't be exciting for long. Because it isn't—exciting." Except it was, the trembling feeling when you handed over the envelope, the copying after hours, no mistakes possible, one ear listening for footsteps in the hall. "You don't have to worry. He's a great kid." He paused, looking over at her. "You never told him?" He moved his finger between them.

"No, of course not. How could I? It was the cover. I was shocked, completely taken by surprise, you remember. I couldn't stand it. I had to leave. It's what we all agreed. It had to stop with you. To save the others."

"I know, but you never—"

"And what good if he knew? I'm *Mutti*. He doesn't want to be in an adventure story with me." She stubbed out her cigarette. "Anyway, there couldn't be any exceptions. The cover story had to hold. For good. A young wife with a baby. So upset, all I wanted to do was go home. To my *Mutti*. And they believed it."

"Not after you moved here."

"Yes, even then. I stayed with my mother for a year. In the West. Nothing suspicious. Then I met somebody, married him." A look at Kurt. "He lived in the East, so I followed him there. I came for love, not politics. A failing of mine. I don't know if they believed that—I wouldn't—but by that time most of the others were safe."

"And now?"

"Now? Oh, like Peter, you mean? Once in, you're never out? That's only if they can still use you. I'm—retired," she said, the word somehow ironic. "Why the look?"

"I'm surprised."

"Why?"

"Because you had the head for it. I never did. I got caught. And here you are."

"Yes, here I am."

"You had the conviction. I never knew anyone who—"

"Yes, well," she said. "But so much time in the West. They don't want you after that. Tainted goods. Who knows how far the infection spreads? How reliable you are."

"It's not Moscow. It's different here," Kurt said, uneasy with this.

"Oh, here, yes. There's nobody more reliable than me. I'm Erich Schmidt's mother. But my orders weren't coming from here. They got me out to protect the others, then—" Another smile. "No pension either. No good-bye."

"You don't need a pension," Kurt said.

"No, they already provided me with that. A husband with West marks. I want for nothing." A sniper's bullet, Kurt ignoring it, a conversation they'd had before. She turned to Martin. "Is anybody left there, do you think? From the group? Or did they roll them all up? Radio silence, we used to call it. When the line was cut."

"I have no idea. You knew them, I didn't."

"Those were the rules. That way there was nobody to give up."

"I wouldn't have."

She fanned away some smoke. "People give people up," she said, starting to cough, the smoke trapped somewhere.

"I tell her she should quit," Kurt said. "Everybody knows it's bad for the health."

Another cough, then a sip of water, under control.

"So two of us out to pasture," she said. "Maybe it's better, when they have no more use for you. Maybe there should be a place for all of us. Somewhere in the country. Where we sit and tell stories."

"But which ones to believe?"

She looked up, a wry smile. "That's right. Which ones? A house of liars, wouldn't it be? In the blood. Well," she said, moving off it, "old times. What's the point? Now it's Peter, his time. So it's good you're here, before it's too late."

"Too late?"

"To be a real person to him. Not somebody in his head."

"It's better for everyone," Kurt said.

"Well, let's hope so," Martin said, not knowing what to say. He looked over at Kurt. "I don't want to step on anyone's toes."

Kurt smiled. "And who brought you here? Who arranged it?" Tilting his glass, an abbreviated toast.

Who did? Suddenly he was back at Invalidenstrasse, a chess piece being moved by someone else. He stood up.

"I should go. If the car's really coming at six thirty." Anxious now to leave.

Kurt stood. "Yes, it's late. So tomorrow we talk. They take Peter to school in the afternoon, so I'll meet you there."

"At the school."

"Yes, we can take a nice walk. To *Neues Deutschland*."

"*Neues Deutschland*?" Sabine said.

"'Distinguished Scientist Defects to the Republic.'"

"No exchange," Martin said.

"No, your own idea, I think. A better story. Then no one asks what was paid for you. Who was exchanged."

Martin nodded. "All right. But why not just have the reporter come to the hotel?"

Sabine smiled. "Maybe the walls have ears. At the Berolina, maybe the trees too."

"Oh, in the trees now," Kurt said, brushing this off. "But Hans is always there. They should charge him for that chair in the lobby. All day, to see who comes and goes."

"He's harmless," Sabine said.

"Hmm, but a nuisance. You swat this fly, it keeps coming back."

"You know who he was seeing?" Martin said to Sabine. "Stefan Schell. Remember, from Göttingen? He's staying at the hotel."

"He's in Berlin? I thought he was dead."

"No, in Moscow. Now there's somebody who would have stories. At your house in the country."

"He was never—"

Martin shrugged his shoulders. "But he worked with Heisenberg. We always wanted to know how far along they were, remember?"

She put her hand on his arm, saying good-bye the way she had greeted him. "You ask him. I'm retired."

Looking at him, the old direct look, where Peter got it, her touch warm on his arm.

"I'll just get your coat," Kurt said, going to the closet, out of earshot, a second alone.

"It's funny, seeing you again," she said, her voice low. "How things turn out. Things you don't expect."

"No. Should I thank you for this? Getting me out?"

"It's not so bad here. They like to watch each other. What the neighbor is doing. But we're building something too." She looked up. "It's important for Peter to have you. For you to have each other."

"And Kurt doesn't mind?"

"Of course he minds." She looked toward the hall, Kurt taking a coat off a hanger. "And he's not retired. Be careful."

Martin raised his eyebrows.

"Not officially. But they have to approve. His arrangements. You need friends to get anything done. So," she said, louder now, "tomorrow. You're sure it's not too early for you?"

"Here we are," Kurt said, helping him with his coat.

"Thank you. For everything."

Kurt nodded. "It's a good start."

"I'll see you in the morning," he said to Sabine, not sure how to say good-bye, a handshake now too formal. But before he could step toward her, she backed away, covering her mouth, another choking cough, and shooed him toward the door. A quick look between them.

"Again?" Kurt said. "You should see somebody about this."

"It's nothing," she said, a gasp, catching her breath, then miming a cigarette. "Bad habits."

———

The East German television studio was in Adlershof, on the southeast fringes of Berlin, out toward Köpenick, an easy S-bahn ride and then an easy walk from the station, but Erich Schmidt went by car, with a driver in a cap and suit. Peter sat between Sabine and Martin, playing guide, craning his head at the window. Through Friedrichshain, across the river to Treptow, patched-up buildings still standing in barren lots cleared of rubble, shells of factories waiting demolition.

"The Russians are over there," Peter said. "In Karlshorst. The old Occupation headquarters. You can see the troops sometimes if you go there, but mostly they stay at their camp."

"Troops."

"To protect the Republic. It's like being in Russia, Kurt says, the language, the food. They're here, but they don't learn German."

More industrial scrubland, pockmarked buildings, allotment gardens. They turned onto Rudower Chaussee, the main road slicing through the town. On their left, the studio, a tall central building with transmitting aerials on top, flanked by wings of single-story admin offices. Behind, acres of sound stages and technical shops, more offices, all of them new.

"You see up there?" Peter was pointing across the street. "That was my surprise. I had the idea last night, but I didn't say. You know what that is?"

Martin peered out. Another new office building, this one with more glass. In the courtyard, visible as they turned onto Am Studio, two giant metal spheres, propped up on steel frames.

"What?" he said, playing along.

"The research institute for the Academy of Sciences. They built it out here. Isn't that lucky? You can work there and we could drive out together. Every day."

"I don't know yet where I'll be. The university, most likely. Research is a young man's game. I'm out of date."

"But you could request it. A position here. They wouldn't say no to you."

Martin smiled. "They might."

"Anyway, you're not so old. You could catch up. It's what you like, isn't it? Research? That's why you worked at those places. Los Alamos. Harwell. And then we could go to work together. It's nice, the car. And the DFF pays, anyway. They wouldn't care if I brought you with me. It's the same to them." Everything thought through.

Martin glanced over Peter's head to Sabine, a parent's look, and for a second, wedged together in the backseat, the fantasy seemed real, they were a family.

"Well, we'll see," Martin said, a parent's answer.

They pulled up to a traffic barrier, a striped pole like the one in Invalidenstrasse, but no machine guns here, just a man with a clipboard who waved them through. Martin wondered what had happened to the boy in the ambulance, probably locked in some basement cell, maybe beaten, Erich Schmidt's just society. Here, at least, no one was trying to leave it. The parking lot was full of boxy Trabants, noisy with delivery trucks.

Inside, Peter was all business, sure of himself, popular with the staff. Waves and smiles but no idle lingering, everybody hurrying.

"New pages," a woman said, handing them to him.

"For today?" he said, not complaining, just planning his time.

"It's not too bad. Mostly you react." She made a face, an exaggerated who me?

"How long do I have?"

"An hour. Take them with you to makeup." She looked at Martin.

"Oh," Peter said, "you know *Mutti*. This is Martin." Not "my father," not ready for that yet.

46

The woman shook his hand. "If you want to watch, stay over there. No talking. The mikes pick up everything."

"I'll show him around," Sabine said. "While you make up. Is that all right?"

The woman nodded. "Don't trip over the wires." Her face deadpan, maybe not a joke.

The interesting thing was how many people it took, holding light meters, adjusting marks, just passing through the sound stage, busy doing something. The set was a living room, about the size of Kurt's but more conventionally furnished, a lumpy old Biedermeier chair, clearly the father's, porcelain figurines, and a wall clock. Where the family gathered and Erich and his scrapes got sorted out and lessons were learned. How much of it did Peter believe? Or Sabine, watching her politics play out, no longer abstract. What they'd fought for, the great experiment. His new home.

During the run-through, the boy who played Erich's older brother, the one who never got into trouble, kept stepping a little past his mark into Peter's spot, never blatant, just stealing a piece of light, the sort of move an amateur wouldn't notice. But Peter threw him a look and stepped around him, a piece of choreography that put him in the center of the shot and blocked the other boy from doing it again. So much for Kurt's theory that he was just playing himself. Martin leaned forward in the visitor's chair, fascinated. Every reaction on the beat, an actor's timing, fluid. But all the audience saw was some young version of themselves, a decent boy tripped up by his own high spirits, grateful for the road map his father supplied out of his lumpy chair. In *Die Familie Schmidt*, in the DDR, everything worked out in the end.

"What did you think?" Peter asked during the break. "The new line, about sharing. Was the emphasis right?" Face earnest, all that mattered right now.

"I thought it was fine."

A quick glance, skeptical.

"Watch out for your brother though."

Peter smiled, conspiratorial. "You saw? He does the same thing every time. It never works and he keeps doing it."

"They're going to do another run-through," Sabine said. "Let's take a walk out back."

"We can see my new lab," Martin said with a smile to Peter, who barely noticed, taking his place with the others.

Outside, Sabine lit a cigarette. "The dream factory," she said, nodding to the hangar-like buildings around the parking lot. "But we can talk out here."

"The walls have ears here too."

"It's not a joke. You forget they're listening and you say things."

"Last night?"

"I don't think they listen to us. He has so many friends. And he checks. Every week. But maybe. The Berolina, yes. A new building, it's easy to put the wires in." She looked up, placing a hand on his arm. "You look terrible. I suppose that's my fault too."

"Nobody said that."

"It should have been both of us. Not just you."

"Then I'd still look terrible and you would too. So what would be the point?"

"No point," she said, blowing smoke. She looked up. "I didn't know it would be for good."

"It wasn't. I'm here."

"For us, I mean. You don't just pick up—it's too late for that." Her brown eyes darting away.

"Then why did you arrange this? It wasn't Kurt's idea. Why did you bring me here?"

"You didn't have to come."

"What choice was there? Prison or—" He spread his hand to take in where they were. "You must have counted on that. A factor in the equation."

"You make me sound like—"

"It's a math term, that's all."

"Oh, math," she said, tossing the cigarette. "Let's go see your lab." She started walking.

He hesitated, still on the steps. "Tell me what's going on. Why be careful of Kurt?"

She looked at him, a question.

"What you said last night."

"Just—be careful of everybody. It's good advice."

"No, you meant Kurt."

"Oh, now you know what's inside my head."

"Not anymore. I used to know you better than anybody."

She looked at him, then started to walk again, Martin following. "So why be careful?"

"Because he always has some idea. You'll see when you get to know him."

"Why will I get to know him? More dinners? Like that charade last night. He's your husband and he's jealous. I'd be too."

"Are you?"

"You're taken," he said, more abrupt than he'd intended.

"Yes," she said, surprised at his tone. "I'm taken. Another exchange I made."

"Do you love him?"

"My god, love. Whatever that is. I don't know."

"Yes, you do," he said, touching her.

She pulled back. "Don't. Someone sees."

"Why did you bring me here?" he said again.

"I told you, for Peter."

49

"For Peter."

"It's the truth. Why else?"

"Maybe you thought you owed me something."

"For going to prison? You knew what you were doing. You knew the risks. You blame me for that? Because I said I didn't know. To save myself and Peter?"

"No, I don't blame you for that."

"Well, then—"

"Do you remember the first night? In Albrechtstrasse?"

"More memories."

"You said we'd never lie to each other. When you told me why you slept with me. To see if we fit."

She was quiet for a minute. "But then we had to do—what we did. It was all lies, living like that. So no one would know. We had to lie to everyone."

"But not to each other."

"No, not to each other." She looked up. "What?"

"Sabine, I know. I've known for a long time."

"Know what?" she said, rattled.

He looked at her, saying nothing.

"Know what?" she said again, her voice stronger, defiant.

"Let's sit," he said, pointing to a bench in the small plaza by the Institute. He looked up at the building. "And what does he think I'm going to do here?"

"I don't know. What you always did. Numbers."

He nodded. "I did a lot of them in prison. Probability theory. Working out equations. Follow the equations and it's there. The proof." He turned to her. "It was you. You gave me away. You told them."

She shook her head, flustered.

"It was you. I know it."

"Know. How can you know?"

"I worked it out. The problem. It couldn't have been anybody else. So now we both know. No lies."

She looked into the street. "How long have you thought this?"

"Years. You locked the cell. And then after all that time, a visitor. From out of the blue. Come to the DDR. So why?"

She looked down. "I didn't lock the cell," she said quietly.

"Yes, you did. I was in it." Another pause. "I know."

She said nothing for a minute, looking at the pavement, then at the glass building, anywhere.

"They had to give them somebody, to save Milner. A distraction. Not a link, a dead end."

"A distraction."

"To keep MI5 away from Milner. They didn't know about you. So then—this bone is tossed to them and they run after it. Away from Milner. Away from the others. They got you, but no one else. That was the logic of it."

"And this bone. You get to toss it. An impeccable source. You made a deal with the Brits."

She said nothing.

"You just did the typing. You knew, but you didn't know. And now you were afraid for your child. You couldn't testify—a wife, after all—but you could slip them evidence. They wouldn't need testimony. They'd have me cold."

She looked at him, her eyes growing wider, the story building like an accusation. "How do you—" she said quietly.

"Probabilities," he said. "And you suggested this?"

"No, of course not."

"But you did it."

"I was ordered. You don't have a choice about these things. You remember what it was like."

"But it was me." Not angry, some physical pain, still here.

"I couldn't—"

"Sabine, ten years."

"We didn't know it would be so long."

"What would have been all right? Four years, five? Never mind, I got lucky. Somebody got me out."

"And that's what you think? It's to make it up to you?"

"No, some other plan. I know you. There's always a plan. So why did you bring me here?"

"It's not something you can make up for," she said, not answering, still in her own thoughts. "Something like that."

"No."

She turned to him. "And you can't take it back. It's done. And after, you think, how could I do that? And then, how could they ask me to do that? What kind of people. But in those days you didn't think about that."

"Ten years. Not even a Christmas card. A picture of him. Nothing."

She nodded, eyes down. "They wouldn't allow it. To keep the story. By then, it's all you know, that life. Whatever the Service wanted. Right then, save Milner. Think about the rest later. And then it turns out you have years to do it. Years to think about it."

"Why now? Tell me the truth."

"The truth. And you'd believe me after this. Whatever I said."

"Yes."

"So you don't learn either."

She stood up, her movements jerky, caged.

"You know what these are?" she said, nodding to the metal spheres. "Labs to test conditions in space. This shape—it offers the least surface area to the atmosphere. Or something like that. Someone told me. They were going to live in these, measure things. Perfect space conditions. The instruments were— And then it turned out their breathing threw the instruments off. There was no point. They had to breathe. It's like this country. They forgot people have to breathe." She turned to him. "But it's still the right experiment. You can live here. Have a life."

"Why, Sabine."

"I thought there would be more time. So you would get to know each other."

He waited.

"It's true, what I said. It's for Peter. I wanted you to come to be his father."

"He has a father."

"No, you. I don't want to leave him with Kurt. You're his father."

"Leave him?"

She turned away, facing the street. "I'm sick."

He stood up, taking her shoulders. "What do you mean, sick? With what?"

"Cancer." A forced smile. "Everyone was right. The cigarettes would kill me."

"How serious is it? Have you seen a doctor?"

"Of course. Don't look like that. There are good doctors here. It's something they brag about, at the Party Congresses."

"And?"

"And there's nothing more they can do." The words as direct as her stare. "I waited too long."

"I don't believe it."

"I know. It's hard at first. I thought I was too young."

"I mean I don't believe there's nothing more they can do."

She ignored this. "So I had to make a plan. It took a long time, to arrange the swap. The British—"

"And what does Kurt say?" Cheerfully playing host.

"He doesn't know."

"What?"

"He doesn't notice things—things about me."

Martin said nothing, at a loss.

"So," she said, picking up the thread, "I wanted more time. For you and Peter. In case Kurt fights for him."

Martin raised his head.

"Don't worry. You're his legal father. Kurt never adopted him. But if you weren't here, he would be the guardian. After I died. So I needed you here. You'd become fond of each other—he'd want to be with you. And a socialist hero. Kurt has a lot of friends, but to fight you—that wouldn't be so easy. But first I had to get you here."

"It didn't take much. One old spy and two kids."

A twitch in her face, not really a smile. "Something would come up, then something else. Always a delay. And I couldn't push too much because I knew what he was thinking. That it was for me, that I was still— And the more I asked, the more he would think that. So it took time. But now I don't have too much. He'll have to know soon. And then what?" She looked up. "You'll take him, won't you? You won't run away, leave him to Kurt?"

"How could I run away?"

"You have an American passport. There's no wall for you."

"Expired."

"But not revoked. You're still a citizen." Something she knew, had found out. "Unless you become one here. Have they asked you?"

"No, not yet." He stopped for a second, looking at her. "So we're back at the beginning. The useful American. Marry him and it's a ticket out."

"You think it was like that?"

"And now what? Get Peter out?"

"No, then Kurt would fight you. And that would be different. Taking a child out of the country. Taking Erich Schmidt? No." She stopped. "But you'll be all right here, both of you. You'll be father and son. You'll be happy."

"You want me to be happy," he said, hearing his voice, the edge in it. "Whatever happened to a 'better world.' I thought that's what you wanted. Why you did it. All of it."

She looked at him, surprised, a razor nick, then turned away. "Well, I didn't get that either. And now listen to us, the way we talk to each other." She took a breath. "But what difference does it make? What you think of me. Just tell me—you'll take him, won't you?"

Martin nodded.

She exhaled, as if she were blowing invisible smoke. "Good. So that's done," she said, bending her head.

He turned her to face him. "We'll see another doctor."

A faint smile. "Americans always want to see another doctor. It won't change anything."

"How—?" He stopped.

"How long?" She shrugged. "I ask but there's never an answer. I'm coughing blood now, so that's not a good sign. Months? He said more radiation probably wouldn't work, the cancer's too advanced. So that means it must be soon, no?" She looked down. "Well, the truth is, I didn't want it. All the side effects and what's the point? They can give you something near the end, for the pain, so that's good. But until then, it's still my life. Don't look like that," she said, reaching up to touch his cheek. "We have to think about him now. You'll help me with him, when I talk to him?"

Martin nodded.

She looked down again, biting her lips. "So look who's here at the end. You know there was never anybody else. All those years. There was never anybody else."

"There is now."

"Yes. But it's not the same. If that means anything to you."

"How is it, then?"

"Like being in a play."

"How do you mean?"

"I play the happy wife, he plays the happy husband. You know the only one who sees the truth? Peter. An actor can tell. If the line readings are off."

"Sabine," he said, reaching for her.

"No, it's finished for us. It's only for Peter now." She looked up at him. "We were good together, though. Even the Service said so. They didn't like to use husbands and wives, remember? Too many complications. But they used us. We were good."

"You were. I just passed papers."

"No, more than that. We were good together."

He looked at her, the damp air curling her dyed hair, the gray roots beginning to come through. "Until we weren't," he said.

CHAPTER 3

Kurt was waiting for them at the school.

"How was *Die Familie Schmidt*?"

"New lines. A whole page. At the last minute," Peter said, in high spirits, still in the fantasy of the new family Keller, making plans on the ride back. A visit to Köpenick, a boat on the Müggelsee. Had Martin ever seen the Ishtar Gate? The grim city suddenly a box of treats.

"No trouble for you, I'm sure," Kurt said.

"No, but they shouldn't do it. At the last minute." He glanced at his watch. "I'll be late. Tell Kurt my idea about the Institute. Maybe he knows somebody at the Academy. Do you?" This to Kurt, but still on his way to the door.

"Why?"

"He'll tell you. It's a good idea."

"What's all this?" Kurt said, watching him go through the door.

"The Academy of Sciences has a research branch across the street from the studio. So we could ride down together, if I worked there. I told him it isn't what I do, but he's not hearing it."

"No, just what he wants to hear. Well, you'll be meeting them

57

soon enough, the Academy. There's a reception for you. But I've already told them you'd prefer something at the university here. That's right, isn't it? They were talking about Leipzig but I said it had to be Berlin. That's what was agreed. Unless you—"

"No, Berlin, that's right. The idea was to be near Peter."

"But maybe not so near as across the street," Kurt said, smiling. "Even with the car." He turned to Sabine, as if this had jogged his memory. "You take the car. We're going to Gerhard for the interview, so we can walk. You don't mind? It's not far."

"To *Neues Deutschland*?"

"No, Gerhard works from his own office." He turned to Martin. "He spent the war in America, one of the exiles. He's very excited to meet you. Come."

Once again, Martin felt swooped up, Kurt's arm around him moving him away. By the time he waved to Sabine, they had already started down the street.

"Peter seems very happy to see you," Kurt said. "You had a good day?"

"It's the novelty of it. It'll wear off. It was interesting to see him at work. He likes it."

"Yes, maybe too much. It's a worry. What if he wants to go on with this business?"

"I thought you wanted him to stay on the show."

"Now, yes. It's important to the Party. But when he grows up—"

"It's a little early to worry, don't you think. I didn't know what I wanted at that age. Did you?"

"No. As you say," he said, conciliatory, not meaning it. "But acting. A boy so clever."

"What were you thinking? A lawyer?"

"Now you're laughing at me. Well, all right, it's true. Why not? Thiele and Son. We could work together." Arranging things.

They had turned onto Unter den Linden, just past the university.

"Where's his office? Gerhard, right?"

"Jägerstrasse. A publisher there. He's a translator. But I think we'll save the interview for another day. *Neues Deutschland* can wait a little."

"Then why tell Sabine—?"

"Sabine doesn't work with me. In my business. I know, it was different with you. But my clients. Sometimes it's very private, things you can't share. Easier not to know."

"So where are we going?" Martin said, suddenly apprehensive. A change of plan.

"To see things. It's natural you would ask for that. We'll walk to the Brandenburg Gate. You see how all the old sights are on this side of the wall, the real Berlin."

"I've seen them," Martin said.

"They'll bring back memories for you, then. All still here. Well, not all. Kranzler's gone. Look." Not making eye contact. "And here the Soviet Embassy. Built after the war, but in the historical style." An enormous neoclassical pile, even heavier than the Stalin blocks on Karl-Marx-Allee, offices for hundreds. "It's an important embassy for them," Kurt said, stretching out the minute, long enough for them to be seen. "And there is the Adlon. You remember that."

Martin nodded. The lobby with the frog fountain, the bar crowd from the ministries on Wilhelmstrasse, Sabine meeting him, running late, breathless through the revolving door.

"So. I'll leave you here. See the Quadriga on the Gate? All repaired. You can go closer, but not near the wall. It's not allowed."

"Am I meeting somebody?" Back in that world, waiting on park benches.

"I don't know. A sightseeing walk only. The rest? I'm not part of that. So have a look." He started to leave, then turned, a glance over at Martin. "Just be a tourist."

But there were no tourists, only a few office workers who hurried past the Gate, the ugly wall behind. He walked around Pariser Platz. The same feeling he used to have making a drop. Eyes out there somewhere, waiting for the flash of an envelope. Every sound magnified, the snap of a twig, footsteps. And then a man walking toward him, a second of relief, the familiar outline, tall with slightly drooped shoulders, the short, military hair, on time as usual. Walking toward him now, the same shoulders, out of the Soviet Embassy and past the hotel, opening a map. Two tourists at the Brandenburg Gate, where there were no tourists.

"Andrei," he said.

The Russian smiled. "A long time, my friend. You've gone gray."

"What are you doing here?"

"I work here," he said, nodding back to the embassy. "Cultural attaché. I've come up in the world. Not that it fools anybody."

"Then why bother?"

"It's important—to keep up appearances. You know how that is. The Stasi know we're here and we know they know. And so forth. But we're not supposed to be here, so we're not. We're—cultural attachés." He smiled. "It's good to see you."

"And you," Martin said, but was it? A door he thought had been shut.

"I'm sorry it's been so long. For what it's worth, I thought we could have done more. To protect you."

"But you didn't."

Andrei shrugged. "I wasn't there. They sent me back. I was your control. Once things started, I'd be the next. So it was safer. You remember the last meeting, I couldn't come."

"At Selfridges. Safety in numbers. I remember." He looked over. "And now? Why did Kurt arrange a meeting?"

"I arranged it. He's the messenger. He made the deal for you, but he's just a messenger. Not one of us."

"You made the swap?"

"The Germans made it. That goes down very well here, choosing the Republic. An international figure. And, to be honest, not a Russian. They have too many Russians already. So."

"But you wanted it."

"It's an opportunity for us. Kurt saw that right away. He has a good feel for that."

"He did all this for you?"

"He asked for our help. To give the Germans our blessing. After all, you're one of us. Even now. So we did, give our blessing. No problem for Moscow. Professor Keller is—retired. Inactive. All yours."

"But still an opportunity for you."

Andrei looked over at him, then nodded. "So, now that you have given me your good directions," he said, folding the map, "let me buy you a cup of coffee."

"Why all the theater? It's not London. You're on home ground here. Soviet territory." He looked toward the wall.

"Yes, but the Germans think it's their home ground, so certain niceties have to be observed. That's what makes you so useful. You're not Soviet."

"Useful."

"We'll have coffee. For old times' sake. I know a place."

They started down toward Friedrichstrasse.

"Are any of them still there? At Harwell."

"From our time, no. We had to start over." He took a second. "You've seen Sabine? She's well?"

"Yes," he said, the lie effortless.

"Kurt said she asked for this. I said, why not come to us herself? An old colleague. But no. She's closed the door on us, I don't know why." He looked at Martin. "An interesting woman. A new husband, but she asks for the old one."

"I think she feels guilty. About not going to prison when I did. So she wanted to do something, to get me out." He looked at Andrei. "Nobody else was."

"My god, to have such scruples. At such a moment. Would she have felt better going with you? A woman with a young child? Well, no matter. You know, the truth is, we have nothing for her to do here anyway. The Germans do it for us. It was different when the West was open, when you could go back and forth. A busy time for us, with the Americans, all of them. But now they're over there and we're over here. They never thought about that when they put up the wall, that it would cut us off too. Now we have more people than we need. Unless they have a special quality." A small nod. "So we meet."

"Why?"

Andrei looked up, surprised at his tone.

"I'll never work in the West again. I'll never have access again. So why?"

"A different kind of access. Only you have it. Here we are. The coffee's not bad."

Martin stopped, putting his hand on Andrei's sleeve.

"I'm not in this anymore."

"Martin. More scruples? Now you? First, listen. Come."

It was noisy inside, the warm air filled with hissing steam and clattering cups and people talking over each other. Andrei led them to a table in the corner, out of the worst of the noise, and sat with his back to the wall, giving the room a quick once-over, Service training. The waitress knew him, nodding when he held up his fingers, two of the usual.

"I'll be your control again, so that's easy. We don't have to get used to each other. The first meeting place will be on the bridge by the Dom. You're interested in seeing Berlin, taking walks. Establish that. So it's not unusual to be there. If I can't stop, the old signal with the newspaper, yes? If you need to contact me, leave a message for Bendler at the Adlon. Not the embassy. We have to assume it's watched."

"By the Germans? I thought you were pals."

"Not everyone from the West is on the other side of the wall."

"And they care if I pay a visit to the Russian Embassy? Let's make it easier for them. I won't. Not any of it. I'm not interested."

"That's not an option." He looked away as the waitress appeared. "Thank you." Then turned back to Martin. "Let's not waste time. We know each other too well for that. The fallback to the Dom is the tram stop at Hackescher Markt. Now the story. Prison has changed you. A lot of time to think. You believed sharing atomic secrets would bring peace—a state of mutual deterrence. But the arms race has made you realize we are farther from peace than ever. So now a disillusion, a regret for having played any part in that. But how to correct it, now that the genie is out of the bottle? How to stop the build up? Governments will never do it. Only scientists themselves can make this happen, can stop it. A moral act."

Martin stared at him, eyes growing wider.

"Yes, I know," Andrei said, a small smile. "Rule number one. Make the story true. Or as close to the truth as possible. You're comfortable so far? With your story?"

"Who wrote it, you?"

"You. Even in Wakefield Prison, conversations like this, someone hears— You took your time. You didn't want to admit this is what had happened. Not peace, a bigger war. Your part in that. But now I think this reflects your thinking, yes?"

"It doesn't matter what I think."

"Of course it does. You have to be convincing. You have to believe in what you're saying."

"Convincing to whom?"

Andrei sat back, toying with his coffee spoon.

"You know, it's one thing to have these thoughts in Wakefield Prison. What harm? You talk to each other, it's like talking to the walls. Unfortunately people have begun having these thoughts in the Soviet Union. That's a different matter. At Dubna, the research institute. First, whispers. Then talk. The morality of what they're doing. Morality. At Dubna. The only morality there is kilotons. To defend the country. This idea to stop work, it's unthinkable. Something had to be done. So, first, you weed out the talkers, the so-called moral scientists, with so much on their consciences. Your old friend Schell, for instance. Time for him to go back to Germany. No more discussions, papers passing from one to the other. So, a solution. He's gone. But now he's here. With the same ideas, no doubt. So where does he whisper? In whose ears?" He opened his hand to Martin.

"You want me to spy on Stefan Schell."

"We want you to listen to him. That shouldn't be hard. You're old friends. You think the same way. In your case, a little more pragmatic, let's hope, but the same. You're not a Western agent—you have ten years away to prove that. Not Soviet either. But a sympathizer at the bottom. Old Reds. Someone he can trust. Who understands his work. It's a special quality, to be able to do that. So he confides in you. After a while, it's like talking to himself, his real thoughts."

"I won't do it," Martin said quietly.

"But it must be carefully done," Andrei said, going on. "Too quick and you scare him away. First, the trust. He'll be suspicious. Here's a man who is a hero in the Soviet Union, a god in the scientific community, abroad too, and these last few years—they make things difficult for him. Not the most intelligent way to handle this. Clumsy, like a hammer. Confiscating papers. Stupid. But now he's here, a fresh start. And who's also here? His old friend. With his own scars, his own story. So we begin slowly. You meet at the Academy reception. A reunion. Then Dresden. He's at Rossendorf and you come to give a lecture. A nice dinner together. Old stories, old times. A friendship."

"I won't do it," Martin said again.

"The lecture has already been announced."

"Andrei—"

"Martin. My old friend. The Service expects you to do this."

"I'm not a spy. Not that kind of spy."

"One day explain to me the difference. But right now we have work to do. I know you're loyal to us. All the years in prison, loyal."

Martin cocked his head, a question.

"We have to listen. Sometimes people—there's a despair, it's natural, and they say things they shouldn't, about other people, the Service. But you never did that. You never betrayed us. No one questions your loyalty."

Martin looked down, following Andrei's spoon as it stirred the coffee, round and round, a grinding down. Listening for years while his life drained away.

"Who did you have inside? I'm curious."

"Martin."

Neither said anything for a minute, the air still, everything else background hum.

"What are my options?" Martin said finally.

"To help us, of course. It's not much to ask. There's no risk to you. Not like before. That was illegal. This is—"

"What?"

"As you say, we're on home ground. We have an influence here. Nobody is going to arrest you for helping us. Instead, the DDR welcomes you with open arms, a good position, a pension, maybe even a medal—your services to the Party. A comfortable life. With your family, who want you here. Good feelings all around. Of course, it could all go the other way. I don't like to think that, but if the Service felt you—"

"They'd make my life hell."

"Nobody's anticipating that."

"And my other options?"

Andrei said nothing.

"I don't have to stay here. I could go back to the States."

"Yes, imagine the welcoming committee. It's true, it's a new government now. Nobody wants to go back to the old days. Spy trials. Old crimes. And no evidence. But now there would be. If the Service were threatened, someone disloyal, we would have to make this available. And then? A trial, I think. They would have to. You understand."

Martin nodded, his neck constricted, feeling hands pressing around it.

"You'd throw me to the wolves. I'd go to prison again."

"Wolves. We want you to be an honored scientist in the DDR. Happy with your family. You deserve this after so many years." He paused. "Schell? He's so important to you?"

"What do you want? In the end. Discredit him?"

Andrei shook his head. "Contain him. What the West wants to do with us. Make him harmless. Already he's gone from Moscow.

So the worst is contained. And it's good for the DDR, someone with his international stature—someone they can send to conferences. Window dressing."

"Like me."

Andrei dipped his head. "So much in common."

Martin looked away, his throat tight again.

"But these ideas of his, in Russia it's impossible, this kind of thinking. And people listen to him. So we have to know what he's doing, what he's saying."

Martin stared at the street, a series of locks clicking in his head.

"Martin," Andrei said calmly. "You can't go back to England. In fact, without a new passport you can't go anywhere. If you do somehow make it to America, you'll face charges. Moscow? The Soviets prefer you to be here. This is your option."

Martin said nothing, listening to the hiss of coffee steam, then turned to Andrei. "What else? Tell me the rest."

"Just keep your ears open. You were always good at that."

"I don't know anybody in Berlin. What would I hear?"

"You know Kurt."

Martin raised his head.

"A man with many interests. So many people to please."

"Including you. What's wrong?"

"Nothing. Just keep your ears open."

"He got me out."

"Yes, and you're grateful." He looked over. "We got you out. You know, I'm looking forward to this, working together again. It was always a pleasure with you. So quick to understand the situation." The words put out to sit on the table, a test question.

Martin met his eyes. "I don't have a choice."

Andrei nodded. "You made it. Years ago."

He walked back to the hotel, detouring through the Gendarmenmarkt, someone who took long walks to see Berlin. Establishing his
story. The bridge by the Dom. The tram stop at Hackescher Markt.
No end of meeting places in a city like Berlin. He felt his throat
tighten again. Changing one prison for another, Digby had said.
Who liked to talk, maybe Andrei's ear there. Not another prisoner,
someone with better access. Why not? What would be his story?
A Yorkshire family, generations in the pits, good trade unionists
and then more, pushed by hard times. Anything was possible. Lis-
teners were everywhere, in old friendships, Göttingen memories.
Kurt had welcomed him to dinner, a family reunion, maybe to
listen to him. Everybody listening, an echo chamber. He turned,
glancing over his shoulder. No shapeless raincoat today. Unless he
hadn't spotted him. But you never lose that extra sense. Call off
the meeting, walk past Andrei, don't take chances. And he hadn't.
Never caught. Until the Service decided to throw him away. He
stopped for a second on the bridge, taking deep breaths. This is
your option.

At the Berolina, Hans was in his usual lobby chair, hat and
coat still on, as if he might be called away at any second to a crime
scene. How long had he listened for the Stasi, their ear at Springer?
Another caught spy, brought home to idle in lobbies, hoping to be
an ear again.

"Herr Keller," he said, standing up and taking off his hat. Same
bald head and ferret eyes.

"Herr—Rieger, isn't it?" Martin said, placing him. "*Neues Deutschland*. How did the interview go?"

Hans shrugged. "A very careful man. I suppose after Moscow—" He let the thought finish itself. "He said to give you his regards."

"Me?"

"Old classmates. You never said."

"This was before the war, Herr Rieger. I'm surprised he remembered."

"Such a famous character?"

"So, the science wasn't a problem?" Martin said, moving away from it.

"Only for me," Rieger said, his eyes signaling a joke. "I asked him what he was working on. Subatomic particles. I didn't even bother to write it down. Who understands such things? My readers? Even if they let you print it. Anything like that, what's allowed?"

"So what will you write?"

"How does it feel to be home?" he said, brushing this away with his hand. "What do you think of the new Germany? Your impressions. The usual."

"Even so, I'll look forward to reading it. It's so many years now." A new idea. "How does he know I'm here?"

"I told him I had met you. I thought, two such scientists at the Berolina? Maybe they know each other. And they do. But you didn't say." The voice suggestive, prying.

"Yes, well," Martin said, not biting. "It was nice to run into you again—"

"Actually, if you have a moment?"

Martin waited.

"Invalidenstrasse."

"The exchange?"

"No, the escape. I'm interested in that."

"I thought the papers didn't run wall stories anymore."

"Somebody climbs over, or digs a tunnel, yes, old news. But here is one man dead. And the other, maybe he envies him. He's at Hohenschönhausen." He caught Martin's look. "Where people are interrogated. Not pleasant for him. And the police investigate. They want to know about the ambulance. So I thought, I want to know too."

"They stole it, I thought."

"Yes, but how? They bribed someone at the hospital to steal it for them. With West marks. Hard currency. So now the police are interested. Who has hard currency?"

"They weren't hospital workers?"

Hans shook his head. "And no loss to the Republic. I went to see his mother, the dead boy. A good boy—of course—but in and out of trouble. You know, officially there is no crime in the DDR—no need—but then, where do you get the bananas, the blue jeans? Without a black market? And who runs it? Thieves like this. But think how much more there is for a thief in the West. You think they're looking for freedom? Better loot. When I was at Springer, we saw this all the time, the crooks coming through. So you take them—who turns a German away?—and call them something else. But if they paid for the ambulance in West marks, they were in the black market. How else? With guns. Not so easy to find here. So now real gangsters. Chicago."

"You went to see his mother?"

"Everybody wants to talk. At first, anyway." He looked over at Martin. "It's a hobby of mine, these stories. What happened? It's interesting."

Martin said nothing.

"So you don't mind? A question?"

"What?"

"The shooting. It was like this, I understand." He leaned over and moved an ashtray on the table, then a napkin, a demonstration. "The barrier is here. The guards. And you were here, yes?"

"I guess. I really don't—"

"Herr Keller, someone shoots at you, it's a moment of sharp focus, no? Usually that's the case."

Martin nodded, seeing the driver's face now, hearing the tires.

"So you and Herr Thiele are here. His car, here. Then the guards. Then here, freedom. So-called. If they make it."

"But they didn't."

"No, the guards shoot at the ambulance. It crashes. The driver himself is shot, the other— Herr Thiele says, call the hospital, and you both get into his car to leave and there's an end to it. It's correct?"

"Yes."

"Good. The guards said it was like this, but it's always good to check. Two sources."

"You talked to the guards?"

Rieger nodded. "For the timing."

"I don't understand."

"Herr Keller, you don't find it interesting that those boys used their guns before they were at the barrier?" He pointed to the ashtray and napkin, his mock-up crossing. "Why not make a run for it? The barrier is up. The ambulance has a powerful engine. Why shoot?"

"The guards had machine guns. They'd be killed."

"Perhaps. But they weren't shooting at the guards. They were shooting at you."

Seeing the face again at the ambulance window, the gun sticking out.

"It wasn't like that. Everything happened at once. Fast."

"So we slow it down, to see the order. They shoot before the guards do. Before they need to. And they shoot at you."

Martin looked at him, a chill.

"Meaning what, exactly?"

"I don't know. That's why I'm asking you. How it seemed to you."

"It seemed like they were shooting at anything. To distract the guards."

"It's possible, yes. Boys that age."

"It was just—all over the place. I'm not sure they knew what they were doing. Except trying to get out."

Rieger nodded. "Amateurs. A piece of luck for you. You never thought—?"

"I wasn't thinking about anything. Just keeping my head down."

"Yes, it's like that. Everyone says so."

"Well," Martin said, ending it. "This help?"

"Yes. Thank you. Everyone agrees. That's important. How it happened. Why—that's something else."

"What do you think?"

"I don't know yet. But as I say, it's a hobby of mine, stories like these."

"Even if nobody's going to print them?"

"Oh, the truth is always useful." He paused. "It's always valuable to somebody."

Die Familie Schmidt didn't film on Saturdays, so it became Martin's day with Peter, shared, at least for now, with Kurt. The excuse was his car, a standard-model Mercedes, rare on this side of the wall.

"It's far, Biesdorf, so this is more convenient."

"He just likes to drive it," Peter said. "People think it's someone from the West. Who? So it's a game we play."

"Be good with Bodo, yes?" Kurt said. "It's serious business for him, these fittings."

"He keeps the pins in his mouth," Peter said to Martin. "Maybe if he laughs, he'd swallow them." Mischievous, having fun.

"Peter?" Kurt said.

"I know. Be like Erich. Why didn't *Mutti* come?"

"He doesn't make ladies' clothes. So it's just the men. We have to get Martin a suit."

"For your party."

"A shaking-hands party. Not much fun."

"Can I come anyway?"

"Peter, what's the answer? You asked—"

"I'm asking Martin."

"Same answer," Martin said quickly, closing ranks.

Kurt glanced over, an amused thank-you.

"Whose hands do you shake?"

"Old scientists. Old teachers. Boring people."

"Tell them one of your stories."

Martin shook his head. "They can't hear. They all have hearing aids," he said, tapping his ear.

Peter giggled. Even better than swallowed pins.

In fact, the pins were in a small cushion on Herr Jahn's wrist, like a watch. Martin stood on a platform while Jahn pinned the trouser length, face rigid with concentration. Selecting the material had taken what seemed hours. Martin had expected Peter to be fidgety, but he had settled into a chair with a magazine, looking up from time to time to watch Martin being fitted, pleased to be there. It was Kurt who seemed impatient, looking at his watch, borrowing the phone to make a call, twice asking Jahn to confirm the delivery date.

"I can't perform miracles," Jahn said, put out by this. "I'm one person."

"But it'll be ready for the reception?"

"Yes, yes, I said so. He's easy to fit. Except the arms are irregular. You see?"

Peter looked up, a smile between them.

"So what do you think?" Peter said in the car. "One is longer than the other?"

Martin held out his arms, stretching. "Both. Orangutan arms."

"We have to make a stop at the office," Kurt said, still preoccupied.

"On Saturday?" Peter said. "Kurt's a hard worker. What about Weissensee?"

"Another day. I'm sorry. Something came up."

"That's okay," Peter said, determined to be sunny. "Look at her." A woman on the sidewalk with a string bag. "She thinks we're from the West. So who are we?"

Kurt's office was in one of the new buildings in Alexanderplatz, facing the Marienkirche.

"Two minutes," he said. "You don't mind?"

"We're fine."

"He works all the time," Peter said, watching him go. "At home too."

He was quiet for a minute. Outside, a man had stopped to look at the car, bending a little to see who was in it.

"Now who are we?" Martin said.

"Martin? Why did you and *Mutti* get a divorce?"

A question he should have expected.

"Well, we thought it would be easier. For her and for you. When everything happened."

"Prison."

"Yes, and the trial. It was a bad time. People weren't always nice. So we made it easier for her to come here. With you." Listening to himself, the rehearsed excuses. "What does she say?"

"She says you wanted it."

"Does she?" Thrown by this. "Well, I think it was both of us." One lie tangled with another.

"And now?"

"Now?"

"Will you get married again?"

"No. She's married to Kurt."

"But you still like each other?"

"Yes, of course. You don't stop liking people. But things change." He took a breath, looking over at him. "But not with children. That never changes. You love them when they're born and then you never stop. It's something in nature, I think. Even the orangutans are like that," he said, about to extend his arms, but then he caught Peter's look. No jokes. "Really."

"But you don't know me."

"You mean things like what do you like to eat or your favorite book? That doesn't matter. You never change the way you feel about a child. You can't. Anyway, I will get to know all the other things, now that I'm here."

Peter nodded. "And you still like *Mutti*." Asking it again. "You'd take care of her."

"Take care of her."

"If she got sick."

Martin looked at him, not sure what to say.

"Sometimes she coughs. I'm not sure why. But if she got sick, who's there? Kurt is always working. Tante Helene's in Babelsberg. So who takes care of her?"

Martin met his eyes, a pact. "We will."

Peter began to smile, then lowered his head, as if a smile would ruin the moment, break the promise.

Kurt took ten minutes and seemed rushed when he got back.

"I'll drop you first," he said to Peter.

"But we have all afternoon."

"I know. It can't be helped. Another time."

"What about Martin?"

"You don't mind to come with me? Some business at the warehouse. I don't like to go there alone. Not a good neighborhood."

Martin looked at him. Why, really?

Peter turned to Martin. "But you'll come back for dinner. *Mutti* said to ask you."

"I don't want her to go to any trouble." Another awkward evening.

"No trouble," Kurt said. "It's Saturday. We'll go out."

"To Ganymed?" Peter said.

"Oh, Ganymed. And what's the occasion?" Kurt said, an easy back-and-forth. "All right. If I can get us in. Saturday."

"You always get in."

"Best behavior, though."

Peter made a little salute. "Erich Schmidt."

"And not too late." The way they talked to each other, the familiar rhythm.

But when the car pulled up to the building in Weberwiese, it was Martin whom he hugged good-bye, a tentative reach, then a real hug, arms around his back, the feel of it sweeping through him, some wall breached.

"Thank you for doing this," Kurt said as they drove.

"What's in the warehouse?"

"Fertilizer." He looked over, a smile. "And some other things. Oranges, medicines. Hard currency items."

"You're carrying West marks?"

"No, no, we have other ways of paying," he said. "It's difficult for us, getting foreign currency."

"Us. The government?"

"I'm the representative. I act for them. They give me a list, what they want. And I make the deals."

"Off the books."

"Well, different books. The West makes it impossible for us to trade openly. You know the Hallstein Doctrine?"

Martin shook his head.

"You can only recognize one Germany. So everyone recognizes West Germany. It's rich, it has the Americans. We don't officially exist to the rest of the world. Except the Eastern bloc. Not a very good source of oranges or medicines. So."

"So you make arrangements. For fertilizer."

"Fertilizer. Coffee. But now it's a problem. I'm trying to make it more efficient. No commodities. Cash."

"Why?"

"Things arrive and then some minister—he can't help it, it's so tempting—sells a little on the black market. For his own pocket. A little here, a little there, and then it's a lot. Sticking to someone's fingers. I'm not a policeman. I don't have time to keep track. So why not eliminate this step? A cash transaction. One account to another. No more temptation. Like this business today. Is it my fault things disappear? Of course it's easier to hide the transaction if it's in commodities. You move cash, there are bank records. Evidence. If anybody wants to look. A possible embarrassment."

"For whom?"

Kurt looked over, as if Martin hadn't been following. "Bonn. The West German government. It's their money."

"What are they buying?"

"Political prisoners," Kurt said, matter-of-fact, another commodity.

Martin took a breath. "Is that legal?" he said, keeping his voice even, trying not to sound shocked.

"Legal. Legal is what the state says is legal. Bonn calls it 'special humanitarian activities.' Does that make it legal? But they can reunite families, get their spies back, maybe some people who want to leave. So for them a humanitarian activity. For us, hard currency, so we can live. But the same arrangement, whatever you call it."

"You're selling people?"

Kurt shrugged. "Bonn's willing to pay. To 'rescue' them. From this fate worse than death." He waved his hand to take in the country. "Of course, prison is not so pleasant, so the prisoners are glad to go. Finally over the wall. And no more expense to us. It's an exchange."

What Kurt had meant at Invalidenstrasse, Martin too distracted to take it in.

"How much? Is there a price?"

"Forty thousand marks," Kurt said easily, a salesclerk. "That's the usual."

"What's that in—?"

"About ten thousand dollars. Of course, adjusted for length of sentence, the prisoner's value to the Republic, and other such things."

"His value?"

"Yes. A worker, forty thousand marks, but a teacher would be more. A doctor even more, two hundred thousand marks, maybe."

Martin imagined them lined up at Invalidenstrasse, each with a hanging price tag.

"And what have they done?"

"Some, real spies. For Bonn. Always caught. Others, activities against the state."

"Such as?"

"Trying to leave. *Republikflucht.* Of course, more of these since the wall," he said, almost breezy. "And many who just want to be with their families in the West. It's good to be able to do something for them. This work, it's not just about the money."

"Am I supposed to know about this? Is anybody? From the sound of it—"

"It's a secret matter, yes. A back channel business. But you're experienced with secrets."

"Not like these."

Kurt smiled a little. "No, with you it was the secrets of the universe. Not some shell game with West marks. But here we are. I don't worry about you. I work with people for years and I don't trust them. But you— It's an unusual situation. When I saw you and Peter today, I thought, here is someone who would never make trouble for me because that would mean making trouble for his son. Everything I do, I do for Sabine and Peter. So our interests are the same." The voice innocent, any threat hidden in silk.

Martin looked out the window. They were in an old industrial area between the Ostbanhof and the Spree, now blocked by the wall, which ran here on this side of the river. The streets near the wall were gloomy and deserted, a dead zone of factories that had survived the bombing but still had broken windows and chains across the doors, warehouses with only an occasional truck at an open loading bay.

"I can see why you wanted somebody with you."

"Well, and your company. So we could talk. It's safe here really." Another minute, not sure how to begin. "You had a good meeting with Andrei?" Finally there, what he wanted to know. Watch your flank.

"Like old times. A tourist with a map. In case anyone was watching."

"Ah," Kurt said, "a little drama." Another second. "What did he want, if I can ask."

"To say good-bye. There's a pension. If I behave myself. The Stasi are sensitive about anyone else operating on their turf. So, see no evil, do no evil. Not even 'sorry' about prison. Just good-bye." He turned to Kurt. "Since you asked."

Kurt held up his hand. "You're right. No questions. That's how we survive here—no questions. But of course I was curious. So it's like Sabine. No gold watch either."

"I can't blame them. I'll never work in the West again—and what use am I to them here? So, good-bye and good luck. At least I'm here, not behind bars. He said you did a good job, by the way. With the swap. I hope they paid you."

"It was for Sabine."

"Still, work. They should pay you."

Kurt lifted his finger from the steering wheel. "Sometimes it's better to make a friend. You need a favor one day, it's there for you. Do a good job, they don't forget."

"We're all dispensable to them. You know that, don't you?" Putting an edge in his voice. "Look at me. Ten years."

"You're angry with them."

Martin turned away, a shrug. "Ten years."

Kurt turned left, the last turn before the wall.

"Ah, there's the good father. Well, not father, I think. Reverend." He pointed to a clergyman standing at the warehouse door, his white collar as conspicuous as a flag.

"A priest?" Martin said, surprised.

"No, Lutheran. He's with the Charities. That's how we get things into the country. The Church is protected in both Germanys, for their good works. It's one country for them. So if they move something from one diocese to another, it's their affair."

"But the money comes from Bonn."

Kurt nodded. "And then it goes to the Charities. For 'humanitarian activities.' And then it disappears. The governments are not involved. Publicly. Come. Reverend Hindemith," he said, getting out of the car. "I hope I haven't kept you waiting."

"No, I wanted to get here early, before anything else disappears," he said, prickly. "Your assistant—"

"Yes, yes, I know, sometimes a little hasty. Abrupt. I talk to her about it." He turned to include Martin. "A colleague. Martin Keller. Reverend Hindemith. Or is it Pastor? I'm never sure."

"You're not a Lutheran?" Hindemith said.

Kurt shook his head. "Or anything else. My parents, their god was socialism. You know what it's like here."

"Yes."

"But it's Reverend? I want to get it right."

"Yes, that's fine. Now, the shipment. Here's the bill of lading at Rostock. The complete inventory. You can see it was all here, what was promised."

"Reverend Hindemith, no one is accusing the Church of stealing."

Reverend Hindemith stepped back a little, not expecting this.

"I've always found the *Diakonisches Werk*—above reproach."

"I should hope so," Hindemith said, still flustered. "But your assistant—"

"Was upset. Now, let's take a look. How much is missing?"

"But we expect the same number of prisoners. You can see here we made a full delivery."

"Of course, the losses are ours. Let's take a look."

The doorbell was answered by a hunched-over custodian wearing a woolen knit hat. Inside it was refrigerator cold. Pallets and forklifts, white fluorescent lights.

"The coffee and some machine parts," Hindemith said. "I don't know what else."

"All the coffee? Well, we'll get Max here to run an inventory."

"But you can see it was all here," Hindemith said, holding out the bill of lading again.

"Yes, yes, all there. So it's since Rostock. DDR territory."

"It's very upsetting, this pilfering. Criminal activity. The Church doesn't work with criminals."

"Except to forgive them, I hope," Kurt said, a glance to Martin. "Herr Thiele—"

"We'll look into it. Maybe it's not what you think. Somebody distributes the goods too early, before the accounting."

"That's called theft," Hindemith said.

"That depends on who's distributing the goods. Maybe a good reason."

An exasperated sigh, skeptical. "The Church can't be put in a position like this. If there was a scandal—"

"I understand," Kurt said. "I have a plan to make this easier. A money transfer. No—criminal element, no opportunity for that. We're setting up the account now. Think how much more pleasant it will be, our meetings. No inventory, just helping people cross."

"And this group?" Hindemith said, holding up the papers again, now a stand-in for the prisoners.

"At Herleshausen, as usual. You'll be there?"

Hindemith nodded.

"Good. It's a full bus this time. You'll want one on your side to take them to Giessen. My god, it's freezing in here. Sorry, an expression. I hope it doesn't ruin the oranges."

"So. There's no problem with this? The numbers stay the same?"

"The same. The problem is ours. But I'm going to solve it."

"We can always rely on you for that," Hindemith said, friendlier now. "A problem? Here's a solution. We could use someone like you in the Church."

Kurt looked up, about to respond, then let it go. "At Herleshausen, then," he said, offering his hand.

While Kurt huddled with Max, Martin walked through the warehouse. Oranges for Berlin housewives. Machine tools for Leipzig. Pharmaceuticals for Halle. A treasury of imports paid for by releasing prisoners from the Republic's never-ending supply. The kid in the ambulance, if he survived. The wall had created a new economy, people for West marks.

"How bad was it?" Martin said on the drive back.

"Not so bad. You need to be a little flexible in this business. One apple goes missing, it's not the end of the world."

"But it's not just one apple."

"No. And it makes us look— It's never on their side. Everything exact. Only ours. So, one of us." He glanced down at the seat, Max's inventory. "It's not just that he takes, it's what he takes. Things the government controls. So the only other place to get them is the black market. That's where he sells, to real criminals."

"You know who it is?"

Kurt shook his head. "I'm not the police. And I don't make

trouble for myself. Some things it's better not to know. So, if an apple goes missing, an apple goes missing. It's the system here. Do I stop living until it corrects itself? If it ever does? I'm living now."

———

Ganymed was on the river at Schiffbauerdamm, next to the Berliner Ensemble, so it attracted an early pre-theater crowd, men in suits and women with teased hair and thick eyeliner, last year's Kurfürstendamm styles. Even at this hour, Peter was the only child, drawing smiles from a few of the other diners, recognized. The room was a throwback to a prewar brasserie, wall sconces and overstuffed settees, and had the table-hopping atmosphere of an elite hangout, people pleased with themselves for being there.

"If I lived here, would I know most of them?" Martin said.

"Most. It's always the same," Sabine said.

"There's Marthe," Peter said, nodding politely, used to this.

"In the old days, it was different," Sabine said. "Canteens. Not even a menu."

"The joys of socialism," Kurt said.

"Kurt," Peter said.

"Well, but you must admit, this is better."

"And still socialist."

"In the summer it's pleasant," Sabine said. "They put tables outside, in the square."

"It's better than the theater, watching the people," Kurt said. "If it's Brecht anyway."

"But it's always Brecht," Sabine said. "It's his theater."

"Sabine loves Brecht. How many times now for *Mother Courage*? How many times can you see one play?"

"A great play? Any number. Anyway, what do you know about it? You always fall asleep." Not really quarreling, familiar ground.

Martin looked at her. A sleeveless dress, despite the chill outside, her arms long and white, a light beige cardigan draped over her shoulders. Hair brushed back, away from her face, more color in her cheeks, either from rouge or high spirits, but a visible sign of health. "You had a good day," she'd said earlier, nodding toward Peter. Now she seemed determined to make the evening go well, to match the soft glow of the room, everyone happy.

"Do you like Brecht?" Peter said.

"I don't know," Martin said. "I've never seen any of his plays."

"Any of them?"

"I've been—away."

Peter nodded. "That's right, no plays there. Did you have television?"

"No."

"What did you do? I mean, what was allowed?"

"Reading. There was a library.".

"But you could get letters."

"Yes," he said, feeling Sabine's eyes on him now.

"And did you have friends there?"

"Peter—" Kurt said.

"Not at first," Martin said, answering him.

"Why not?"

"They thought I was a traitor," Martin said. "They have their own hierarchy inside. I was at the bottom. Or near it anyway."

"Should we start with something to drink?" Kurt said, looking for a waiter. Around them the room was filling up, people clustered near the door, waiting for tables, the noise rising like waves of warm air.

"It must have been lonely for you there."

Martin looked at him, disconcerted. "Well, it's supposed to be. It's not really a place to make friends."

"Imagine the conversations," Kurt said, an off note. Peter shot him a look.

"Sabine, how nice. And with all your men." A woman with her hand on Sabine's shoulder, on her way out.

"Marthe," Kurt said, getting up.

"No, no, sit. I don't mean to interrupt. Peter, so big, you keep growing." She looked at Martin.

"Marthe, this is Martin Keller, my—"

"Yes, I know. Everybody knows. And both at the same table. You don't often see that. And everyone friends."

"Why not?" Kurt said.

"Well, that's right. All adults. Except you, *Liebchen*, but look how tall already. You're staying in Berlin?" she said to Martin, an excuse to look at him, take him in.

"You can help us convince him," Kurt said. "They want him in Leipzig, at the university, but I think Berlin would be better."

"Well, Berlin is Berlin. Sit. Sabine, call me, yes? I never see you anymore."

"I promise."

"You're leaving so early?" Kurt said.

"You know Karl. To bed with the cows. Like a farmer. Yes, I'm coming." This to a man near the door who now dipped his head to Kurt. "So call," she said to Sabine, patting her on the shoulder again as she left.

"She says the same thing every time I see her," Peter said. "So tall. You keep growing."

"Well, you do keep growing," Kurt said, still standing, watching her go, Karl waiting with a coat at the door. He touched the table, about to take his seat again, when his eye caught someone else in the crowd. He stiffened, a reaction, so that Martin followed his look. A man who'd just come in, still in his coat, scanning the room, then seeing Kurt, surprised, not looking for him, but now not looking away, eyes locked on him. Younger than most of the other men in the restaurant, but confident, in charge. Martin watched his face change, the man's eyes now motioning to Kurt to come to the door, a kind of command. Come.

"Excuse me, I'll be right back."

"You're feeling all right?" Sabine said, but Kurt ignored her, heading across the room, and now the waiter arrived, handing out the tall menus, so that when Martin put his down again, he could no longer see Kurt, just the sea of heads stretching to the door.

"Can I have the Wiener schnitzel?" Peter said.

"Oh, and leave half of it on your plate like you always do. Eyes too big for the stomach."

"I thought it was a celebration."

"You know, when I first came back to Berlin, it was impossible, Wiener schnitzel," Sabine said. "You couldn't get it anywhere. Well, we couldn't. Things are so different now. Still shortages sometimes, but better than before."

"So can I have it?" Peter said.

Sabine rolled her eyes and nodded, a mock defeat. "But we should wait for Kurt to order. He always does this. He sees somebody and then he disappears."

"It's business," Peter said. "He sees a lot of people in his business."

"Business."

"Anyway, you can talk to us," Peter said.

She smiled, softened. "What could be nicer?"

"We have to take Martin to Köpenick."

"Yes, all right. When it's warmer. We can go on the lake."

"You've done your hair differently," Martin said, looking over at her.

"No," she said, pleased. "Just a brush. I'm too lazy to change it."

"It looks nice."

"*Mutti* always looks pretty. She was an actress. I think she should come on the show. My aunt. Who comes to take care of us after the accident."

"No, I don't have the energy for that."

"*Mutti* gets tired," Peter said, confiding.

"That's right," Sabine said, a weak smile. "So no TV." A glance to Martin. "What is it? Something wrong?"

"No, no, I just saw somebody."

Hans Rieger at the door, handing his coat to a waiter and looking around the room, spotting them.

"Who?"

"Hans Rieger. *Neues Deutschland.* I met him at the hotel. I think he's coming over. Careful," he said to Peter. "He wants to interview you." Where was Kurt?

Rieger looked around the room again, then started toward them, a broad smile.

"It seems I'm the first to arrive, so I can say hello." Everyone exchanged nods. "A family dinner, all together, but where's Papa?"

"In the men's room," Martin said, an instinctive answer.

"You mind if I sit?" Rieger said, taking a chair before anyone could object.

"He's been a while. I'll just go see if he's all right," Martin said, wanting Kurt there.

"It's such a pleasure to meet you. I never miss *Die Familie*

Schmidt. Well, who does? Such a success." Hearty, settling in. "Did you think it would be like this when it started?"

"No interviews at dinner," Martin said, but pleasantly, a wag of the finger.

"At dinner, no. But a conversation, that's permitted?" Planted at the table. Where was Kurt?

"Of course," Sabine said, taking over. "Such a long time since we've seen you." Leaning forward, their heads close, so that Rieger didn't even look up when Martin left.

Only one man at the urinal in the men's room, not Kurt. Not in the bunch of waiting people at the door. Where else? Outside, some misty lights on the river, no one in the square, night coming on. But where else would he have gone? Maybe a companionable cigar. But the man's look had been sharp, not an invitation. Surprised to see him. Come.

There were lamps along the front of the theater, but no one waiting. Too early. No one in the street either, which swung around the theater to form a service cul-de-sac. But in the quiet an odd thud. Martin followed the sound. At the corner, lighted by the theater, an alley of dumpsters and trash cans, a tarp flapping at a building site, where the sound must have come from. Sand and bricks, a scaffolding on the building opposite. Now a grunt, the sound of someone hurt. Martin turned the corner. The man in the overcoat holding Kurt up against the side of a rusty dumpster, hand at his neck, the thud again of a head hitting metal.

Martin ran toward them, unthinking, blood rushing through him. He grabbed at the man, turning his shoulder. "Stop it." Barely seeing Kurt shake his head, eyes panicked, grabbing at his throat, suddenly free as the man let go to deal with Martin. "Fuck off." A growl, not even a word, and Martin felt himself being slammed against the dumpster, head hitting the hard steel, a sharp pain. "Fuck off," the man said again, his fingers on Martin's throat now. A cough, Kurt gasping for air. "Leave him alone. He's not in it." "Fuck," the man said, shoving Martin again, just to show he could, the violence more out of control, sparks shooting out of a fire. Kurt grabbed at the man's coat, and now three of them were pulling at each other, a scrum, the man swatting them away, a brawler, no rules. Martin raised his arm and brought it down on the side of the man's head, a quick smash, pure instinct, Cain's jawbone. "Fuck." The man staggered slightly, finding his balance, then roared, slamming Martin against the metal again, this time harder, going for the kill, arm up against Martin's windpipe. "Stop it," Kurt said, a harsh whisper, not wanting to be heard. Still no one in the street, no footsteps. The man pressed his arm harder, Martin's chest heaving, desperate now for air. And then, no more distinct than a blur, he saw Kurt bend to the ground and bring up a brick, not hesitating, and smash it down on the man's head. The man pitched forward, arm dropping, a kind of dazed, pointless movement, but still standing. Kurt swung the brick again against his temple and this time the body started to slump, away from Martin, and slid to the ground. Martin clutched his throat, gulping air, watching Kurt drop to his knee and bend over the body, fingers on the man's neck, feeling it, lifting his head from a small pool of blood. And then, looking around the street, he lifted the brick and smashed it down again, this time on the man's face, pulp.

"Jesus Christ," Martin said, his stomach suddenly churning, dizzy with nausea.

Kurt looked around again. "Help me."

"What?"

"Help me lift him." He nodded to the dumpster.

"We can't—"

"Quick. Before anyone comes. Grab his feet." Already lifting him under his arms. "He's too heavy for me."

Sleepwalking, just moving, Martin bent down and grabbed the man's feet. "It's too high," he said as they began to hoist the body up to the rim. "We can't swing him over."

"Get his head over first. Then push. We can do it."

Martin switched his position, helping Kurt lift the torso, then pushing the legs up after.

"On three," Kurt whispered.

They heaved together, feeling the body pull away from them as it went over, carried now by gravity. A loud thud as the body hit, muffled by garbage bags.

Martin leaned over, hands on his knees, taking deep breaths. An old woman by the river, not stopping, too far to see anything. Still no one in the square.

"Who was he?"

"Nobody. A crook. They won't be surprised he ended up this way." He looked around the cul-de-sac again, then pulled out a handkerchief. "Here. There's some blood." He started wiping the side of Martin's head. "Just a little. There. No one will notice. What about me?"

Martin looked at his face, the moment eerily intimate and trancelike. He nodded an okay.

"Hans Rieger is at the table," he said stupidly, the first thing that came into his mind.

"All right, hurry." Another look at the street. "They won't find him. Not today. We're all right."

"Kurt—" he said, feeling his fingers begin to tremble.

Kurt took him by the shoulders. "There was a line at the men's room. So, a little time. But show nothing in your face, you understand? Rieger, he's always looking." He squeezed Martin's shoulders again. "We can do it. We have the same interests."

Inside, the noise and heat came at them in a rush.

"Let me go first," Kurt said, beginning to cross the room, putting his hand out as he reached the table, playing host.

Martin ducked into the men's room and splashed some cold water on his face. He looked up in the mirror. How you looked when you killed somebody, what showed in your face. But had he? Too late now for technicalities. The minute he grabbed the man's legs and heaved, he'd become part of it, complicit. So now I've done this. Murder. Not the abstract killing that haunted him, the bomb and its chain of guilt. Not any of that, a brick in the face, pulp. He wiped himself, steadying his shaking hands on the washbasin. We can do it. Hadn't he done it before? All the time at Harwell, the secret of who he was put away in some compartment, not connected to the rest of him, smiling at parties, dinner at someone's house, betraying but not betraying because that part of him was somewhere else. But this was different. A real body, not a number.

"I've ordered some wine," Kurt said at the able. "Hans is joining us."

"For one glass only," Rieger said, holding up a finger. "While I wait. But maybe he's not coming." He looked at his watch. "It's not polite to be this late. And no message. But what can you expect? From such a person."

"Who?" Peter said.

"My dinner companion. Herr Spitzer. Ah, I see your father knows him."

A twitch in Kurt's face, involuntary, so that Martin knew now too. Not late, not coming at all. He pressed his fingers on the tablecloth. Keep still.

"I know of him," Kurt said. "Everybody does. The notorious Herr Spitzer."

"Why is he notorious?"

"He does bad things," Rieger said, talking down to a child. "What they call the black market. The boss, in fact. Or so they say. No friend of yours, I think," he said to Kurt.

"I don't know him." A cool reply, returning a serve. Martin felt his head turn from one to the other, following the play.

"But he knows you. This plan I heard about. Money transactions. He won't like that. Nothing to get his hands on if that happens. A loss of business for him."

"He has plenty of other business. Anyway, what plan? Where did you hear that?"

"Not from you. Discreet as always. It's lucky not everybody's like that. Or I'd be out of business." Smiling, with a nod to Peter, a joke.

"If he does bad things, why are you having dinner with him?" Peter said. The right question, stopping the ball in midair.

"Well, it looks like I'm not," Rieger said, looking at his watch again, then back at Peter. "I have to talk to people in my job. Not always nice ones. That's the way you find out things."

"What are you trying to find out?"

"Peter—"

"No, it's all right. Herr Spitzer knows a lot of things. But tonight I wanted to ask him about someone who used to work for him. You remember," he said to Kurt. "The boy in the ambulance at Invalidenstrasse."

"He worked for Spitzer?"

"Once. I'm not sure if now. That's what I wanted to find out."

"But he was going over to the West."

"And maybe he had help."

"And Spitzer's in that business now?"

"Maybe an old favor."

"What business?" Peter said.

"*Republikflucht*," Rieger said.

"Oh, like Matty."

"Yes, but he's not on television. No one knows where he is, in fact. Or at least nobody tells me."

"But I thought you said—" Martin started.

Rieger nodded. "Yes, Hohenschönhausen for questioning. But now somewhere else. It's remarkable how that happens. People just . . . disappear."

"But someone must know," Kurt said.

"Yes, someone must. Maybe you would inquire for me."

Kurt held up his hands. "You have better contacts than I do. I'm just the lawyer. For the exchanges. They give me a list, that's all."

"Maybe they'll want to exchange him. That would make a story, yes? He finally gets to the West, the man who shot at you. And it's you who gets him there."

"Shot at him?" Peter said.

"Herr Rieger," Sabine said.

"An incident at the wall," Kurt said calmly. "No one was hurt."

Martin looked at him. No one hurt, people dead only when you want them to be. Spitzer still walking around somewhere, not lying in a dumpster outside the Berliner Ensemble. Rieger sipping wine, toying with Kurt, unaware his source had vanished, end of story.

"Yes, but a family dinner, excuse me," Rieger said now. "I must leave you to it. Good luck with the Wiener schnitzel," he said to Peter, evidently something they'd discussed earlier. "Sabine? If I may? Very kind of you to share your family with me." A bow, courtly, almost theatrical.

"I hope you find your friend," Peter said.

"My friend. If he does turn up," he said to Kurt, "tell him he should learn better manners."

Kurt held up his hands again, a mock protest. "I don't teach Spitzer."

"No. What does he need with manners in that business?" Pleasant, a worldly shrug.

He started across the room, and Martin saw, his fingers no longer gripping the table, that they were going to get away with it. Rieger would even be their alibi, sharing a bottle of wine while Spitzer met his underworld fate. What criminals did, put bodies in dumpsters, cover for each other. A quick glance at Kurt, who had picked up his menu, ready to see the rest of the evening through. Martin heard the thud again, the body sliding out of their hands. But nobody else had heard it. Nobody knew. Except them. Nobody else could give them away. And he realized in that moment that it didn't matter anymore who was guilty, who had actually done it. Something else had happened. Kurt's life was in his hands now. And his in Kurt's. Something only they knew. Like a marriage.

CHAPTER 4

It was a long drive to Herleshausen, first down to Leipzig, then west through the mountains to the border, the last stretch pitch-dark in the dense woods. There was no real reason for Martin to go, except that Kurt had asked, another trip he didn't want to make alone. A chance to see the exchange at work, as if he were being brought into the business.

"Hindemith is usually there. Just to make sure."

"Of what? How many?"

"And which ones. No substitutions at the last minute. He doesn't trust us. They give us a list of people they want, we negotiate, we agree on the names. He wants to make sure they get who they paid for. This group tonight, I thought it would be interesting for you. Some of them are part of the exchange for you."

Martin said nothing for a minute, watching the dark trees streak by.

"Have they found his body yet?" he said finally.

"I don't know. The police haven't said. You have to understand, this kind of criminal, it's an embarrassment for them. They're not supposed to exist. In the workers' state." He took a breath. "It's all right. Don't worry."

"But they will find him. There. Where we were."

"No, where he was going to meet Hans. Something happens to him on the way? Nothing to do with us. Men like Spitzer—it's no surprise. This is how they live. Everything in the fists. Well, you saw."

Martin nodded. "I can still see it."

"There's no good in that," Kurt said quietly.

"I know." He turned to face him. "Why did you kill him? He was out."

"And then he wakes up and tracks you down like a dog. He has to. It's his nature. At first, he's sending a message, something in the alley. But then you surprise him and it's something else. He can't walk away—too late."

Martin looked at him. The way it had happened now, Martin the trigger.

"What message?"

"Stay out of my business. He was stealing from the supplies. He thought I was trying to stop that. But he got—excited. You have to act at such a moment," he said easily. "You or him."

"And now where are we?"

"We're here." His eyes left the road for a minute. "No one knows," he said, his voice calm, not a threat, a reminder. Martin looked away.

They drove without talking for a few minutes, Kurt turning the knob on the radio to find the weather report.

"We were having dinner at Ganymed. Everyone saw."

"With Hans," Martin said, as if he were practicing, committing it to memory.

"Yes, with Hans. Lucky for us, not so lucky for him. I think his story died with Spitzer, no? The interesting thing is that he doesn't understand nobody wants such a story here. He's still in the West. He took money from the Stasi, so now he's here, but his head? Back there with Springer. Ah, here we go. Please, no rain." Changing the station, moving on. A second of static, crackling, then a low, flat Saxon voice promising a cold evening. "It's always cold in the mountains."

Martin followed him, away from the alley. "Why go all this way? Why not Friedrichstrasse?" Not really caring, making conversation.

"There are people at Friedrichstrasse. But there's nobody at Herleshausen. A castle and a village." He looked at his watch. "Already asleep. The checkpoint's not even in town. A few kilometers north. So, no one."

"But it's not a secret. Too many people—"

"Well, an open secret. Some people know, but not how many, how much is paid. If you're the prisoner, you're grateful to be out. You don't ask questions. Or your family. The West German government? There is no such program. Nobody has to explain the money. They know but they don't know. Germans are good at that. So, Herleshausen. In the woods. At night." He was quiet for a minute. "I was born here, in the East. I know what this country is. But think what it can be. If we survive. So, what price?" He turned off the radio.

"You never wanted to go to the West?"

"Me? No. The Nazis killed my father. And who's with Adenauer in Bonn? Nazis. You can make a life here too, without Nazis."

"How did you meet Sabine? She was in the West."

"With her mother. But in those days, people could go back and forth. Live in the East, work in the West. I was a lawyer here, but I had business in the West too. Like now. So we met." A minute. "How does she seem to you?"

"What do you mean?" Martin said, surprised, a skidding effect.

"Is she like before?"

"She seems happy, if that's what you're asking."

"Good. You know, sometimes you worry."

"About what?"

"I don't know exactly. We have a good life, some privileges. But I think sometimes she's—I don't know. Sad a little. Maybe she misses the old excitement, with the Service. I was worried, when you were coming, that you'd remind her. Of happier times."

Martin turned to him. "They weren't happier. They were different. She's happy now, with you and Peter. I didn't come to change that." •

"No, no, I didn't mean— It's just—she's not an easy woman."

Martin said nothing, uncomfortable. Why didn't she tell him she was sick? Her husband. What did they talk about? Would she ever know about Spitzer? No, they'd both lie to her. We have the same interests.

The border crossing was a simple road barrier and a guardhouse, just big enough to keep the guards out of the cold, all of it bathed in harsh overhead lights that made the surrounding woods seem even darker. A bus was already parked on the side of the road, passengers filing out, their movements awkward, slightly blinded by the lights, their names being checked off a clipboard. All of them were dressed in a suit and hat, what Martin imagined was the standard issue prison release suit, hidden by bulky overcoats. He thought of his own release, each minute suspended, not to be trusted until it had passed, the sound of doors closing behind you. A few of the prisoners were stamping their feet in the cold and smoking cigarettes, looking down the road as if there were something to see in the dark, some welcoming sign. What they'd dreamed of for years. Not a wall this time, just a stretch of road, the other side so close now you could taste it. Any minute, unless something went wrong.

Reverend Hindemith was standing next to the bus with his own clipboard, double-checking names.

"Everything all right?" Kurt said to him. "Cold tonight. Where's your bus?"

"Any minute. Yours was early. They must be eager to go."

Kurt shrugged, not rising to this.

"What happens now?" Martin said.

"They go to Giessen, the refugee center. Welcome to the West and here are a few questions. A debriefing. The good reverend wants to make sure we haven't slipped a few spies into the group."

Hindemith smiled. "It's not hard to tell. Just look at their eyes. They look back, something's up. The others are too afraid to look. Only at the ground. The Karl-Marx-Stadt prison look."

"A scientific method," Kurt said.

But they were, in fact, looking at the ground, or down the road, not at each other. Martin remembered milling in the yard at Wakefield, almost a social occasion. Here the prisoners seemed apprehensive, trying not to be noticed. He wondered about the boy in the ambulance, transferred somewhere to have the fear beaten into him.

"There's young Kennedy. Like the family, but not. My client. Herr Kennedy, come meet Martin Keller. You're being exchanged for him."

Tall and athletic, no more than twenty, the smooth face of a young boy, quick rabbit-like eyes. He put out his hand, a tentative shake.

"Your father will be so happy," Kurt said. "A long process. But here we are."

"Exchanged," the boy said. "I don't understand. You're American?"

"Yes."

"And you want to come here?" His voice soft, almost a whisper, not wanting to be overheard.

"Yes."

"A different experience, Herr Kennedy. Yours was not so pleasant, but now that's all over."

The boy looked directly at Martin, serious. "Don't. Whatever they've told you. You don't know."

"And then what happens to you?" Kurt said. "Martin's here so you can go. Should I reverse the process?"

A look in the boy's eyes that went through Martin, more than dread, an animal about to be struck.

"Not everyone begins by breaking the law," Kurt said. "It's not a picnic after that, no."

"What did you do?" Martin said.

"I helped some friends. Who wanted to get out."

"A car trunk. Amateurs. Of course they were caught. Seven years," Kurt said, nodding to the boy, the sentence and the person the same. "Your father was so worried. But someone sent him to me, so we started the process and finally— So now it's *auf Wiedersehen*. I wish you luck. Please give my best regards to your father, yes?" Motioning him toward the other prisoners, now forming a line.

The boy glanced at Martin again, about to say something, then looked away and went to join the others. A matter of minutes now and it would be over, everything different down the road.

"A nice boy," Kurt said. "One foolish mistake. The father is a very prominent lawyer. Many contacts in Washington. So a priority on the list. You don't come cheap," he said, pleased, almost a joke.

"How much did he pay you? The father."

"Just the usual fee," Kurt said. "Of course, in dollars it's more for me."

Hindemith was now leading the group through the barrier to the bus waiting on the other side. The same formality as at Invalidenstrasse, guards ready in case someone made a run for it. Where, the dark forest? They were free. But nobody said a word or threw a hat in the air or even looked back.

That night, in bed, not really dreaming, just letting his mind drift, Martin saw himself in line with the prisoners, heading for the new bus, every step one more step away, lighter, until he was running. And he knew that the only real thing in the ritual exchange had been Kennedy's sharp, knowing look. All the others—Kurt, Reverend Hindemith, Sabine, everyone—had gone through the looking glass, into an arbitrary world of euphemism and six impossible things before breakfast, a country that didn't exist, where people were sold for oranges. Where he was going to spend the rest of his life. He could feel himself sweating under the covers, the way he used to sweat in prison, and he threw them off and went over to the door to make sure it was bolted. That first night he had left it open, but now he felt safer with it locked. What Digby had said, a new prison. But how could he leave? Any of them? Their lives were here. So you made the best of it, pretending it was a real place. Until someone looked you in the eye.

———

Andrei was waiting on the bridge in front of the Dom, right on schedule and evidently not tailed, since his newspaper was folded.

"So how are things?"

"Fine. Lots of time with the family. Peter's getting used to me, I think."

"Good, good." He lit a cigarette. "And Kurt?"

"Friendly. He took me to one of his exchanges. At Herleshausen."

"Not as exciting as yours, I hope."

"No. Off one bus and onto another. I don't know what he wanted me to see, exactly."

Andrei shrugged. "Maybe how important he is. You know, at the exchanges it's only him there. The public face. He acts for the Stasi, but you don't see the Stasi. Only him."

"And he's not Stasi?"

"No. It's a delicate position. He's protected by them—you'd have to be, to do this work—but Ulbricht and the others in Pankow don't like the idea of the Stasi running everything, a secret government, so it's good to have somebody independent. "

"How do they know he's not really Stasi?"

"It's been looked into." He drew on the cigarette. "So. The Academy reception. Schell is coming. He's looking forward to seeing you again. So be sure to make contact there. I don't know how much time you'll have—there'll be a crowd—so maybe dinner while he's still here in Berlin. Catch up. Make plans to see him in Dresden. You know what to do. We're particularly interested in his friends at Dubna, if he mentions them. Any so-called concerned scientists."

"That's going to take some time. Build up a little trust."

Andrei nodded. "You'll manage. You have your speech ready? For the toasts? There are always toasts."

"I wish I knew what I'm being honored for. Being a spy?"

"For coming here. Another brain for the DDR. Someone who

can work with Schell. And his colleagues. Atomic energy for peace. You know they burn lignite here. Think how much nicer the air will be when the power plants are nuclear. How much cleaner. It's important work."

"Work with him. He's in Dresden."

"Yes. At Rossendorf."

"And I'm here."

Andrei took a last puff, then tossed the cigarette. "You can see the boy on weekends. That's how it would be here anyway. You're not living with them, having dinner every night. So it will be the same."

Martin took a minute. "This has been decided?"

"It's important that you be at Rossendorf. Your old friend Fuchs is there too."

"He's not a friend."

"Well, you can get to know him better."

"Kurt promised me Berlin."

"I know." He paused. "It's not far. We need you there."

"What changed?"

"Before we had a general interest. In Schell. Now we know there were papers prepared at Dubna. For an international audience."

"Know how?"

"Someone told us. So now it's serious. We have to know what they say."

"Why not just send him to the Lubyanka and ask? You've done it before."

"The bad old days?" He shook his head. "Not with him. There would be a protest—exactly what we want to prevent. No, a more subtle approach." He took another breath. "It's important."

"And after? I come back to Berlin?"

"Of course. If you like."

"No, if you like. And why should I believe you?"

Hah "Who else? We'll always look out for you. You know that."

———

Everyone arrived on time, an almost comic display of German punctuality. The German Academy of Sciences had several research institutes, but its headquarters were in Jägerstrasse at the Gendarmenmarkt, and people were spilling across the square from all sides, down from Unter den Linden, around the corner from Hausvogteiplatz, making a bottleneck at the doors. Cars, unmistakably official, were pulling up at the corner, but most people had come on foot, many with canes. It was an old crowd, white-haired and hunched over, a few with SED lapel pins. The Academy prided itself on casting a wide net—Humboldt had been a member and, in happier times, Einstein—but most of the members now were postwar, appointees acceptable to the new regime, technocrats with a sneaking sentimental affection for their historic old building, with its staircases and wallpaper and an assembly room so large that it might have been designed for parties. A string quartet had been hired and waiters in tailcoats, passing trays of canapés and sparkling wine. A buffet table was set up along one wall, crowded with people filling plates for dinner. Martin smiled to himself. Academic parties the world over.

Kurt had handed him over to Jürgen, the Academy head's assistant, who led him around the room making introductions. The director's toast had been early and his response modest and grateful. Now he had only to be pleasant and get through the evening, be the curiosity the others would talk about. How did he like Berlin and was this his first time in the East? No one mentioned his other career, something from another time, when such things happened. There were photographers for the official welcoming glass of *Sekt* with Schilling, the Academy head, whose easy manner seemed at odds with his pressed suit and military posture.

"I understand you'd like to join our team at Rossendorf."

Understand how? Martin wanted to say, but what would be the point? How did the Service do anything?

"I hope that's possible."

"Oh yes," Schilling said. "I have to consult with Professor Schell, but I don't foresee any difficulties. You're old friends, yes?"

"Yes."

"So that's pleasant. And it's your field, nuclear research. You'll be doing important work there."

"For peace this time."

Schilling looked at him, not sure how to react to this. "Yes, of course, for peace."

"They're working on other things at Adlershof, I think. So convenient, but—"

"You've been to the institute?"

"I was nearby, visiting. So I went to see it."

Schilling's smile stayed in place, but his eyes darted off to the side now, suspicious. Not somewhere you dropped in.

"Next time someone will take you."

"A look only. An impressive facility."

"Really, Dr. Keller. It's your choice. If you prefer Adlershof. We're honored to have you."

"No, no, Rossendorf. It's my field after all. Or was."

"You'll catch up," Schilling said, genial, a man used to working the room. "And look, another colleague. Dr. Fuchs, Dr. Keller, but I think you already know each other."

"Many years ago," Fuchs said.

"Klaus," Martin said, shaking his hand. "How nice." Bald now, but the same rimless glasses and whispering voice. Martin remembered him at Los Alamos, the shy bachelor at the edge of the party, retreating, not quite there, betraying them all. But so had he.

"Dr. Keller is going to join you at Rossendorf."

Fuchs tipped his head. "You would be most welcome."

"No *Sekt* tonight?" Schilling said, indicating Fuchs's empty hand.

"Not for me. Have you met our new director, Professor Schell?"

"I was hoping to see him tonight," Martin said, looking around the room. "We were at Göttingen together. If he remembers."

"Ah," Fuchs said, noncommittal.

"Excuse me. You two must have so much to catch up on. I should say hello to Professor Bauer." Schilling slid away, a practiced art.

"Do we have so much to catch up on?" Fuchs said with a smile, mischievous. "We never knew about each other at Los Alamos."

"No."

"Not even the same control. But that was for the best. As it turned out. We were never caught."

"Not there, no."

"I know what it's like for you, these first days," he said, suddenly just the two of them. "People don't want to think about it, what we did. Something might rub off. But it gets better."

"Did it, for you?"

Fuchs shrugged. "I was never bothered by it. It was the right thing to do, that's all that mattered." Sure of it.

"Do you like it here?"

"Yes, well enough. It's safe."

"Safe?" Martin said, for a second not sure he'd heard correctly.

"No FBI, no more army intelligence, with their questions, trying to trap you. All those years, not knowing if— But now it's safe. You can breathe."

Martin looked at him. Everything inside out. He thought of the prisoners' eyes.

"You'll see," Fuchs said. "At first people will be suspicious, because you've just come from the West."

"The West? I was in prison."

Fuchs nodded, taking the point. "But not here. It's not a personal matter. With so many enemies, they have to be careful."

"They really think the West is—"

"Of course. A unified Germany. Under America. With a gun pointed at the Soviet Union? Destroy everything we've tried to accomplish? They try, but they don't succeed." He looked directly at Martin. "It was right, what we did. Now the Russians help us here. And that's right too. A Communist world—that's what we worked for. So welcome. You're safe now."

Martin looked away, hoping no expression showed in his face. He must have thought this once too. Had he? Fuchs was smiling a little now, still sure.

"I see you're married," Martin said, looking at the ring on Fuchs's finger.

"Yes, very soon after I got here. For me, it's a happier life."

"Congratulations."

"Well, Klaus, do you remember me?" Sabine suddenly there with a glass in her hand.

Klaus hesitated, clearly not sure. "Frau Keller?"

"Well, Thiele now," she said. "We divorced."

A step back, not expecting this, the way a scarecrow would move. "Of course I remember."

"Oh, now you're being polite. It's all right. We all change."

"No. A dinner at the Bethes. I remember it clearly." As if he were being tested.

"All of us so young," Sabine said. But not tonight. She looked older, drawn, the blush in her cheeks at the Ganymed gone. "I wonder, did we think then that we'd be here one day, at the Academy. The guest of honor, no less." A quick smile at Martin.

"The question was whether the Academy would be here," Martin said.

"No, I knew we would prevail," Fuchs said, so humorless that Sabine looked up, surprised. "History is a powerful force and history is with us."

"Still, do you think?" Sabine said.

"Of course."

"Well, I hope you're right. It would be terrible if history switched sides. After all that."

Now it was Fuchs who was at a loss, blinking instead of replying.

"Bodo Jahn," she said, reaching up and fingering Martin's lapel. "Very stylish."

"You like it?" A couple getting dressed to go out.

Sabine nodded and started to say something but covered her mouth, stifling a cough.

"Are you all right?" Martin said.

"Sorry. This stupid cough."

Fuchs took this as an end point. "Well, I have a train to catch. I hope you feel better. Dr. Keller, I will see you at Rossendorf. I look forward to our talks." He made a half bow, the scarecrow now erect, and backed away into the crowd.

"What an odd duck," Sabine said, the cough subsiding. "Where's Rossendorf?"

"Near Dresden. A nuclear research center."

"Oh yes, you're giving a talk there. Kurt told me."

"Well, now something more. The Academy wants me to take a post there."

She looked up. "I thought you said you'd never do that work again."

"It's not weapons. Reactors. To make energy."

"It's always weapons, one way or the other. Just tell them no. They can't make you do it."

"I want to do it," he said, as effortless as breathing.

Sabine stared at him.

"I'm a guest here. I have to go where they want me to go. It's not far."

"The point was to be here."

"I know. But I can't be here all the time. I'll still see Peter."

"Kurt can fix it."

"No. It's been decided. Anyway, it's the most logical place for me. It's supposed to be an honor." He turned toward the noisy room.

"Will you be a professor? Professor Keller. You always wanted that."

"I don't know. I suppose so."

"And now you won't have to see me. Another point. Only when you drop off Peter. That will make it easier for you."

"Listen to you."

"Why? Am I so wrong?" She looked up. "You asked for this?"

"We'll talk later."

She covered her mouth again, the cough back, reaching for a handkerchief.

"That doesn't sound good."

"Well, it wouldn't, would it?" She looked down at the handkerchief. "No blood. So that's something."

"See another doctor. You can't just—"

"Just what?"

"Do nothing. They have better treatments now. Chemicals. Radiation—"

She made a wry face. "I think we've both had enough of that. Maybe that's why I have this. We were all exposed. That would be a joke—to pay this way." She wiped the corner of her mouth. "Anyway, who would I see? The Charité has the best doctors in Berlin."

"You all right, Sabine?" A woman's voice, coming from behind Martin. "It's going around. Hilde had it. She still can't shake it."

Sabine started coughing again. "Some air, maybe. Excuse me." The words coming in gasps. She waved her hand between them.

"I can introduce myself," the woman said, stepping around Martin. "Ruth Jacobs." She held out her hand, an American handshake, a flat Midwestern voice. "Do you need anything?" she said to Sabine.

"Just some water. I'll be back," Sabine said, leaving. "Martin Keller."

"Everybody knows that. He just made a speech. A pleasure." She nodded to him.

Middle-aged but not gray, her hair swept back in a utilitarian cut, like sleeves rolled up to do a job. Lively, observant eyes, confident, a woman who could run an office.

"You're American," Martin said.

"Mm. So what am I doing here? I married into it. Gerhard was in the States during the war, and when he came back, I came with him. Not much fun in those days. Freezing. You'd sell your soul for a bucket of coal. But I stuck it out and it got better."

"What made you stick?"

"You mean was I a true believer? We all were. I kept my passport, just in case though. Still have it, in fact. Brecht always said, keep a foreign passport. He had an Austrian one. I can't remember why, but he kept it till the end."

"You knew Brecht?"

"It was a smaller town in those days. And Gerhard knew him in exile, so we saw quite a lot of him. Gerhard Jacobs. He's interviewing you for *Neues Deutschland*."

"Right. Jacobs. I'm sorry—"

She waved this off. "I wanted to do it, but they said Gerhard."

"You're a journalist too?"

"When they let me. Which isn't often. Stories with a woman's angle, whatever that is, I wish someone would tell me. So mostly it's stringer stuff. *Il Messaggero*, of all places."

"A Western paper?"

She shrugged. "Not much gets through. I had a piece in the *Daily Worker* once and only half of it ran."

"But you stayed."

"I have a husband here. So I'm here. Not very many of us now. Americans, I mean. I know what it's like, in the beginning."

Martin looked at her, an echo of Klaus with an entirely different tone.

"If you need any help. Who to see, anything like that, I can get you in the right door." She took out a card. "Feel free. Off the record." She slid the card into his hand, seamless, a magic trick. "Don't worry. It's Gerhard's too. Same number. You'd have a reason to have it. If anybody asks."

"Thanks. So far I just leave everything to Kurt. You know, who arranged the swap."

"Sabine's husband. And you're the ex. I'd love to do that story.

Talk about the woman's angle. No, I meant American connections, if you need to see somebody."

"Are there any? I thought—"

"Officially, no. We don't recognize East Germany. Unofficially, though, there's the Political Affairs Division. Of the US Mission. Eastern Affairs Section." She caught Martin's look. "I know. It's a lot of doors. That's why the offer," she said, indicating her card. "For us, it's still 1945 and this is the Soviet Occupied Zone and we're holding down the fort on Clayallee. A military command. The Russians do the same in Karlshorst. And the DDR doesn't exist. But the Americans here do, and sometimes they need help. So the Mission's their unofficial embassy."

"I'm the last person they'd want to see."

"Why? You're still an American. You never renounced your citizenship."

He looked at her. "How do you know that?"

"I made a guess," she said quickly, not blinking.

"Clayallee's in West Berlin, isn't it?"

"But you can get word to them. If you want to. Or flag down one of the missionaries." She smiled. "Military Liaison Mission. Another holdover. So the Allies could coordinate the Occupation. They're in a big lake house in Potsdam. American soil, American flag, just like an embassy."

"What do they coordinate?"

"Not much. Mostly they take the car out for a drive and snap pictures. Soviet installations, whatever looks interesting."

"Aren't they followed?"

She nodded. "Faster cars. Once they hit the autobahn, they're usually okay."

"And the Soviets put up with it?"

"They've got their own liaison mission in Frankfurt. Handy for

running agents in West Germany. Worth a little Wild West here."
She smiled again. "Welcome to the DDR."

"And you just happen to know all this."

"It's not a secret. Not a big one anyway. I used to be a reporter.
Before they put me on the woman's angle. So if you need an American contact—"

"Why would I?"

Another shrug. "No idea. But if you do." She paused. "You
might change your mind. About being here. I might have, if it
hadn't been for Gerhard. You never know."

"I bought a one-way ticket here," he said, looking at her.

"They'll be relieved to hear it. Maybe you don't see it," she said
carefully, explaining something. "It's a little bit of a risk for them
too, bringing you here. Good propaganda. They've even got Gerhard lined up for the story. So, special. But think of the propaganda
value for the other side if you went back. You came, you saw, you
left. Another win for the West."

"A small one."

She smiled. "It's a small country. Sensitive."

"And so far very kind to me." He motioned with his hand to
take in the party.

She raised her eyes. "They gave Brecht his own theater. And
he still kept his passport. Nobody ever played it better. They were
never sure about him. But they didn't want to lose him. So, push-pull."

"I'm not Brecht."

"No, but hang on to your passport anyway. It's your Get Out
of Jail Free card. If they stop being nice. When are you seeing Gerhard?"

"I'm not sure. Kurt's arranging it."

"The fixer," Ruth said. "Look at him. All cozy with Schilling.

You have to hand it to him. An Academy reception, no outsiders allowed. But there he is."

"You disapprove?"

"Oh, who am I to disapprove? But I'm fascinated. By how he does it."

"Works for both sides."

"Plays the system. You know, he grew up here. First the Nazis, then the SED. He's never known anything else. And look how he thrives in it. There used to be a real sense of something new here. The new Germany. I know, it's a laugh, maybe even then, but it felt that way. Not cynical, not yet. About something. And now that's all gone. Now it's a place for Kurt. And people like him. Not bad. Amoral. I look at him and I see what's happened to us. And why did it? Well, listen to me. Nice to have new ears, I guess."

"And why did it?"

She looked over. "I used to think it was the Stasi, the listening, what it does to people. I don't think it's that, though, not now. I think it's the lies. Ulbricht, the old Stalinists, they always told lies. Maybe they had to. Now we all do." She took a breath. "Well, you see why I don't get many assignments. Buy me a coffee sometime and we'll solve the other problems of the world."

Martin smiled. "Be a pleasure. And tell whoever asked you to talk to me that I'm fine. Not going anywhere."

She held his look for a second. "So suspicious. But I guess you'd have to be, given everything." She cocked her head, a gesture. "It's funny, you don't look like somebody who– I guess that's what made you good."

"Not that good. I was caught."

She looked up. "But that's another story. And here comes Kurt." Then, a quick look. "Keep the card anyway. Just in case. Kurt, we were just talking about you."

"Nice things?"

"Martin said you're arranging an interview with Gerhard."

"Tomorrow. And nobody else, please," Kurt said, raising a finger. "You know it makes him nervous."

"Since when?" she said, but pleasantly, the way they talked to each other. "Oh, and now look." Glancing over his shoulder. "I thought you said Gerhard had an exclusive."

They turned to follow her gaze. Hans Rieger at the door, looking flustered, scanning the room. Martin raised his head, alert, a deer scenting something in the field. Back in it, the old training like a reflex: don't look alarmed, face blank, take a sip of wine, smile.

"What is he doing, coming here? He's not on the list."

"As if that ever stopped him. He probably used Gerhard's name." She laughed a little to herself. "How can you look like a weasel and not *be* a weasel?"

"A rival?" Martin said.

"He should be so lucky," Ruth said. "He's in a sweat about something. Do you mind?" she said, excusing herself. "I can't resist."

"What do you think he wants?" Martin said, voice low, into the glass.

Rieger was still scanning the room, frustrated, when Ruth blocked his line of vision.

"He's looking for somebody."

Kurt turned back. "Let him look. So. How are you holding up?" Party talk.

"She's a nice woman."

Kurt nodded. "Very loyal to Gerhard. Everyone wonders why she puts up with it."

"With what?"

"His women. You wouldn't think, to look at him. But she stays. Even when he was in prison."

"For what?"

"After the Slánský trials. If you'd been abroad, you were—contaminated. Infected with capitalism. People who'd fled Hitler. So they locked you up. Then Stalin died and it was all right again. Three years. And she stayed. But Gerhard's a little crazy too. After, when you could go to the West—just take the S-bahn—he stayed. After prison. You know what he said? The Party had made a mistake but now it was corrected. Three years, a correction. So that's the kind of man he is. Now I think it's a little bit difficult for them. She used to work in the West, before the wall, so they had West marks. But no longer."

"Worked where?"

"A publisher there. Like Gerhard here. A translator."

"No children?"

Kurt shook his head. "Gerhard's the child. She stays for him. Hello, he's seen us."

Martin watched Rieger make his way to them, sidling through clusters of people, still in his coat, his face red from the heat. Martin clutched his glass.

"So you've heard?" Rieger said, skipping a greeting.

"What? You seem upset."

"Spitzer. They found his body. Killed."

"Killed? How?"

"Beaten to death."

"Well, it's not such a surprise, is it? A man like that. When was this?"

"Saturday. That's the point. I wanted to warn you. I've given your name."

"My name?"

"He kept a diary. Well, a datebook. And the last date was with me. Dinner at the Ganymed."

"But he never showed up."

"Yes, yes, that's what I told them. But you are the proof. We were there together. You don't mind, my giving them your name? You can vouch for me."

"You want me to be your alibi?" Kurt said, his voice silky, his whole face alive with the irony of this, the tangle of it. Martin looked away.

"If you would say—"

"Of course."

Rieger exhaled, a little breath of relief. "Thank you. It's a great favor."

"No, it's just the truth. He never showed up. Surely they don't suspect you."

"They don't know. And there's my name in his book. And I was asking about his friend. You remember, the boy in the ambulance."

"The one who disappeared."

"So there's that too. Another mystery."

"It sounds like a story for you."

"Not now," Rieger said, holding up his hand. "Just tell them I was waiting, that's all. Drinking wine, yes?"

"Yes. Just as you say. Martin will back me up. Two witnesses." A glance at Martin, enjoying this.

"You would do that?" Rieger said.

Martin nodded.

"Thank you. Both. Yes, two witnesses." Another breath of relief.

"So that's that. Why don't you have a drink now? I'm sure the Academy wouldn't mind. Now that you're here. How did you get in, by the way?"

"I said I had a message for you," he said, a flush in his cheek, embarrassed.

"And you did. So I can vouch for that too," Kurt said, smiling, everything fine.

Martin saw the legs sliding over the edge of the dumpster. They were going to get away with it.

"Have you seen Sabine?" he said, eager now to get away. "She's disappeared."

"Probably having a cigarette," Kurt said, grabbing a glass for Rieger off a passing tray. "Here you are. That's better."

Martin started for the door.

"No," Kurt said. "Not in the street. A lady doesn't. Try out back." He pointed to a door on the other side of the room. "It's Berlin. There's always a *Hinterhof*."

"Thank you, Herr Keller," Reiger said, his new ally, everything inside out.

She was standing away from the light, near the corner of the courtyard.

"You all right? I was getting worried."

"I've been putting two and two together. It's too noisy in there to do that."

"Which two and two?"

She looked up at him. "You're working for them again, aren't you?"

Martin said nothing.

"At first I thought maybe Kurt had arranged it. To get you out of the way. But then I thought, no, he likes to keep people where he can see what they're doing. Anyway, he doesn't have enough influence to do that, send you to Rossendorf, not unless you wanted it."

"Why would he want to get me out of the way?"

"And you don't want it. Stop," she said, holding up her hand. "I know you. You didn't want to do it even when— So not you.

Then who? Who wants you to do this? Who could make you? Two and two," she said, meshing her hands together. "Who's the new Andrei?"

He looked at her for a minute, not saying anything. "The old one."

"My god," she said. "But why? They can access anything you can access. It's not a foreign country here. It's their country. A least for this. What papers can you pass to them? Their own papers. So what—?"

"I don't know."

"No, you don't say. There's a difference."

"What do you want me to say? Do you think this was my idea?"

"No," she said, lowering her head. "I thought we were finished with that."

"I thought so too. Do you want me to say no to them? Here? As long as I'm here, I have to—"

"And who brought you here? Yes. I should have thought before—" She looked up. "You don't think it was my idea, do you? My fault, but not my idea."

"Fault. They saw an opportunity, they took it. It's what they do. You know that."

"Yes," she said, almost a whisper. "I know that. What opportunity?"

He looked away.

"At least before, we could talk." She rummaged through her bag and pulled out a cigarette and lit it. "I know, I shouldn't, but what's the difference now?" She drew on the cigarette. "Before, during the toasts, I thought, that's how it should have been. You, not Schilling. And I'd be standing next to you. Frau Keller and her distinguished husband. I thought you knew everything. Because I didn't know it, what you knew. My brilliant husband. Who looked at me like— Why wasn't it us up there?" She exhaled. "But it wasn't. I got everything wrong, didn't I?"

"I never said that."

"You listened to me. It was exciting, in the beginning. My brilliant husband, but he listens to me."

"I agreed with you."

"With my argument. The logic. But you never wanted to do it. Now I can see it. Then, all I saw was—well, who knows what I saw. It feels like a dream now. But you never wanted to, not really. You don't want to do it now. So listen to me again. One last time. Don't."

"I can't. Not here. They can do anything they want to me here."

"What would they do?"

He held up his fingers. "Which one? Let's say, this one. They pick me up on espionage charges. They say I was turned at Wakefield. So, Hohenschönhausen. And then I disappear, somewhere into the system. It would be that easy. All they'd have to do is pick me up."

"You're American."

"You think they'd set up a swap for me? Get Kurt to arrange it, another one? How many years would that take, do you think, even for Kurt? And meanwhile—"

"All right," she said, stopping him.

"Where do you think we are? In *Die Familie Schmidt*?"

"And this is how you'll live? Doing all that again?"

"No, raising our son. Trying to protect him. Isn't that why you wanted me to come? So I'm listening to you again. He's what matters now. If I have to—then I have to. How important can it be, compared to what we did before? If you can live with that—"

"But you didn't live with it. It ate you up. I watched it happen to you. When it was over, I think you were relieved. Even though it meant— And now it's starting again." She dropped the cigarette and stepped on it.

"Sabine. It's done."

She twisted her mouth. "'We'll talk about it later.' We used to talk about everything."

"Except once."

She looked away. "Yes, except once."

A door opened across the courtyard, the party noise spilling out with the shaft of light. Another smoker. The flick of a lighter, still not seeing them, an audible exhale. A man, bulky, not as old as some of the guests. He saw them on the second gulp of smoke, then leaned forward to see better.

"Martin, it's you?" Coming over to them now. "My god. I've been waiting for a chance all evening. And you're making speeches. Who would have thought?" With them now, putting a hand on Martin's shoulder. Not a hug, but more than a polite shake, fond.

"Stefan."

"Sabine?" Schell said, surprised. "But I thought you—weren't together."

Sabine smiled. "We're divorced. But still friends. Like in a play. How good to see you," she said, holding out her hand, not sure a kiss would be appropriate.

Stefan took her hand and raised it to his lips, a courtier. "*Gnädige Frau,*" he said.

"Oh, *gnädige.* Old anyway. How did we get to be such an age?"

"You look the same."

"Liar," she said, pleased. "Let me look at you."

But it was Martin who was staring, a piece of his past, barely visible in the courtyard light, a ghost. With the same full cheeks and wiry hair, receding now, the kind eyes earnest. All of it came back in a rush, the late nights at Göttingen, the complaints about one teacher or another, the guarded talk about the future, what to do when war came, the visit to Liesl's parents' house, needing a buffer, too nervous to go by himself, self-conscious looks across the table.

"And Liesl?" he said.

"Dead," Stefan said simply.

"I'm sorry."

Stefan nodded. "So strange to see you again. I never thought I would. You were on the other side of the world. Take a globe, spin it, literally the other side. Heisenberg said you'd never come back, the ones who left, but here you are. So he was wrong about that too." A twinkle in his eye, baiting the lecturer again. "Such different paths and now both back in Berlin," he said, sentimental. "So much to talk about. Well, but now there's time, yes? When we're at Rossendorf."

Sabine looked up. "You're not in Moscow? I thought—"

"I was. For years and years. But now here. And now our paths cross again," he said to Martin. "My old friend."

Sabine raised her head. "You're at Rossendorf," she said softly, her eyes growing wider, looking at Martin, a stage moment.

"Yes," Schell said.

"So you'll be working together," Sabine said, still looking at Martin.

"Oh, getting all my secrets," Schell said, playful. "Except I don't have any, not anymore. They don't trust me. So if that's what you're after—"

Martin put up his hands. "No secrets. That was . . . another time. A different time."

Schell nodded. "You know, I used to thank you. For all the help you were giving us. Of course, I didn't know it was you. Just someone helping. So we could catch up. Those days. Beria like a madman. Hurry up. And then it turned out that all the time it had been you, my old friend. I couldn't believe it."

"It wasn't all me."

"Yes, yes, the others. But you were—Martin. I knew you. And then everybody knew. I'm sorry about what happened to you. We needed the help, but you were the one to pay. But we did it. We built Stalin his bomb. And then later I wondered, do you feel it too, like me? That we have the blood on our hands." He raised his hands. "You never intend it, but then it's here. So easy. Then how do you get rid of it?" He made a washing motion. "That's not so easy. Or maybe you don't feel that. I'm sorry. I don't mean to assume—"

"I know what you mean. It's there."

"For all of us. It was there from the beginning. Even when we thought it was right, what we were doing." He stopped, a sudden quiet, Sabine just looking. "But tonight it's a party. For you. So no more talk. Plenty of time at Rossendorf." Another look from Sabine. "I'd be interested, how you feel now. What it was like in—that place. Everything. But do you know what I'd really like? Seeing you, both of you, I thought, let's go to the *Kneipe*, you remember, the one with the good beer? Some beer again, not this fake champagne. Schilling thinks it's elegant. So now that's you—elegant. But I know better."

"You shouldn't say things like that," Sabine said. "About the blood. It'll get you in trouble."

"Oh, trouble. I'm already in trouble. Why do you think they sent me here? It's supposed to be a punishment, not being in Moscow. Hah."

"Punishment for what?"

"Seeing the blood," he said, holding out his hands again. "Talking about it. Bad enough to think it. We thought we were making the peace," he said to Martin. "If both sides had it. But now look.

More and more. Bigger. Who can stop it now? And you think if only we'd never started. But it can't be too late to stop it. If someone would take responsibility." He stopped, catching himself, and put a hand on Martin's shoulder again. "It's so good to see you. To have someone to talk to at Rossendorf. The others there, how many are Stasi? Watch what you say. But you— So come. We'll have dinner. Really talk."

"Yes," Martin said, not looking at Sabine. "Really talk."

CHAPTER 5

Gerhard Jacobs used a tape recorder because, he said, "I take notes and then I can't read them afterwards." They were in his office on Jägerstrasse, not far from the Academy, an old high-ceilinged room cluttered with piles of paper and galley proofs, stale with pipe smoke. Jacobs was pudgy, the slack body of someone who never left his desk, and took his time between questions, refilling and tapping his pipe. Standard interview questions, easy, and then, seemingly from out of nowhere, "Did you ever have second thoughts about what you were doing? The ethics of it?"

Martin took a minute, watching the tape spools turning lazily on Jacobs's desk.

"At the time, no. The orders were very clear. One state having this terrible power alone posed a threat to everybody. Not just the Soviet Union, but everybody. With two, you could make a balance—one deters the other. It's fragile, yes, but it can work and the proof is, it has worked. Twenty years later and we have peace. Would that have happened if America had kept its atomic monopoly? Who could afford to take that chance? The bomb was too dangerous to be owned by anybody."

"And now?" Jacobs said quietly.

"Now?"

"Yes, how do you feel now?"

"Well, it's a very different time now. Maybe it was inevitable, maybe not, this arms race. Maybe it's human nature. But the result is that things are more dangerous than ever. The balance is threatened by one side, then the other makes more weapons. Then more," he said, hearing Schell's voice, realizing that this was for him, one strand in a web of sympathy. "This is not a matter one person can effect, some secret that needs to be shared. Only international cooperation can work."

Jacobs glanced up.

"And who better to lead that effort than the Socialist Republics? Who wants peace more? It's time for us to talk to the West. But it's also time for them to listen. The ethical question now is how do we not blow ourselves up? And how many answers can that question have?"

Jacobs nodded, a hint of a smile, and switched off the tape recorder. "Very eloquent," he said.

"Will any of it get through?"

"I think so. Not the arms race, but the Socialist Republics, yes, they like to hear that. Who wants peace more?"

"Why not the arms race?"

"Herr Keller, they don't want to end the arms race. They want to win it."

"Could I have a transcript copy? I'm giving a speech and I want to use some of the language."

"Of course. I'll send one over to the Berolina after it's typed."

"Before the blue pencil."

Jacobs smiled. "In this case, red. But yes. Thank you for this.

It's nice to have someone with the old spirit again. Sometimes, you know, you're so busy living day to day—what's in the shops, who's on the television?—that you forget we are part of a larger historical moment." He made a sweeping motion with his arm, taking in the piles of paper with the history. "Sometimes I think cynicism is a bigger threat than the West."

Martin looked up at him. Someone they'd put away for three years.

"Well," Martin said, hands on his knees. "Is there anything else you'd like to know?"

"Off the record? Many things, but we have enough for the piece. Where is Kurt today? He's usually here, the mother hen."

"There's a photo shoot with Peter. His son," he said, the word somewhere in his throat. "So he's playing hen there. *Stern*."

"*Stern*? Here, in the East?"

"The show's popular in the West."

"So. A Socialist Shirley Temple," Jacobs said, enjoying the joke. "Who would have imagined?" He looked up. "But it's your child, yes?"

Martin nodded.

"And how do you feel about that? With Kurt—"

"I'm glad Peter had such a caring father. Now he has two."

A little smile. "The machine is off," Jacobs said, pointing to the tape recorder.

Martin raised his eyes toward the high corner of the room. "Maybe not all of them."

"Maybe not. After a while you forget. It's too much work to remember. So, all right, a caring father. But someone who likes playing with fire too, I think. And sometimes you get your fingers burned. Of course, he must have a protector with—" He stopped and cocked his head toward the ceiling. "But protection comes and goes. And where does his money come from? They protect," he said, another nod to the ceiling, "but they don't pay. So where?"

Martin thought of the warehouse, the stacked pallets, then Spitzer's face at the Ganymed door, just a movement of his head.

"He got me out. That's all I know."

"Yes, of course. And me this interview. So we're both in his debt. One more question? You don't mind? For me, just curiosity. I hear you're going to Rossendorf. Don't worry, we don't say that in the paper. Such things are secret."

"What's the question?"

"Given how you feel, how can you work at such a place again?"

"They're not making bombs."

Jacobs said nothing.

"It's my field. It's all I know."

Jacobs nodded. "So, no ethical problems?"

Show nothing in your face. "No. No ethical problems."

———

He hurried across the bridge toward Alexanderplatz, where they had scheduled the photo shoot. Jacobs had been plodding and Martin thought he'd be late, but they were all still at the World Clock when he got there, standing around and arguing. Peter, in his Erich Schmidt clothes, seemed bored, someone with better things to do.

"They want to take pictures in the Gendarmenmarkt, but Kurt says we don't have permission to shoot there. Only Alexanderplatz and Karl-Marx-Allee. Berlin today. You know what they want—to show the bomb damage, then everybody thinks East Berlin is all like that."

Martin glanced at the clock, six hours earlier in New York, everyone still asleep, no bomb damage anywhere.

"Joachim, this is Martin," Peter said to the photographer, a way to interrupt the impasse.

"Another agent?" the photographer said, a needling glance to Kurt.

Peter shook his head. "A friend," he said. Not father, still sorting out his compartments. "Maybe we should start?"

"Yes, but we'll need more than one location. This is *Stern*, not some—Party paper."

"Well, a different party," Kurt said. "I'm sorry. Our permission is for here. You have plenty of places for pictures. Look at the TV tower, the tallest in the world when it's finished."

"But it's not finished yet. The clock gives me nothing. A department store?"

"Karl-Marx-Allee, then."

"Everyone shoots there. It's the only street anybody ever sees."

"But it's where Erich Schmidt lives."

"All right. Let's do that end of the square, with Karl-Marx in the background. Any problems with that?"

"No," Kurt said, annoyed. "You wanted the World of Erich Schmidt. This is his world. He doesn't go to the Mitte. Why would he?"

"Or the wall."

Kurt looked at him. "Or the wall. The arrangement was for Alexanderplatz only."

"Nobody told me. And if you want this to run, you'd better talk to someone about opening up a little."

"It doesn't matter to us if it runs. What do we gain?"

"More exposure. In the West."

"To what end? Our transmitters won't go any farther. Peter doesn't work in the West. This was information only for people who enjoy the show."

"Right, information only. A profile in *Stern*. Want to see the waiting list?"

"I'm not on it." Kurt took a minute. "Something may be possible. What do you need?"

"How about Potsdam? We're calling him Erich the Great. Fun to have him at Sanssouci. A new Friedrich."

"You're joking."

The photographer shrugged. "I just take the pictures. Why don't you see what you can do?"

His tone dismissive, to an assistant, but Kurt nodded.

"It's not possible today. You can come back?"

"If you get us another pass. All day. I've never seen Sanssouci. I'll need to look it over."

"It's very nice," Peter said, making peace. "Martin, have you been?"

"A long time ago."

"Oh, with *Mutti*. It's in the East, but west of Berlin. So if you go west from West Berlin, you get to the East." He laughed a little, a schoolboy conundrum. "So you'll come?"

Still planning expeditions, Martin still a visitor.

"Let me get permission first," Kurt said. Then, to the photographer, "The palace grounds only. Not the town. I'll call you. Now, we can begin here?"

The photographer and his assistant began moving equipment toward the far end of the square.

"How was Gerhard?" Kurt said.

"Friendly."

"Good."

Martin lowered his voice. "Have you heard from the police yet?"

Kurt shook his head. "Maybe a waiter vouched for him and they don't need us. It's just Hans making a drama."

"Still, police."

"Don't worry," Kurt said, putting a hand on his shoulder. "There's no connection."

Spitzer at the door, not even a nod, just a look on his face. Come.

"What's that?" Kurt said, louder. "Makeup? He's a child." The assistant stopped, brush in midair. "A child's skin doesn't need makeup."

"It does if you want it right," the photographer said, adjusting a large reflector disc. "Christ, look at those clouds. You ever get any sun over here?"

The assistant dabbed at Peter's cheeks with the brush, but lightly, trying not to make a fuss. "There you go, handsome."

A few people had stopped in the square, intrigued by the reflector discs.

"Look, it's Erich Schmidt."

Peter smiled and waved to them, in character.

"Sometimes I wonder, can this be good for him?" Kurt said to Martin. "All this attention."

"He's okay. It's a job. He sees that."

"He doesn't need a job. He has me."

Martin said nothing, letting the words settle.

"I wish that one knew *his* job," Kurt said, jerking his thumb toward the photographer. "We'll be here all day and I have things to do." He looked at his watch. "*Ach.*"

"Busy day?"

"There's another exchange. Lists to go over. All of that takes time. And here we are, taking pictures in Alexanderplatz. *Quatsch*."

"I can stay if you like. Get him home."

"I don't like to ask." He looked again at his watch. "Maybe. Let's see how it goes. Sabine said you saw Schell at the reception. How was that?"

"Hard to believe it's twenty years. People don't change."

"Well, they don't get better anyway."

"I'm going to Dresden. He wants to show me around."

"I'm sorry about this. I know I promised you Berlin. When we made the arrangement. But the Academy—"

"Things change. I still have weekends. For Peter. If that's okay with you."

"Of course."

The exaggerated politeness of an Asian ritual, as if they were bowing to each other.

"Martin, you know you're welcome anytime. It's a little unusual, but it's okay, no? Oh, and now what?" he said to the photographer, who was walking toward them, snapping pictures. "His father too? There's no permission for that. Just Peter. Erich."

"Not you," the photographer said, then turned to Martin. "I didn't recognize you before. I didn't know it was you."

"And there's still no permission," Kurt said. "It's not allowed."

"How long have you been here?"

"Not for interviews either. Just the boy."

"Okay, okay," the photographer said, letting his camera fall on its strap. "What's the connection?"

"Friend of the family," Martin said, indicating Kurt. Not Peter's father, a story for *Stern*.

"I thought you were in jail."

"I got out."

The photographer looked at Kurt. "One of your swaps?"

"Are you finished here?" Kurt said. "It's getting late."

"Finished for now. Let me know about Potsdam."

"And the film?" Kurt said, extending his hand. "There was no permission for anyone else."

"But now they're all mixed up on the roll. You can have yours. Souvenir of the shoot. You even get the TV tower behind. I'll bring them with me to Potsdam. Don't worry, *Stern*'s not interested in you. Just *Die Familie Schmidt*."

It took another half hour to get the equipment packed up and loaded in the car. Kurt had insisted he drive them to the checkpoint, a controlled visit. "It's not tourists, photographers from *Stern*. They promise one thing and then something's in the magazine that shouldn't be there."

"Peter and I can walk," Martin said. "It'll do us good."

Kurt lifted his head to protest, then nodded. "Yes, all right. It's not too far for you?"

Peter rolled his eyes. "Bye, Joachim. See you at Sanssouci."

"Erich the Great," the photographer said, grinning.

"That wasn't so bad," Martin said as they walked toward Karl-Marx-Allee.

"No, but it's boring. The standing around."

"Do people always recognize you?"

"They think I'm Erich. It's the same person to them. With Kurt too sometimes. He's nicer to me since I'm Erich. He says it's good for all of us."

He said nothing for a few minutes, working something out.

"What?" Martin said.

"You said you would be here. To help take care of *Mutti*."

"I will be."

"No, you'll be in Dresden. She told me." He looked at Martin. "You didn't."

"It's not for a while yet. It's for my work. I'll be here on weekends."

"She needs you all the time."

He turned to Peter. "What's wrong?"

"The cough is worse. I hear her, in the night."

"Peter, if she needs me, I'll be there. I told you that. You believe me, yes?" He waited for Peter to nod. "But now she's still okay and I have to work."

"Are you going to be a spy again?"

A lightness in his stomach, leaving a step and not feeling another one beneath.

"No. Scientific work. It's difficult to explain. I don't even know exactly what yet."

"I thought you would live with us."

"No, Kurt and Sabine are married. It's their house."

"But she asked for you. She made him bring you here."

"She wanted to help me. Get out of that place."

"You don't see it, the way it makes her happy, all of us together." Another step, nothing beneath.

"Sometimes we see what we want to see."

"I'm good at seeing things. Beate says so. On the show. She says I have a clear eye."

Martin smiled. "You're eleven years old."

"Twelve. Almost twelve."

"Twelve."

"So what's going to happen?"

"What do you mean?"

"You said you'd help, if she gets sick," he said, picking the same scab. "And now you're leaving."

"I'm not going far. And I'm not leaving. I have to do this. Just for a while. Make myself useful. So I can stay here."

"That's good. You're leaving so you can stay." The hint of a smile.

"It's like Potsdam. Go west to go to the East."

"If you kept going, you'd be in America."

Martin looked at him, trying to sense what was being said.

"I guess. Long way to go, though."

"You're American."

"That doesn't mean I'm going there."

"We're not allowed to leave. But you could go." A question. "You could see your family."

"They're dead, Peter."

"All of them?"

Martin stopped walking and looked at him. "You're my family. I'm not going anywhere."

"Even if *Mutti*—?"

"Even then."

Peter thought about this for a second, then nodded. Martin took a step forward, expecting a hug, but Peter lifted his arm instead and took his hand, formal, a handshake to seal the deal, Kurt's son.

Afterward Martin walked up the hill to Volkspark Friedrichshain, with its old fountain lined with fairy-tale statues. He doubled back through one patch of trees, the way he'd been taught, but no one was following. Not since that first day, in fact, the man in the bulky coat, almost as if someone had decided he wasn't worth the effort. Andrei was waiting by Little Red Riding Hood, his short, bristly hair not unlike a wolf's.

"So you made contact."

"A reunion. Just what you wanted. Old times, the *Kneipe* where we used to drink. Very like his old self, in fact. He hasn't changed."

"Suspicious of you, do you think?"

"No. The opposite. I've been out of it for so long that I don't have any strings attached. Not in Moscow, not here. Someone he can talk to."

"Excellent."

"I thought you'd think so."

Andrei looked over at him, but said nothing.

"I did an interview with *Neues Deutschland* and pretty much said what he says, so he won't have to waste time fishing for my 'beliefs.' I also got a transcript, so he can see what I said before they cut it. Socialists for peace. International cooperation. An end to the arms race."

Andrei smiled. "Be careful or we'll have to start watching you."

"I'm going to Dresden so he can show me around. Then dinner."

"A fast worker," Andrei said.

"Mm. I'm staying over, so it'll be a long dinner, brandy after, lots of talk."

"Excellent," Andrei said again.

"It would be even better if you told me what I'm supposed to be looking for—listening for. I know, civilization and its discontents, but what, specifically? He seemed just the same to me. A good man. So what's changed?" Not mentioning the blood on his hands, playing Andrei now.

"A good man. It's not a field that requires sensitivity. Pragmatism would be better."

"So what, exactly?"

"There's a conference in Geneva. Atoms for Peace. He's been invited."

"Don't let him go if you're worried."

"That's not so easy. The invitation's been offered. Everyone in the scientific community is aware of it. And he has friends there. And you know how it is, some of them would like to embarrass the Soviet Union."

"So he sends his regrets. Something keeps him at home. You've done it before."

"And if he sends a paper to be read instead? What then? Then he's a martyr. Another Pasternak."

"That depends on what's in the paper."

"Exactly."

"And he's going to tell me."

"We can't take any chances. One: if he attends the conference, does he plan to defect? Two: what does he say?"

"Do you really think he'd defect? Stefan? After all these years? A good Communist?"

"Maybe you could tell us."

"Maybe."

"His wife is dead. We have no one we can hold behind now."

"To make sure he comes back," Martin said, the spittle in his mouth suddenly sour.

"So. Have dinner and see what's on his mind."

Martin looked at his watch. "And the next meeting?"

"The U-bahn at Eberswalder Strasse. The wurst stand under the arches. It's good."

"By the way, I don't think I've been followed. I thought—"

"You won't be. We told them so many people on the street, it gets clumsy. Of course, they don't like this, even a polite request, so keep an eye out in case they do it to spite us."

"One more thing, then? Since you're so well-connected?"

Andrei raised his eyebrows.

"The morning of the exchange, there was a shooting."

"An ambulance. I remember."

"The driver was killed, the other kid was taken to Hohenschön-hausen and then he disappeared. Would you find out where he was sent?"

"You have his name?"

Martin shook his head. "The police report will have it."

"And why?"

"Well, he took a shot at me, for one thing, so I'm curious."

"Schell is the assignment here."

"I'll connect the dots later. I have a hunch."

"A hunch."

"It's a simple favor. It shouldn't be hard to do."

"The Service doesn't do favors."

"I'm not asking the Service. I'm asking you."

Andrei took a second. "Because he shot at you? A wall jumper? Maybe you were just in the way."

Martin nodded. "There were two of us by the car." He looked over at Andrei. "You gave me two assignments."

———

Schell met him at the train station with a car and driver.

"I thought, first, a look at the old city. I've only had a glimpse myself since I got here. Then, Rossendorf. It's convenient having the driver, but I think he also listens, so be careful in the car."

"Let's walk, then. It's not far."

"Ah, you've been here."

"Before the war."

"Now look," Stefan said, leading the way, a crab's walk, skittering and hunched, someone who spent the day bent over a worktable.

The bombing raid that leveled the city had been nearly twenty years ago, but much of it was still in ruins, worse than Berlin. Prager Strasse, the main artery into the old city, was a patchy field, with a few Soviet-style buildings under construction and the *Schloss* at its end a pile of jagged walls.

"The Zwinger is almost finished," Stefan said, "the restoration. And the Opera. They can't do everything at once. There's so much. And where does the money come from?"

"My god," Martin said, looking around the square, some of the walls still streaked with scorch marks, as if the stone itself had burned. Around the corner the Frauenkirche was a pile of rubble. He remembered the last time he'd been here, walking along the Elbe with Sabine, the city like a baroque stage set.

"And these were conventional bombs. Not the ones we have today. Now there'd be nothing. Nothing." They stood looking for a few minutes. "Well. Come. I'll show you where we make them."

"I thought Rossendorf wasn't a weapons facility."

"It's not. Research. To make them better, more powerful. And then you have this. But how do you stop, when you're already part of it? When do you say no?"

"Stefan—"

"Yes, I know, forgive me. Heresy. But it's useful to see how it ends. The theoretical work. For us only numbers. But this is how it ends." He took a breath. "Come. We'll save the porcelain collection for another day."

"It survived?"

"It was hidden. Like us. Heisenberg's team. We were protected. But the Russians came anyway. Remember, nothing in the car. I know he listens."

Instead they talked about Göttingen, happier times, Martin glancing toward the front seat, imagining the driver's report. Sentimental memories, now notes for the file.

Rossendorf was a suburb east of Dresden and the Institute a gated compound surrounded by woods. There were factory-like buildings with offices and labs and parking lots and a smokestack over the central boiler room, a self-contained village. A sentry at the gate checked IDs. His new home. But which of them hadn't been guarded? Los Alamos, remote on its mesa, Harwell, country house brick, but still patrolled, then Wakefield, real bars, not metaphorical ones. He had spent his whole adult life behind one fence or another. Could he really do it again? But he wouldn't have to live here, just report for work and listen, like Stefan's driver.

"Where do people live? Dresden?"

"Some. More in the town here. We'll find something comfortable for you, don't worry. It's easy with one. A family would be harder."

They had lunch with some of the staff, including an almost silent Klaus Fuchs, then toured the labs and had introductory meetings with the other scientists, a make-work afternoon.

"Why don't I get you settled in at the club and give you a little time for yourself. We'll have dinner there later."

"The club?"

"Dresdner Klub, and it's exactly what it sounds like. A smoking room and a library and all the rest of it. Except the waiters don't wear gloves."

"A socialist club."

Stefan smiled. "Terrible service. It's a retreat for intellectuals.

So look how far you've come. Professor Mannheim wouldn't believe it."

The club was in the spa town of Weisser Hirsch, a nineteenth-
century villa posing as a castle high on a hill overlooking the Elbe
and the city off to the west. The wood-paneled interior reminded
Martin of the Union League Club in Chicago, where he'd once had
an interview during that time after Los Alamos when he thought
he'd teach at a university, before the Service had a different idea.
There was an elegant dining room with starched linen tablecloths
and silver and, even better, an adjoining terrace with a view. A
world away from their walk down Prager Strasse, the dusty gray
buildings, women lined up at the shops.

It was still too cool to eat outside so they had a quick, shivering
drink on the terrace, then went back in, Stefan nodding to a few
people on the way to their table. A restaurant murmur with the occasional tinkling of cutlery. The menus had stiff covers, like books.

"So you were impressed? With the facility?"

"Very. No expense spared."

"It's like that in Russia too. Only the best for Dubna. Never
mind the shortages."

"Lucky for you, though."

"Yes. We could do our work. The work becomes everything.
You don't see the rest."

"Los Alamos was like that. Exciting. Just to see if you could do
it. Later? We didn't think about that. Well, some did."

Stefan looked at him. "Such different paths. And here we are
at the same place. You know, since the reception, when I saw you,
I keep thinking about those days. Göttingen. What if this. What if
that. But we can't change it now."

"No."

"Tell me something—you don't mind? I always wondered. Did Sabine know?"

"No," Martin said, not even hesitating.

"And yet she came here."

"She met somebody else. From here. It wasn't the politics."

"Somebody else," Stefan said, almost to himself. "When I think of the way she was with you."

Martin shrugged. "She needed somebody to take care of her. She had a child. And I was—gone. Who knew for how many years. In those days they didn't have these swaps. You were there for good."

"Still, a divorce."

"I never blamed her for that. It was the right thing to do."

Stefan looked down, embarrassed. "And none of my business. Excuse me. A curiosity, that's all. How things turn out. So, we should order. The blue trout is excellent."

Martin smiled, closing his menu. "You're the expert. In fact, you're my boss now, aren't you?"

"Not yet. But try the trout."

He placed the order with the waiter.

"What about you?" Martin said. "What if, what if. How was it, during the war?"

"How was it," Stefan repeated. "Like walking on eggshells. Heisenberg protected us, but still. You had to watch what you said." He looked up, a wry smile. "Good training for later. But I was safe. Not a Communist, not then, not anything. German. That's what I told myself, to get through it. I was German, that's all. But of course we were working for them. You couldn't get away from that—we were working for the Nazis. What made it possible is we never thought we could do it, make the bomb. We thought it would take years and by that time—"

"We always wondered how close you were."

"Not so close. Speer didn't believe in it. So we never got the money." He looked up. "We never asked, either. That's how we could live with it. That's my theory, anyway. So there's a what-if. What if we'd been able to do it? What then? It's interesting to think, what would we have done? Given Hitler the bomb?"

The waiter came with the wine.

"And after?"

"After? The Russians came and scooped us all up. Another what-if. What if I'd been captured by the Americans? Maybe we would have worked together. When you were—" He stopped. "Huh. Maybe you would have spied on me."

Martin took a sip of the wine.

"I never knew you were a Communist," Stefan said. "How long?"

"At Göttingen. They were against the Nazis. Nobody else seemed to be. So. But it had to be secret. I would have told you, but I couldn't."

"They would have killed you, the Nazis. I know. Huh, it's funny. I always thought Sabine might be, not you. I'm not a very good judge. So you did this for them, copied the plans."

"I thought the Soviets deserved to know. They were allies, why not share it with them. Anyway, that's what I thought. I don't know that I think that now. But now is a little late. In the end, did it matter? Stalin was going to get his bomb anyway."

"It gave us two years," Stefan said simply.

"Two years. But you pay with fifteen."

The trout arrived, curled from cooking and deep blue.

"So that's me," Martin said. "After that Harwell and then prison and then they made the swap. So it's years since I've done the work. I hope this won't be a problem. I don't want to let you down."

Stefan dismissed this with his hand. "The brain doesn't go to prison. At least I don't have to worry about our secrets. Unless you're working for the Americans now." A twinkle in his eye, enjoying the tease.

Martin smiled. "I'm retired. From both sides. Every side."

"Oh, from every side. Wouldn't it be wonderful. Anyway, the secrets are not so tempting. You'll see. America is years ahead. The first reactor here wasn't operational until '57. So we're still playing catch-up. On the other hand, that means we have a lot to do. So we can lose ourselves in the work." He looked up. "I'm glad you're here."

"And you?" Martin said. "Are you Soviet now? All those years there."

"Still German. Like with Heisenberg—no party."

"So they finally sent you back."

"They sent me here to get rid of me. Another Siberia. But it looks better to come here. Home to Germany. A reward for all your good work. But not really home. Such a strange place—everybody listening. It's like Russia that way. Everything means something else. At Arzamas we had 'secretaries.' Not bodyguards, secretaries. Wherever you went. Except we never went anywhere. Once you were at Arzamas, you didn't leave."

"How long were you there?"

"Years. 'Los Arzamas' we called it," he said, a little smile. "So just like you. The same paths, then."

"But that means they must have trusted you, to send you there."

"By then, yes. Not at first. At first I was like all the Germans. We were sent to *sharaski*—you know *sharaski*?"

Martin shook his head.

"Special institutes set up in prison camps. No problem with security. We had our own housing, we weren't with the prisoners— we would have died and they wanted us to work—but still, it was a camp. Still slave labor. Reparations for the war. And do you know what? We were grateful. They could have shot us, but they wanted our brains. So that was the trade. We survived. And when they were finished with us, they sent us home."

"But not you."

"Well, by that time I knew too much. I was at Arzamas. We were doing important work. Of course, all Russians, no foreigners, not even Germans from the *sharaski*, but I had a specialty and Sakharov asked for me, so they couldn't say no. Liesl hated it. You know there's a monastery there, the original Arzamas, and Liesl said the bells made her crazy. And the isolation. Hundreds of kilometers from anywhere. Nothing to look at but birch trees and this old monastery. I had my work—our team was given the Lenin Prize. A team prize because I was foreign and it should go to a Russian. But poor Liesl. Anyway, finally, begging and begging, they reassigned me to Dubna. So now at least we had Moscow. But was it any better, I wonder. She never learned Russian, not really. We never had friends, just each other. The Germans we knew had gone home. But me they were never going to send back. So it wasn't a very good life I gave her. And then she got sick," he said, his voice trailing off, following some memory.

Martin said nothing, giving him a minute.

"So why do they want to get rid of you?" he said finally. "Now, I mean."

"Now? They think I'm a bad influence on my colleagues. Like Sakharov, some of the others. After Liesl died, I didn't have to be careful anymore. What did I have to lose? For years I said nothing. That Lenin Prize? That was after we developed the hydrogen bomb. A great achievement, technically. And it gave us parity again with the Americans. I confess to you, we were proud to receive it. And after? Back to work, make it bigger. I think that was the first time I started thinking—what were we doing? It was already big enough. To destroy everything. But now, even bigger. A madness. What

JOSEPH KANON

if they actually use it? And who's to stop it? They want a bigger bomb, but they don't make it. We do. So what is our responsibility? They won't stop. But what if we stop?"

"What if," Martin said quietly.

"Yes. So another speech, excuse me. But if not us, who?"

"Stefan, this kind of talk—"

"I know. Gets me in trouble. And my old friend looks out for me," he said, another smile.

Martin smiled back, feeling his stomach clench.

"Don't worry. You know what it says on the Lenin Prize, the medal? A hero of the Soviet Union. A hero for making the hydrogen bomb. So they're careful with me."

"Plenty of heroes ended up in the gulag."

"In the old days, yes. Now, exile in Rossendorf. It doesn't matter so much what the Germans say to each other. Just keep him out of Dubna. But even in Dubna they have ears. You just have to get their attention."

Martin looked up, his stomach tight again.

"Don't do anything foolish," he said.

"That's what Liesl used to say. Keep your head down."

"Still good advice."

Stefan nodded. "But I don't know what it means anymore. What's foolish? She would tell me, but now she's not here."

"What can any of us do? One person."

"Well, that's what I've been thinking about. What? Get their attention. Not some whispering on the coffee break. Really get their attention. I could never do it before. I had to be safe for Liesl. They use the family that way—as hostages. And you don't want them to get hurt, so you do what they say. If you go somewhere, you come back. You say what's approved. Nothing foolish. But now their hostage is dead. And I'm in this place. Not Germany. Not Rus-

148

sia either. So where is my home now? Nowhere. It doesn't matter where I am. If I come back."

"Come back from where?" Martin said, alert.

"Anywhere," Stefan said. "And you. It's the same with you. Where's home now? Not here. Why did you come here?"

"They got me out of prison. So I came."

"No, I mean here. Why come to Rossendorf." Looking closely at him now. "To do this work again. After everything."

"It's what they want." He looked away. "'No' isn't an answer. So you separate. Just give me equations to solve. Don't tell me what they're used for."

Stefan nodded. "That's what I used to say. So we're alike that way too." His eyes well-meaning, somehow avuncular. Not young anymore, the wiry hair sticking out in tufts. "And then one day you can't say it anymore."

Martin waited.

"This child Sabine has—it's yours, yes?"

"My son."

"And what do you say to him, when he asks someday? Why you do this work? How do you answer him? You know, we never had children. A tragedy for Liesl. But for this one reason I was glad. How would I explain myself? For making these bombs. What explanation could there be?"

Martin looked at him, his stomach suddenly moving again, some fist squeezing it.

"I don't know," he said.

Stefan reached across the table, putting his hand on Martin's arm. "Forgive me. I don't mean you alone. All of us. All of us have to answer for it." He took his hand back, a resigned smile. "After the generals. Come. Shall we have a brandy? It's not too late. And so good to talk to you."

Martin got up and followed him to the smoking room, the white tablecloths and bulky suits passing in a kind of background blur. And then, walking behind Stefan's hunched shoulders, the unruly wiry hair, Martin suddenly knew he couldn't do it. He felt a shortness of breath, as if someone had just punched him, and then the pressure on his lungs, his ribs closing around them. Andrei's face. Do what you have to do. And suddenly he couldn't. What do you say to him when he asks someday? I betrayed everybody. I kept doing it, after I had any reason to do it. Andrei wouldn't let me go. I was still useful, one of them. For good. Unless I betrayed them too. But no one betrayed the Service, no one. Only play them, if you could, play for time. Work both sides, like Kurt. To do what? I don't know, but I can't do this. Looking again at the sprigs of hair bobbing in front of him. A man he hadn't seen in twenty years. Do what you have to do. But what do I say? I did those things. But I won't do this.

"Are you all right?" Stefan's voice, oddly far away.

"Yes. Just lost my breath for a minute," Martin said. "I'm fine."

"Would you prefer I didn't smoke?"

"No, no, it's nothing."

"Liesl hated the smell. You and your cigars, she'd say. Outside. But of course in the winter it wasn't possible."

They found a corner with two club chairs and a stand-up ashtray and ordered brandies.

"I read the interview with *Neues Deutschland*, the copy you gave me."

"The uncensored one."

"Yes. It'll be interesting to see what they take out. You never know. What's the fashion this week? At least your man seemed intelligent. My interview—why did they even want it? The man knew nothing about science, nothing."

Martin smiled. "Hans Rieger."

"Yes. You know him?"

"I met him. One of Kurt's contacts. He was a crime reporter for Springer, but he was working for the Stasi on the side and got caught, so now he's here." He looked up, another smile. "Science reporter for *Neues Deutschland.*"

"Ouf. They're all working for the Stasi at that place. Whether they know it or not. Ah, here we are," he said, lifting a brandy from the waiter's tray. "*Prost.*"

"So what did you think of the piece?"

"I thought how alike we were. I'm in Moscow and you're in England and yet we think the same. The same conclusions. No wonder we became friends."

"That's funny. I remember us always arguing."

Stefan smiled. "Well, maybe it's true. But after that, the same. You'll see. I brought something for you." He pulled a folded paper out of his pocket. "Some remarks I'm preparing. I'd welcome your thoughts. Any comments."

Martin glanced through the speech. An international association of concerned scientists. Information exchange. A slowdown to the arms race. Treaties.

"You can't say these things."

"Not here, no."

"Or Moscow."

"No. A conference."

Martin looked up at him. What Andrei wanted. Handing it to him. "Where?"

"In Geneva. They're calling it Atoms for Peace. A nice thought, no?"

"And they're letting you go?"

"Oh, because I'm such a dangerous character? The truth? I

don't know. They don't have the hostage anymore. On the other hand, I'm not representing Russia. East Germany. And just having me speak gives them recognition. They'd do almost anything for that. Almost. So maybe yes, maybe no. We'll see."

"They'll want to know what you're going to say."

Stefan nodded. "An approved text. Not this. They won't know about this."

"Unless someone tells them."

"That's why I'm asking you. I don't trust the others. They're here too long or they're like Klaus, a believer. It's a religion with him. First Luther, then the Party. It's the same impulse. He would have to report it—a matter of conscience. But I'm not asking him."

Martin said nothing for a minute, back in the dining room, waiting for his breath to come.

"I can't be involved in this. Any trouble."

"I understand. There's the boy."

"You realize none of this is going to happen," he said, putting his finger on the paper.

"I know. But just to say it, that's already something. How else do we start?"

Martin took another second. "I'm sorry. I never saw this. If anyone asks later. Put it away."

"Some notes for a talk. Not the plans for the atomic bomb. If they ask you, tell them. Tell the truth."

"I won't be used against you. And I won't go back to prison. Put it away. What makes you think you can take it out of the country?"

"This paper? No. It's here." He tapped the side of his head. "So let them search." He put the paper in his pocket.

"You do this, it's like throwing a hand grenade at Rossendorf. We'll all be—"

"So your advice is, don't do it? Don't give such a talk? So we can go on as before."

Martin said nothing.

"A hand grenade," Stefan said wryly. "You think it would have such an impact? One speech? You're right, I didn't think about Rossendorf, just myself. So I'm sorry for that. All the questions. But nobody knew about it." He looked over. "Not even you. So an inconvenience only. For me, of course, it's different."

Martin raised his head. "You won't be able to come back," he said quietly.

Stefan looked away. "You know, I think you're right. One speech? Is that enough to get anyone's attention? Dubna, for example. Will they hear the speech? So how to do it? Actions speak louder than words. So, an action they would hear."

"If you defected," Martin said, the final piece.

"As you say, it will be difficult to come back, after the speech."

"I haven't heard this. Any of it."

"Of course not. Speculation only. A general conversation. Would such a thing get people's attention?"

"Everybody's."

"So it's something to consider. In principle."

Another sip of brandy. "Why are you telling me this? It's some kind of test?"

Stefan smiled. "A specialty of yours, I remember. Always prepared. Up late. Me, I would just walk in and take my chances. But you were ready. No surprises."

"You don't want to take chances with this."

"No. So maybe a little test. I wanted to see your reaction. Would anyone hear? We're in our own little world here. So I ask you. And you say yes."

"You didn't need to ask me that. What else?"

"So you could prepare. A new exam. If such a thing happened."

"Prepare."

Stefan looked at him. "Don't take this job. I know you came for me, but if I'm not here? Klaus Fuchs would be in charge, at least for a while. Your old friend from Los Alamos. He's already jealous of you."

"Jealous. Why?"

Stefan shrugged. "He thinks he was the only one. Not the Rosenbergs, not you. A strange thing to be proud of, but he's a strange man. So think how unpleasant. And you're right, they would question you. My old friend. More unpleasantness. Stay in Berlin. You had no idea I was thinking of this. I can call Schilling at the Academy, say we talked and the work isn't suitable. Better a post in Berlin. Then we're not connected. You pass the test."

Martin sat up, suddenly light-headed. Everything inside out again. Andrei's face.

"I can't," he said.

"Can't?"

"I mean, it wasn't my decision."

"I'll talk to Schilling."

"It's not just that." Use anything. "It's better—for Peter. For me to be a weekend father. Until he gets used to me. If I'm in Berlin all the time—it's hard for Sabine."

"Well, Leipzig, then."

"You don't want me here? I was looking forward to it. Working together. This other thing—who knows if it will happen?"

"But if it does, then it's too late."

Martin shook his head. "I'll be as surprised as anyone. You never said a thing." Another knot, tangled.

"Of course I would like you here," Stefan said, visibly touched now. "This idea—it was for you—"

"I know," he said, finishing the brandy, safe again.

"I can still warn you. So you have time to prepare."

"Stefan, don't say anything more. To me. To anybody. They must be watching. Both of us."

Stefan looked around, a mock concern. "And what do they see? Friends having a drink. An innocent moment," he said, lifting his glass.

Martin smiled a little. "An innocent moment," he said, hearing himself.

CHAPTER 6

Klaus Fuchs was waiting on the platform, reading *Neues Deutschland*. Martin's first impulse was to duck, but Klaus had looked up and seen him, so there was no avoiding a meeting. A gray day, overcast, with the promise of drizzle, a morning alone to think, not field more questions on the train.

"Back to Berlin?" Klaus said. "A short visit."

"Really just to see the place. Stefan wanted me to meet some of the others. Don't let me interrupt. You probably have work," he said, nodding to the briefcase at Klaus's feet.

"Yes, but later. Right now I'm reading you, in fact." His watery eyes lively behind his glasses, making a joke.

"Ah, the interview. They ran it. Well, don't believe everything you read."

The eyes clouding now, not a joke. "But it's *Neues Deutschland*."

"How do I sound?"

"An idealist. And a good socialist. It's true, no?"

"It must be, if it's there." Still trying to be light.

Klaus looked at him, not sure how to take this. "It's what's been agreed. It's important for Party discipline, for everyone to follow what's agreed."

"Could I have a look?"

Fuchs handed him the paper.

"I suppose it could be worse," Martin said, giving it a quick scan. "Newspapers. You never sound like yourself. Don't you think?"

"I don't know. I don't give interviews."

"Not even when you arrived? You must have. It was news."

"The Party requested it, yes." He paused, hesitating. "You don't mind a criticism? It's true what you say here, the general outline. But also a little misleading. When you were—passing information, they already had it. I gave them everything. You were a confirmation. So there's no reason for these feelings, any guilt. They already had everything. If you had never done it, it would have been the same."

Martin looked at him, another scarecrow pose, rigid with conviction.

"I didn't know that. Why did they want me to do it, then?" A capital crime.

"To make sure maybe. That it was accurate. But they already had it." He took a step back. "You had a pleasant visit?" Awkward, not used to small talk.

"Very. They put me up at the Dresdner. Quite a pile. I had no idea."

"What?" Fuchs said, genuinely puzzled.

"That there were such places here."

"Oh, places of luxury, you mean. Not so many. But ours are for the people, not businessmen and Nazis."

Martin looked at him. Did he really believe this? A man of faith. First Luther, then the Party.

"Here comes the train," Martin said, relieved. Or would they have to sit together all the way to Berlin? "Are you waiting for someone?"

"No. Why?"

"That man over there keeps looking at you. I thought maybe—"

Fuchs swiveled around, then turned back, embarrassed. "It's for my protection," he said.

"Is that why he's so obvious? So everybody will know?"

"We all have one at Rossendorf. For our protection. You don't mind if I do my work on the train?" He held up the briefcase. "It's not polite, but I need to prepare—"

"Of course. I'll finish this, if you don't mind." He nodded to the paper. "See what the Party line is today." A deliberate barb, Fuchs reacting as if he'd been jabbed. Martin looked up. "Do you ever disagree? What then?"

"Then I try to understand the reasons."

Martin waited.

"I wanted us to work on reactors. That was my dream. The energy of the future. But the Republic has no money for such an investment. And plenty of cheap coal. So I understood the thinking." His voice soft, still filled with disappointment.

They sat across the aisle from each other, not speaking but aware of any movement—a shuffling of papers, the snap of a briefcase lock. Martin stared out the window, the drizzle finally there, turning the landscape hazy, gray houses and pale green fields, allotments with toolsheds. If you had never done it, it would have been the same. But he had done it. And now this. So clear last night in the dining room, but now cloudy again, like the day. Andrei would want details, not just what he'd said, his mood, what he was thinking. Martin could do that, a kind of card trick, the real card unseen in his palm, but who was he doing it for? Stefan? A man who made bombs and now wanted to make up for it. Maybe for himself, making up for everything. Doing the right thing. By betraying Andrei, which only a fool would do. Or Stefan, which was like betraying himself. How many half stories could you juggle before one of them misses its turn, falls to the ground? He looked again through the condensation on the window. A made-up country, but the land rushing past was real. What if the train kept going, switching tracks in Berlin? But where did he want it to go? Except back.

Fuchs walked with him down the platform.

"I'm sorry for the work," he said. "We didn't get to talk."

"We will. At Rossendorf. Here's your paper."

"No, no, it's for you. Something for your scrapbook," he said, trying to be pleasant. He slowed. "What I said before, I hope you won't think– Of course what you did was valuable. I'm sure the Party was grateful. It's just the way I express myself sometimes."

Martin nodded, an end to it.

"Can I drop you somewhere? We can share a taxi."

Before he could answer, Andrei came into view over Fuchs's shoulder, holding a newspaper, his meeting signal. A day early. His being here jarring, a disturbance in the air.

"No, I'll walk. It's not far. We'll see you again soon, I hope."

Fuchs tipped his hat, oddly formal, and headed for the taxi rank. Martin quickly looked down the platform. No one. He started for the station hall, expecting Andrei to intercept him. What was wrong? Slow down. But he was outside the station doors before Andrei appeared.

"A coffee? No, not here. They watch the station café. I know a place."

"I thought it was tomorrow, the meeting."

"It was. But I had the time."

"Something wrong?"

"No. Come." He cocked his head back toward the station. "That's something you don't see every day. Two famous spies. On the same train. What did they say to each other, I wonder." Having fun with it.

"Nothing. He had some work to do."

"A shy man. I remember."

"From when?"

"By reputation."

"You took a chance, letting him see you."

"No, we never met. There was nobody to recognize. Nobody on the train?"

"Not that I noticed."

"And you would have."

"He had a tail at Dresden. Maybe they're tag teaming him."

"I doubt it. They watch at Rossendorf. But it's probably not worth the expense to follow him."

"So he's not one of yours anymore?"

"Not for years."

"Why not?"

"When he confessed, he confessed too much. Names. We had to scramble to save the network. An amateur." He looked over. "Not like you. You always saw what needed to be done. And you never told them anything. The Service doesn't forget that. Here we are."

Another coffee shop with hissing steam, another corner table, Andrei's routine.

"So why the meeting? I thought this was against the rules."

"This once. I wanted to see you. First, how did it go in Dresden?"

"Just the way you wanted. Old stories. Very pleased I'm coming. Comrades. You saw this?" He pushed the copy of *Neues Deutschland* toward Andrei.

"Very inspiring."

"He thought so too. Which is what we wanted."

Andrei took his coffee from the waitress.

"And the talk?"

"Memory lane mostly. He misses his wife."

"Geneva?"

"Yes. He was pleased to be asked but he's not sure if he wants to go."

"Why not?" Andrei said, surprised.

"He won't really know anyone there. He'll have to read something from an approved text. Somebody with him all the time—he says in Russia they call them 'secretaries.' So is it worth the bother?"

"You believe him?"

The first line to cross. "Yes. But I think he'd still like to go."

"Why?"

"He'd be representing East Germany. Rossendorf. He's happy to be here, back in Germany. Apparently in Russia people were a little—standoffish. And the authorities here would like it. They think it's an honor."

"So you think he'd come back? If he went?"

Another line. Martin nodded. "It's home. And where would he go? He's still a Marxist. Whatever trouble he got up to in Russia, my sense is that it was about fixing the system, not leaving it. But you'd know more about this than I would."

Andrei looked at him for a second. "So, Geneva? Your view."

"If you tell him not to go, he won't be surprised. Business as usual. If he does go, he'll behave himself. And come back. And the East Germans would like it. I think it's a political question, not a security question. So. Is that what you couldn't wait to hear?"

"And maybe he says what he thinks you want to hear."

"Maybe."

"So you'll keep listening."

Martin nodded. "Now, what's wrong? Why the meeting?"

"Nothing wrong. You asked me to get some information for you. I thought you'd like to hear it."

"Information."

"Your assassin. If he was. His name is Karl Hitzig. Not a nice boy. Lots of bad company. After Hohenschönhausen he was transferred to the prison at Karl-Marx-Stadt. The old Chemnitz."

Martin looked up. Where the swap prisoners had come from.

"Apparently he was going to be part of an exchange. Of political prisoners."

"Political prisoners?"

"Anyone who tries to get over the wall is a political prisoner. That's why they have so many. You might ask, who would want such a person, all the time in trouble, but apparently his mother is in the West. You're always a good boy to your mother. Now the interesting part. Who arranged for this transfer? Our friend Kurt."

"How do you know?"

"A source. Nothing in writing, of course. Kurt never leaves a fingerprint. That's why we use him. Why everybody uses him, I suppose. So we can say we don't. Now let me ask you something. Why did you want to know this?"

"He shot at us. Everyone thought it was random, part of the escape. But he shot first, so he meant to shoot somebody. Me? Why? I think he was shooting at Kurt. But why? And then why exchange him? A man who tried to shoot you? How much would the mother pay? Not even Kurt—" He looked up. "Could somebody talk to him? Hitzig?"

"Not anymore. He's dead."

Martin stared at him. "Dead," he said flatly, taking this in. "How?"

"With a knife. Something shaped like a knife, anyway. Prisoners can be ingenious about such things."

"Do they know who?"

Andrei shook his head. "No fingerprints this time either."

"But Kurt wasn't—"

"No, not anywhere near. I checked. It made me curious too, this question of yours. You have good instincts. So what was bothering you? Maybe something we could use."

"Against Kurt? That wasn't—"

"Against? No. But information is always useful. Sometimes it brings him closer. So what did you suspect?"

"I don't know. I just like things to make sense."

"I remember. Your famous gut feeling. When something was wrong."

"Protect yourself first. Isn't that what you taught me?"

"From Kurt?"

"That doesn't make sense either."

Andrei lit a cigarette. "Sometimes things don't. Sometimes it's a fight in prison. No sense to it, like caged rats. It can happen that way. Or an escape at the wall, everything goes wrong. No sense." He looked over at Martin through the smoke. "Stay close to Kurt. There's always a mistake. Then you'll know."

"And then what?"

"Then you protect yourself. The way I taught you."

He walked back to the Berolina, his head buzzing. How long can you juggle before something misses your hand and falls? Why not save Stefan from himself and keep him at Rossendorf, out of trouble? A word to Andrei would do it. Protect yourself. In prison it had been easier—stay alive, get through it. But now it wasn't just him. Keep juggling, keep it going. The life he had, too late for any other. It would be different for Peter, a real future. He came out of Alexanderplatz onto Karl-Marx-Allee and stopped. Stalin's future, already passed. Not this. He owed him something more than this. A stepfather who could kill as if he were swatting a fly. A father who helped him, to protect himself. Andrei seeing nothing, his eyes fixed on the balls in the air.

Hans Rieger was waiting in the lobby, slouched in his usual chair, hat pushed back to take in the whole lobby.

"Ah, Herr Keller, I've been waiting for you. You had a good trip?"

"Yes, fine."

"Good. Well, here's more good news. I was so grateful that you and Herr Thiele would vouch for me to the police. But now no need. You won't have to see them. But so grateful—"

"Why? What happened?" A small alarm, hairs rising on the back of his neck.

"They found a witness."

"A witness?"

"Yes, a woman who was passing." The old woman by the river, head down. "She saw two men at the dumpster. Not me. She said definitely not me. So it's a relief, yes?"

"She saw them?"

"Not well, in that light. But a different body type. Not me. But here's something interesting. No coats. No hats. So possibly men from the Ganymed. Imagine, this could have been happening while we were drinking our wine. A murder, steps away, and none of us had the faintest idea." He made a dramatic shudder.

"Two men?"

"Two. She saw them from behind and from the side. The police don't say about the faces. Maybe a sketch artist. But definitely not my body type. So no trouble for you, and I'm so grateful that you would help."

"From behind," Martin said. "But would she recognize them if she saw them again?" Had they turned? A glimpse at most.

Hans shrugged. "The way these things happen, they'll have her look at pictures. Spitzer's associates. Of course, with that element, the police often have photographs. In the arrest file."

But Martin was thinking of another photograph, taken for *Stern*, the TV tower in the background, two men. Whom she couldn't really have seen, not closely enough to identify, just shapes and body types. But what if? And it was at that moment, looking at Rieger's weasel eyes, that he knew everything would go wrong, the balls finally dropping from midair, rushing down in a kind of eddy, taking Martin and Kurt and everyone else down with them. He could die here. Prison. He felt it rush through him, a wave of nausea. And then an odd clarity. You always knew what needed to be done. And now he did. It wasn't possible to be careful anymore, hide behind the juggling. He had to save himself. It was just a question of doing it right. No mistakes possible, a different kind of juggling, all the fuzziness in his head wiped away.

He noticed Rieger looking at him, reading his face, and willed himself calm.

"Well, let's hope she finds them. It'll be a great story for you. Now that you're not in it."

A resigned shrug. "It's what they like in the West. Not so much here."

Tante Helene was really Helene Bosch, an old theater friend of Sabine's whom Martin had met once or twice when they were young in Berlin. Now, forty pounds heavier, she was a wardrobe mistress at the DEFA studios in Babelsberg, next door to Potsdam. *Stern* had decided they wanted Erich the Great in a frock coat, the new master of Sanssouci, so she and Sabine spent the morning rummaging through trunks.

"Remember this?" Helene said, holding up a maid's uniform. "If I could get into it now."

"At Adlershof the costumes are all numbered," Peter said.

"Oh, everything up-to-date. Here too. This is the spillover. They don't want them anymore, but I can't just throw them out. Here, do you want to be a Russian soldier? Our glorious comrades." She held up a uniform, modeling the hat herself.

"No, I want to be Friedrich the Great."

"I know, I know. Here, try this." She turned to Martin. "And you? Are you part of this costume party too?"

Martin held up his hands, then looked around the room crowded with piles of clothes and stuffed suitcases. "How do you find anything?"

"I have a system. Oh, Peter, look. I take it in just an inch here, and perfect. Ten minutes."

"You sew too?" Martin said. "I don't remember that."

"You weren't looking at me," she said, brushing back her long hair. A blowsy woman with alert eyes. "It was good to know, sewing. In the war if you couldn't sew you had nothing to wear. And now, what do they sell? Frump clothes. I miss the West. For the shops."

"You moved here?"

"To keep the job. Before you could live in West Berlin and take the S-bahn out. Not a bad ride. But now it's impossible, and where would I work in West Berlin? There's only one DEFA and it's here. You want to see it before you go? They still have the sound stage where Lang shot *Metropolis*. Of course, now they argue, which one? Those were the days, when it was UFA. But even later, we were always busy. Now it's all television, out in Adlershof, with Erich the Great." This with a wink to Peter. "That's the future. But to me, there's nothing like Babelsberg. So I'm here."

"My god, look at this," Sabine said, holding up a dress, glittering with spangles.

"You know who wore that? Zarah Leander. A nightclub scene. Imagine, a nightclub in Berlin, when really the bombs were coming down. Well, that's the magic of it. If you see it, it must be true."

Martin looked over at her. "A trick of the eye."

"Well, at UFA it *was* true. Every detail. You had to be careful with the details, or you'd spoil it. Look at this, hand sewn. With the war going on."

"We have a little time," Sabine said, glancing at her watch. "Would you like to see the studio?"

"It's not as nice as Adlershof," Peter said. "It's old."

"Like me," Helene said, smiling. "Practically a silent picture."

"That's one thing you'll never be," Sabine said. "Silent."

"So come," Helene said. "I can't believe Kurt trusted you with his precious car. What will they think at the gate? Helene in a Mercedes. A new boyfriend maybe. Little do they know." She touched Peter on the chin. "I'll bring my makeup box. Everybody looks the same in *Stern*. Red faces. For health, I suppose. But you have to look like a king."

Peter was right, the Adlershof studio was newer, the paint still fresh, but Babelsberg had the same factory look, this time with red brick sound stages in a park of trees dotted with smaller utility buildings. The magic was all inside, the nightclubs that weren't real. Except to Helene, a perfect guide, telling stories about Lubitsch and Dietrich as if they'd been personal friends. Peter looked bored, his day-to-day world, but Martin took it all in, the workmen waving to Helene, a group of extras dressed as soldiers on a smoke break, the sound stage suddenly barracks, Babelsberg a camp. If you see it, it must be true.

The air was turning warm, early spring with trees in bud, a perfect day for the shoot. He watched Sabine enjoying the outing, comfortable with Helene, her whole manner looser, happy, the way she used to be. How could she be ill? There had to be more they could do, not just bow to the inevitable. Even if you just bought time. Something he hadn't really faced, the idea of her gone for good.

"It's like old times," Helene said to him. "The way you look at her."

"You're imagining things," he said. "She's a married woman."

"Yes. To you."

They drove from Babelsberg to Sanssouci, early enough for a short walk in the park, through the obelisk gate down the main allée, the palace up the hill on their right, terraces of vines rising up to it like steps.

"It's a mistake, though, in the design," Sabine said. "It's foreshortened. You can't really see the palace from below, just the top."

The photographer was late, some trouble with the guard at the gate, and was still fuming when they met at the Grosse Fontane, his assistant weighted down with camera bags.

"It's impossible, the East. How can you live here? A pass for everything. We have the permission forms, but no, where are your identity papers. As if they could read them. Maria they wouldn't let in. So we'll have to do the makeup ourselves."

"Tante Helene can do it," Peter said, matter-of-fact. "She's at DEFA."

"Hah." Almost a grunt, squaring off for the match to come.

"Do you like the coat? She found it."

"Hah," he said again, but softer this time, a professional acknowledgment. "Yes, fine." He took out a list. "All right, the palace, of course. But also the Orangerie and the Chinese house. And maybe something in the park? Where the trees are out?" He looked around. "Nice. The light is good."

They started at the fountain and worked their way up the terraces. By the time they had reached the top, Helene and the photographer had found a working rhythm, changing clothes while he adjusted the lenses, a quick touch-up with the brush, a different angle. Peter posed and waited, not complaining, used to it. Martin and Sabine busied themselves trying to stay out of the way.

"We'll be hours," Helene said to them. "We haven't even started at the Orangerie. Why don't you show Martin the town in your fancy Mercedes. You can be alone for a change. Talk." A sly edge to her voice, matchmaking.

"Really, Helene—" Sabine said, but in the end they went.

"Just don't go near the Glienicke Bridge. I hear they're stopping cars there these days. Nervous fingers." She pulled a trigger in the air.

They drove through the old garrison quarter and then the

Dutch village, dollhouses of brick with gables, then along the Neue Garten, the Jungfernsee glistening in the distance.

"So now he's the face of the DDR," Sabine said. "In *Stern* anyway. You don't mind, do you?"

Martin said nothing. How do you start? A private moment, what he'd hoped for, but how do you start?

"It won't last much longer," Sabine was saying.

Don't waste the time alone. Start.

"That's the Cecilienhof. Where they had the conference. See across the water? The villas? So big. It was all the servants, I suppose. They had to have rooms for them." They turned off on a street that led to the water. "The Hohenzollerns built some here."

Another silence. Sabine glanced over at him.

"Helene thinks we have so much to talk about," she said.

"We do."

"Something's wrong?"

Another turn and he saw the flag, just where Ruth Jacobs had said it would be. The Military Liaison Mission, a white stucco villa behind high iron gates, the American flag flying in front. An odd jolt, seeing it. American soil, just behind the gates. Guarded by East German soldiers. Out of reach, no closer than the long trip home.

"What is this place?" Sabine said.

"I don't know," he said, hedging. "Pull up and we'll ask the guards."

"Just like that."

"It's a simple question."

But the guards didn't want to answer it, waving them away, the villa enemy territory.

Martin had just rolled down his window when another car drove up, a Zil with special plates, Cyrillic letters. The guards came to attention and swung open the gates to the gravel driveway. Martin watched, curious, as an American officer came out to greet the Russian and then, surprisingly, his wife.

"What's the occasion?" Martin said to the guard.

"Lunch," he said and then, catching himself, "Get going. It's not permitted here."

A last look up at the flag.

"Funny, seeing it here," Martin said to Sabine.

"It must be something diplomatic. To be in the East. Maybe from the war. Shall we go back? There's nothing to see, really. Houses."

"Not yet. Let's take a walk. The park we passed. I want to talk to you."

"About what?"

"This and that."

"Oh, something serious. All right, the Neue Garten. It's nice on the lake."

They parked on the street and crossed the broad lawn to the water. A woman in a hat walking a dog, no one following.

"Are you still American? Technically?" Martin said. "Did you renounce citizenship when you married Kurt?"

She looked at him, thrown for a second. "I didn't do anything. They gave me an East German passport. You had to have one to go back and forth to the West. When that was allowed. Can you be both?"

"No. So you're East German."

"What difference does it make?"

"I just need to know your status, that's all."

"This and that." She stopped. "What is it?"

They had reached the pathway along the lake. A few more people, all of them old, pensioners with canes.

"I need to know to plan."

"Plan what?"

"We're going to do a job together."

"For Andrei?" She shook her head. "I'm finished with that, I told you."

"No. For us. We're going to leave. With Peter."

For a minute she said nothing, just stared at him. "Leave. And where are we going?"

"America."

"America. Should we meet you at Friedrichstrasse? Get on a train? Are you crazy?"

"No, we can do it. I just have to plan it right."

"Plan it right. People get killed doing this."

"That's one argument for doing it." He looked at her. "We did it before. Zoo Station. You thought they'd stop you on the train."

"That was different. The Nazis weren't looking for us."

"The Stasi aren't looking now. Not for me. I'm in *Neues Deutschland*."

"How do you know? They listen everywhere," she said, turning her head, as if they might be in the trees.

"Sabine, I have to leave. I can't stay here."

"Why? Because of Andrei? Now you don't like the work?"

He shook his head. "I can't tell you now. I will, but right now, I just need to know. Will you come? I have to know—to plan it."

"You'd risk your own child?"

"He'll be safe, whatever happens."

"Oh, safe."

"You want him to stay here? Be a poster boy for a country nobody else thinks exists? That's what you want for him?" He paused. "I won't leave him here with Kurt. Kurt's—"

"I know what he is. Maybe better than you. You know, if you

wait, you won't need me. I'll be gone and you can do what you want. He'll be yours."

"I don't want to wait. I want you to come."

"So I can die there?"

"So we can have whatever time we have." He took her shoulders. "Sabine, we can do it."

"How? Dig a tunnel?"

"No."

"How, then?"

"I'm going to make an exchange. Like Kurt."

"His pupil now. You think he's going to swap you back?"

"No, it's my swap. Nobody knows. Just you. So if anything happens, I'll know—"

"You don't have to say that to me."

Martin looked away.

"Why tell me anything if I'm so— Or am I part of the trade? What do they give for me?"

"I need you to help. Peter will listen to you. He has to come now. I can't come back for him."

"So it's for him. I thought maybe—ouf, maybe for one minute. But of course it's for him. Why would I think—?"

"Stop. For all of us. We all go."

"Even though you hate me."

He took her shoulders again. "You're my wife."

She looked down, shaking her head. "I divorced you."

"But I never divorced you. We'll get you better. I don't know for how long. But how long do we have now? We can still save something. And Peter. You can help me. We were always good together." He looked at her. "We'll be happy."

"They'll put you in jail."

"Maybe. Let's see what kind of deal I can make."

"And you'd risk that too."

"I have to. I have to leave."

"Why?"

He shook his head. "Not yet. It's better if you don't know. You have to trust me."

She turned away, facing the lake. "And Peter? What do I say to him?"

"Now? Nothing. It's not safe."

"And later? It's a crime to leave. He believes that. It's what they say on the show."

"He knows you're sick. He's worried about it. We're going to see a new doctor," he said, the words slowing. "We're going as a family. Together. He wants that."

"Yes," she said, looking down. "You hate it here so much? I thought you agreed to stay with him."

"I did. Then something happened. Now we have to do this."

"I wanted you to have him. That's why—"

"I will. And you." He looked at her. "We can be a family."

She stared at him for a minute, then turned back to the water. "A family who don't love each other anymore. He'll see through that. Even a child."

"We can start over." He put his hand to her hair, stroking it. "All of us. Sabine, look at me."

"Oh, start over," she said, almost a whisper, then suddenly put her hands up to the sides of his face, holding it there, something she used to do. "And we have so much time. Start over. After everything."

He felt the blood rush to his face, her hands warm.

"After everything," he said, looking at her, talking with his eyes.

"You believe that?" she said, her hands still on him, but her eyes darting away, skittish.

"It's why I came."

Another stare, direct, like the one from the couch, then she dropped her hands, self-conscious, and stepped back. "We should be careful. They're always watching somehow. And if Kurt sees—"

"He thinks we couldn't stay away from each other. He half thinks that now. Sneaking around—it's a good cover."

She looked at him and then, surprising herself, laughed softly. "For the job," she said. "He's so busy watching us he doesn't see—"

"Anyway, it's true. We couldn't stay away from each other." He glanced up. "We still fit."

Another look, but backing away now. "And what is the job? What are we really doing?"

"Does Kurt bring work home or does he leave everything at the office?"

She took another step back, eyes wider. "You want me to go through his papers."

"Does he bring them home?"

"Sometimes. And what am I looking for?"

"Ernst Spitzer. Any reference. Probably on a company roster, not alone. Then the companies. Any payments."

"You're making trouble for Kurt? I won't do that."

"He made the trouble. I'm just putting a deal together."

"If you do this, they'll blame him. He brought you here."

"Kurt can take care of himself."

"And me. I made him do it."

"But you won't be here."

"I haven't said yes."

"Yes, you did." He looked at her. "We'll be a family."

She hesitated. "And that's what you want? When this gets worse—"

"What?"

"The cancer. Then it's someone you have to take care of. You want that?"

He nodded. "You're my wife."

She looked away, not meeting his eyes. "And what makes you think the Americans will want you?"

"The Republic did."

She smiled a little. "No. I did."

By the time they got back, the photographer had finished at the Chinese House and Peter was in his own clothes.

"He was an angel," Helene said. "You had a good drive?"

"Oh, Herr Keller, I almost forgot," the photographer said, taking out an envelope. "You wanted these. Not such good quality, but since you asked for them—"

"I had to promise. No pictures, no interviews, unless the authorities give permission. Part of the arrangement. You understand."

"This place. Everyone's afraid of his own shadow."

"That's what they say in the West," Peter said, "but it's not true."

"Well, maybe not," the photographer said, not wanting to argue.

Martin flipped though the photos, surprised again seeing himself, someone older. The TV tower, Alexanderplatz in the background, then with Kurt, a series of fast shots, two men, then two men turned to the side, the photograph like a moment in a lineup.

"Thanks," he said. "Sorry. My one chance to be in *Stern* too."

"You can still be in *Stern*, anytime you like. My editor said he'd do an interview. He likes spies." He handed him a card. "If you can get the okay."

Martin put the photographs back in the envelope. Evidence. What the woman would have seen. In coats this time, but standing side by side, the same angle. He looked at the card. "We're not allowed to call West Germany."

"Kurt can," Peter said.

"Everybody's agent," the photographer said.

"What do I owe you?" Martin said.

"On the house."

"You kept the negatives?"

The photographer looked at him, slightly thrown by this. "They're with the rest of the Alexanderplatz roll. I didn't know—you need them?"

"No," Martin said, backing off. "Just curious." Buried in a photo file drawer in Hamburg. "I'll let you know about the interview."

The photographer nodded. "Reuters keeps a man in East Berlin. He can always get through to me. They listen but they don't block the line." A glance to Peter. "If you'd rather not bother your agent."

CHAPTER 7

He read a newspaper in a café while he waited for her to come out. Another gray day, moist, Jägerstrasse still slick from last night's rain. The lights were on in Gerhard's office, but the windows too high to see through. She'd been there almost an hour, enough time to run whatever errand she'd come for, unless they'd lingered over coffee, some late morning routine. When she did appear, her swept-back hair covered with a kerchief against the damp, she moved quickly, full of purpose, maybe late filing a story for *Il Messaggero*. Martin threw some coins on the bill saucer and followed.

She headed up to Unter den Linden and then east across the bridge. Why not just catch up and talk to her now? But he was drawn into the rhythm of a tail, invisible, a voyeur's curiosity. Another street, trams passing, the Marienkirche, then the station. At Alexanderplatz she took the stairs down to the U-bahn. Tailing was tricky on the subway, more easily spotted, but now he wanted to see if he could do it. She seemed oblivious, not even looking around. So much for everybody here looking over his shoulder. He stood by the door in the next car, out of her line of sight.

The U5 took them east, running under Karl-Marx-Allee. Not where she and Gerhard lived. Another errand. Above them, the Stalinist blocks were flying by, Weberwiese, where Sabine was waiting for Peter, the bookend towers of Frankfurter Tor. Then they were under Lichtenfeld, somewhere he'd never been.

She got off at Magdalenenstrasse to an almost empty platform. Martin turned, looking at the station map, then followed. She was facing straight ahead, her walk steady, all business. Outside he found himself in a neighborhood of old apartment buildings, broken by the office compound across the street, two, no three buildings around a gated courtyard. She passed through the entryway, evidently someplace familiar to her. Black cars parked inside, long rows of windows, a fortress, the streets around nearly empty. People walking took the other side of the street, as if proximity alone could get them in trouble. He thought of his prison, the weight of it, and knew, even before he saw the nameplate, what this must be. State Security Service. Ruth was paying a visit to the Stasi. By appointment? A report on the neighbors? But why do it in person? He looked up, expecting cameras, but the wall seemed clean. Who would come this close? He walked to the corner, just someone in the street, and turned up the slight hill, circling the compound. No barbed wire or turret guns or packs of guards, like any office building, a place to keep files. He reached Normanenstrasse, ordinary buildings, people living here across the street, the compound part of the daily landscape. Until the summons came, the office visit, just a few questions.

He kept walking, trying not to draw attention in the quiet street. She must be with someone by now. Answering questions? Making a report? Was there any difference? Part of the system, like everybody else. Someone who'd stayed. But not what he'd expected. Think it through. Not an informer meeting on a park bench. Someone who never looked to see if she was being followed. Offering him her card. Someone who knew where all the doors were.

There would be no excuse for lingering in the street, not here, so he circled back to the U-bahn station and waited there, hunched in his coat. A train pulled in, blocking his view of the entrance, so he didn't see her, coming from behind, sliding onto the bench next to him.

"It's not what you think," she said.

A second to get over his surprise. "What is it, then?"

"An arrangement. My old friend Johannes. He has to okay any article. He likes to send the final copy himself. To be sure."

"To *Il Messaggero*?"

"Anywhere. He likes to go over everything."

"And have a little visit."

"As you say."

"And talk about mutual friends?"

"Not so many these days." She took a breath. "My beat was the foreign community, what people were up to. That's the way things worked. Once you did it, they threatened to tell your friends you were doing it, so you kept doing it. Afraid they'd find out."

"You talk about Gerhard too?"

She smiled. "They didn't need a report on Gerhard. There was nothing secret about him. The heart always on the sleeve. A man of principle," she said wryly. "But he'd been in prison. And stayed. So who would question his loyalty?" She looked down. "And if there was any question, they had all the information about the women. That they could share with me. He thought I didn't know. So they didn't have to worry about Gerhard. It wasn't always like this. In the beginning it was different. But this is what it is now. I visit with Johannes. That's how we live." She looked up at him. "So, now you? Why were you following me? Who are you working for?"

"Nobody. Myself."

"I can believe it. So clumsy on the train. Why didn't you stop me in Alexanderplatz? People run into each other at a station. It's natural. But you came all the way out here. Why?"

"To see where you were going. If I could trust you."

"Well, you got your answer. You can't."

"On the other hand, I can't trust anyone else."

She looked over. "Trust me to do what?"

"A favor. You told me you knew where all the doors were. I need an introduction."

"An introduction," she said carefully. "And what makes you think I can do that?"

"You know a lot of people. Here, there," he said, nodding, then cocking his head. "Both sides. But you kept your passport."

"That doesn't mean much." She paused. "An introduction to whom?"

"Someone who can run interference at State. The Agency used to have a base of operations in Berlin. I assume they still have it."

"Run interference," she said.

"Someone they'd listen to. Not a desk clerk. Who could make a deal."

She raised her eyebrows. "Why don't you ask your friend Kurt? Isn't he the expert? He made a deal for you."

"Because I don't want to ask him. I'm asking you. Can you do it?"

She hesitated. "A deal for what?"

"I'd like to keep my passport," he said, looking at her.

"What?"

"It's expired. I want to renew it."

"You're traveling somewhere?"

"Not immediately. But I may. I want to be like Brecht. Keep my options open."

"You know, in the end he wrote a poem praising Stalin. That was the option he had." She faced him, interested now. "Where do you want to go?"

"There's a conference in Geneva. People I work with are going. I may want to go too. If I don't have my passport, I have to travel on East German papers, which would mean renouncing American citizenship. I'd like to hang on to it."

"Geneva. So. You're leaving us so soon?"

"If they invite me. If I can travel. If."

"Kurt will be disappointed," she said, ignoring this. "After all the trouble he took to get you here. A black mark against him maybe. You're aware of this?"

Martin said nothing.

"And that's why you came to me."

"Just to open a door. You don't have to be involved in any of it. I can't go to West Berlin. I have to meet someone here. So I need someone who knows someone."

"A risk for her. If she did this."

"But a good deed. And no one knows—unless you told Johannes. Would you have to? Is that the rule?"

She shook her head. "No rules. He's not interested in you. I'm not sure why. I thought at first, maybe you have a protector. You know, the way Kurt is close to Koch. But maybe it's all the personal ties here. A child. People like you don't leave. Or maybe he's waiting, to see how he can use you."

"Or maybe he knows I could go to prison again if I leave."

"Geneva isn't America."

"But I'd still need a passport to get there. Can you do this?"

She looked at him, then smiled to herself. "And you ask this at Stasi headquarters. Right under their noses." She turned at the sound of the approaching train. "Tomorrow at the Adlon. The lobby bar at six. You're reading a newspaper with your drink. Someone will contact you."

"Who?"

"I don't know yet who they can send. If there's nobody, I'll turn up so you don't sit waiting. All right?" Another look. "I'm just opening a door. I don't want to know what happens. I don't want to tell Johannes. A quiet week. Like so many others."

"Thank you."

"Good luck. By the way, you know in Geneva they'll have someone watching. Wherever you go."

He nodded. "If I go."

"Better get in the other car," she said as the train pulled in. "And be careful of Kurt. Don't make trouble for him."

"No trouble. Who's Koch? His protector?"

"Number three, some say number two. Mielke's like a brother to him. So if you go against Kurt, you'll have the Stasi to deal with."

"One more thing," he said as he pushed the button to open the doors. "If you knew I was following you, why didn't you get off? Not show me—"

"So you'd know where I was going. And think what it tells me. If you still want my help, knowing that, you're willing to take a risk for it. It must be important. More than a passport."

———

The Adlon bar was full of Russians from the embassy nearby, men in gray suits and wire-rimmed glasses, loud and burly. The Germans, Party functionaries up for a night or two from Leipzig or Chemnitz, huddled in quiet clusters, as if they were sheltering from the noise. There were no obvious Americans. Martin would have to wait it out, let the contact approach him. He folded the newspaper smaller, half-turned on his bar stool.

The voice was so discreet it was almost inaudible, a whispering near his ear, the man short, unobtrusive.

"Pay and go to the men's room, then out the side door to Wilhelmstrasse."

Gone before Martin could acknowledge him, a gray suit now crossing the lobby to a corridor of shops.

Martin paid and followed. No one in the men's room except the bored attendant. No doubt on the Stasi payroll, listening over the splashes of urine and trickles of running water, men talking among themselves. Outside, on the street, the man seemed taller, less hunched. He was lighting a cigarette.

"Ed Nugent," he said. "Shall we walk a little?"

They passed a building site, apartments replacing a bombed-out ministry.

"They were all here. Goebbels. Hitler down the street. Now they're building playgrounds. Except who wants to live this close to the wall? So it's a real estate problem. Only in Berlin. I understand you want to renew your passport. I have to say, I'm surprised. Considering."

"Considering what?"

"Who you are. What you did."

"That was a long time ago."

"Yeah, well, so was the war. Hard to forget, though. Me, I wouldn't have made the swap. But the Brits had their reasons, I guess. So shoot. Why the meeting? Kind of thing could get you in real trouble, meeting with us."

"You have a direct link to State? They'd have to be involved. Not just you."

"Involved with what?"

"Another swap."

"Who's being swapped this time?"

"Me."

"That was quick." He turned his head, taking in the street. "Not all it's cracked up to be, huh?"

"We don't have a lot of time."

"All right. I'm all ears."

"Three passports. Me, I'm expired, but that's easy to renew. My wife's citizenship lapsed when she married an East German, so she'll need a new one. My son was born in Britain to two American citizens, so he's legit. He just needs to have one issued to him."

"Three passports."

"And immunity for me. From prosecution."

Nugent looked at him. "In your dreams."

"Nobody cares anymore except Hoover. I went to prison once. I'm not defecting to do it again. Three passports. Immunity."

"That's it?"

"No, one more thing. I don't want any money. But I'd like a little protection. Until we see how the Russians take this. And I want access to a top cancer doctor. Maybe military. Whoever the Agency would use if they wanted the best."

Nugent looked over. "For you?"

"No."

Nugent dropped his cigarette, staring at his foot as he put it out.

"And what do we get?"

"Plenty."

"Your information's ten years old."

Martin nodded. "History. But the kind of history the Agency likes. A full debriefing. Who, when, how."

"I thought you said nobody cares anymore."

"The Agency will. Some of it, they can close the file. Strictly history. Some of it's still alive, so they get some leads. You'll have to trust me on this. They'll want to hear it. That's one. Then there's the propaganda value. Atomic spy defects. The minute I get here, I'm asking to come home. Huge embarrassment for the East Germans."

"They've already got plenty to be embarrassed about."

"Not like this. They're trying to set up a nuclear program with a nice place for me and I'm walking away from it. That's a hard one to explain. Somebody giving the whole country the finger. The West Germans will have a field day."

"Why not go to them, then?"

"Because I'm American. And so is my son." He looked over at Nugent. "He's also Erich Schmidt on *Die Familie Schmidt*. When his mother defected, the actress who plays his mother, it was a national scandal. If he does it, it'll be like—I don't know, Andy Hardy turning Red."

"Andy Hardy. A little out of date."

"You pick the example. I know it won't mean much at home, but here—the West Germans will owe you."

Nugent said nothing for a moment, looking away.

"You'd have to get yourself out. We can't exfiltrate. There are a lot of unwritten rules here and that's number one. In the old days, you could snatch somebody on the street. Both sides did it. But not anymore. Somebody tunnels out, we welcome them with open arms, but they do the digging. There are certain—sensitivities."

"Understood. No help."

"Well, not exactly. Get to West Berlin and we'll do the rest. We just can't put people on the ground in East Germany." He paused. "If we do this."

"Okay. But you need to decide fast. I don't have a lot of time."

Nugent looked at him, curious. "Want to enlighten me—why?"

Martin shook his head. "Everybody knows just his piece, that's all. That's how we did it at Los Alamos. Compartmentalization."

"A fancy word for 'mind your own business.'" He looked up. "But you didn't."

Martin let this go. "It's the only way this works. There are a few pieces. Somebody will betray me. The only way I can protect myself is by keeping the pieces separate, so they only betray part of it."

"What makes you sure somebody will?"

"Somebody always does. If you don't plan for it—" He trailed off.

"And you think the Agency would?"

Martin shrugged.

"But you came to us anyway."

"There isn't anybody else. Not for this. So. We're clear? I get us to West Berlin and you—"

"That's not so easy these days. I don't suppose you want to tell me how you're going to do it. Or is that another compartment?"

"Has to be."

"Some advice? Don't use forged papers. They spot them right away. Even ours."

"My son has the most recognizable face in East Germany. We have to go as ourselves."

Nugent looked over, thinking about this. "That's quite a trick, then. I wouldn't give you odds on it."

"Well, we'll see. How do I contact you?"

"Emergency? Same way. Our mutual friend. Otherwise you don't. They've got you at the Berolina, right? We'll find you."

"We have to move on this."

"I heard you before. Couple of days. Bound to be some conversations."

"They're going to start with your report. So what do you think?"

"What do I think? I think the Agency could make a lot of trouble for itself. And not get much for it."

"The Agency doesn't have to do anything except meet me on the other side."

"And take care of you. And explain what it thought it was doing, getting you out. They'll all think we did it. The Russians will for sure. Turning their people. From ten years ago. What's the percentage in that? The East Germans will have a fit. Nobody's going to believe you did this yourself. So we're in their backyard, making trouble. What do they do? The usual—make trouble in ours. And for what? Some stories for the files? If true. For all I know, you're a double." He held up his hand. "Don't bother. It's possible. We'd be crazy not to suspect it and we're not crazy. That crazy anyway. And meanwhile you're in the papers. For about ten minutes. Which doesn't buy us much propaganda—you might be overrating your appeal just a little. It was a while ago. The kid, that's something else. We could do something with that. So you balance it out and what do you get?" he said, moving his hands like a scale.

Martin waited a minute. "And that's your report?"

"Look, I'm just trying to show you how they'll see it. This isn't something you want to go back and forth with. You decide and that's it. One way or another, this is going to piss people off. Just when we're trying to get them to calm down. So is it worth it?"

Another minute, Martin quiet. "Let's add something to the pot, then."

Nugent raised his head.

"Two defectors."

"You and—?"

"Stefan Schell."

Nugent looked down the street, as if he thought somebody was listening.

"You serious?"

"Delivered, tied up with strings. In time for the Geneva Conference. Where he'll give a talk about arms control. What Uncle Sam wants to hear."

"How—?"

Martin held up his hand. "Another compartment. All you have to know is I'll deliver him. Part of the deal."

"Another passport?"

"No, he'll want to stay in Germany."

"The Russians aren't going to like that."

"Not even a little. Would that be enough propaganda for you?"

"You've talked to him?"

"We're old friends. Don't worry, it's for real."

"Why didn't you mention this before?"

"You like to be wanted for yourself. But since the pot wasn't big enough—"

"Anything else in your back pocket?"

"That's it. Let me know. We should turn around here. They don't like you getting close to the wall."

They started back up Wilhelmstrasse.

"Tell me something," Nugent said. "Kurt, the guy who arranged your exchange—you know we've worked with him. He know about this?"

"No."

"And his wife is coming with you?"

"She was my wife first."

"That's a hell of a compartment you've got him in."

———

"I need your help with something," Kurt said. "If you don't mind."

They were in the studio car on the way to Adlershof to pick up Peter.

"What?"

"I have a prisoner exchange coming up and Hindemith wants to go over the inventory. Man wouldn't trust God. Anyway, you know the warehouse. I have a meeting, so it would be a help if you could let him in, show him around. He'll want to check the manifests—you remember."

"When?"

"Tomorrow."

"Yes, okay."

"Good. Old Max could let him in, but it makes him nervous, people poking around, and Hindemith likes to snoop. He needs a watchdog."

"What is it this time? More oranges?"

"Medical supplies. Surgical equipment we don't make. You listen to Hindemith, it's gold. If he'd just deposit cash in our account and let us buy the stuff ourselves, he wouldn't have to go through all this. Well, soon." He glanced up front at the driver and lowered his voice. "Hans told you?"

"About the witness? A lucky break for him—"

"Very."

"You're worried?" Martin said, his voice even lower.

"No. What could she have seen? But I don't like this 'no coat' business. They'll start talking to everybody in the restaurant. Maybe someone saw—"

"There was a lot going on."

"And who notices? You get up, you're going to the men's room. Still."

"There are other restaurants in that street."

"But they'll start with Ganymed. Well, keep your head. All they've got is an old woman who didn't know what she was looking at. And they don't know when. Hans thinks we were sitting together all the time. That's how he remembers it. Our alibi," he said, shaking his head. "Christ, Spitzer. He was always trouble. Even dead." He turned a little in his seat, a pivot. "How do you like these?" he said, touching his glasses.

"They're new?"

"Italian."

Martin looked at him. A minute ago they were at the dumpster. "Right in style," he said.

"But not too much, no? Can I get you anything tomorrow?"

Martin looked blank.

"The meeting's in the West. Is there anything you'd like? Something from KaDeWe? I won't have much time, but—"

Martin shook his head. "Thanks, no, I'm fine. You just come and go?"

"It's business for the state. I have a special visa. The lawyer from the other side is a West Berliner so we have to meet there."

"What do you mean?"

"A technicality. A West German citizen could cross to the East. But a West Berliner is not officially a West German citizen—he's a resident of an occupied zone. So no passport, just a West Berlin identity card. You can't cross the wall now with that. So I go to him." He shook his head. "Berlin. Another way we tie ourselves up in knots. Look at Friedrichstrasse. All the lines. The passport control. Like rats in a maze. I don't have time for that. So I drive. And you know it's good for the car. It's better to get it serviced in the West. They have the parts. Peter disapproves. 'We have everything we need here.' That's how he says it on the show. But he doesn't say no to the presents either."

"So it's easy for you, to cross."

"Well, they know me. They know I have business there. And they know the car—not so many like it on this side. Sometimes they don't even check my papers," he said. "A salute and I'm through." His voice pleased with itself.

"I thought there were lines at all the checkpoints."

"Not at Invalidenstrasse. It's VIP only."

"Where you exchanged me."

"Yes. Not so exciting tomorrow, let's hope."

"The ambulance, you mean," Martin said. "I wonder what happened to the kid, the one they took away." To be knifed in prison. Waiting.

"No idea," Kurt said, his voice even. "A cell somewhere." His face smooth behind the Italian glasses, the lie easy.

"I guess," Martin said, moving on, as if the lie had worked.

"Look, there's Peter," Kurt said. "They must have finished shooting early."

Sabine and Peter were waiting on the sound stage steps, Peter in East German jeans. They were finally going to Köpenick, an afternoon on the water.

"You look like a film star," Peter said to Kurt, nodding to the glasses. "Where'd you get them? The Ku'damm?" Almost an accusation.

"No. As a matter of fact, the Exquisit shop on the Linden. You like them?"

Peter shrugged. "Let's go. Do you know how to row?" he said to Martin. "I'll show you."

Köpenick, only a few kilometers east, was part of Berlin but seemed like a village from another, slower time. There was a small baroque old city, a *Rathaus* with a clock tower, and a pretty yellow stucco *Schloss*, all of it surrounded by water, the rivers connecting to a chain of lakes broad enough for sailing. There were boats to rent near the *Schloss* and Peter ran ahead to pick one.

"He's like a little boy again," Sabine said to Kurt. "Remember how he used to play in the water?"

Kurt nodded. Martin imagined a snapshot of the three of them, Peter filling a pail with sand, Sabine and Kurt half drowsing on a blanket. His parents.

"Come on," Peter was saying now. "Kurt, you row us out and then we can switch."

"Aye, aye," Kurt said, steadying the boat as the others got in, then taking up the oars.

The boat was barely large enough for four, Sabine and Peter wedged in front, Martin facing them in the stern. Almost immediately they were in the breeze, hair blowing around them in wisps, the light falling on the waves in flashes as they swelled. Sabine leaned back, her face to the sun, and Martin saw another snapshot, the beach at Wannsee that hot summer before the war, her hair short so that she didn't mind getting it wet, shaking like a puppy as she walked out of the water, a quick smile as he wrapped her in a towel, his.

"Let's head down to the Langer See," Peter said.

"So far?" Kurt said. "I don't know if I'm strong enough." An old joke between them.

Peter smiled. "I'll help you."

Martin leaned back. What were they doing here together? Two

families, but one ten years too late, no small talk, no private jokes. Not enough room for both. Why not let the others float in the sun, the family Thiele. For a second Martin felt a prickling of dread for what he was about to do, upend all their lives. Maybe Peter would see another snapshot later, that day on the lake when we were still happy. All sunshine and breeze, what was visible. But hadn't Sabine sent for him, a mother protecting her own? His substitute father was laughing now, everything bright in the sun, but only a few minutes ago he'd lied about having a man killed, eyes innocent behind his Italian frames. The happiness was a trick of the light. Do what you have to do.

"When do you go to Dresden?" Kurt said, maybe feeling the boat crowded too.

"Soon. They're finding me a place to live."

Sabine opened her eyes, paying attention now.

"Be careful," Kurt said, genial. "They'll want to put you in bachelor quarters. Cheaper. Hold out for something nice. You have a certain standing."

"Big enough for two," Peter said. "So I can come visit."

Sabine looked at Martin, uneasy. "Yes, big enough for visits," she said, now part of it too, all of them lying.

"Well, but not by yourself," Kurt said. "On the train."

"Maybe he can use the DFF car," Sabine said. She turned to Peter. "We'll see," she said, as if it might happen.

"I've never been to Dresden," Peter said. "Maybe they can write it into the show, a trip there. Then we all can go."

"We'll see," Sabine said again. "Isn't this nice? On the water?" Moving them somewhere else.

"An Academician, after all," Kurt said. "You should have a good flat, maybe even a house."

"No, I wouldn't know what to do with a house. "

And what would they have in the States? No Academy there. No Rossendorf job either. Things to think about later, the escape so absorbing that everything else seemed like clutter. Just get across, the rest would take care of itself. He looked over at Sabine. Don't worry, I can do this. But she was looking away, uncomfortable.

When they reached a stretch of open water, Kurt put up the oars and lay back in the boat, using the life preservers as cushions, his head lying against Sabine, something they'd done before.

"We'll drift," Peter said.

"I'll get us back," Kurt said. "The current's not very strong here."

"Remember last time. You fell asleep."

"No chance of that today, with all the noise," Kurt said, playful, waving his hand toward Peter.

Martin looked at them, easy with each other, Sabine smiling at no one in particular, the boat rocking them. How often had they done this? Ten years together. But she'd agreed to come, willing to walk away. Her eyes were half-closed now, squinting in the sun, not the girl at Wannsee, someone else, another man's head resting in her lap. She must have loved him once, or had he only been useful, the way Martin had been useful? She opened her eyes, as if she'd overheard his thoughts, looking straight at him, no one else in the boat, two people with a secret. But Kurt had secrets too, different secrets, the air suddenly heavy with them, everything that wasn't being said. And then Kurt shifted, trying to get comfortable, and raised his arm to get the cushion behind his head, and as he brought it down, Martin saw the brick in his hand again, smashing down on Spitzer, a secret that couldn't be contained in a glance but spread like a net until it caught everybody. They couldn't stay here. It had to work.

Sabine started coughing blood when they got back from the lake, a desperate heaving, something that couldn't be hidden. Kurt drove her to the Charité, quicker than calling an ambulance, Peter next to her, his face white and drawn. At the emergency door she was rolled away on a gurney, the coughing subsiding, as if she had finally used up all her breath. It was after he'd talked to the doctor that Kurt called Martin.

"I can't leave here. Will you stay with Peter tonight? I don't like to ask the neighbor."

"I'll be right there."

He found them both in the waiting area, an open room at the end of the hall overlooking Luisenstrasse, their faces blank with shock, people at an accident.

"Can I see her?"

"They gave her something to sleep," Peter said.

"What happened?"

"The doctor said 'complications,'" Kurt said. "What kind of diagnosis is that? Complications. Come, she's down here."

"We're not supposed to," Peter said.

"Just for a minute?" Martin said, asking permission. "You come too."

Peter shook his head. "Only a minute. She needs to sleep. The doctor said."

The room was three doors down the hall, only half-lit, quiet except for the audible hiss of oxygen and the click of a monitor. Her face was gray against the white pillow.

"Sabine," he said, as if she could hear through the drugs.

"The doctor says he thinks it's spread, but that's not the problem. I mean, it will be the problem, but not the problem tonight. I don't know—" Kurt said, his voice drifting, vague.

Martin stared down, a different kind of X-ray, into the past. The last time he'd seen her in the hospital had been when Peter was born, her face sweaty and pink, an exhausted smile. Happy.

"I have to stay. But Peter—it's not good for him, he's already— You can see it in his face. You don't mind? There's a guest room. He'll feel safer with you. The studio car picks him up. He's all right after that." Making plans, ticking off items. "I'll have to cancel my meeting. But Hindemith—well, you can still see him. We need to get that done." He stopped. "She could die. Then what?" A boy's voice.

"You knew she was ill?"

"I'm her husband. She didn't want to say, but I found out. You know, you have to keep your eyes open. And I have good connections."

Martin looked at him, thrown by this. "You mean you had her watched?"

"Oh, so shocked. At least it was me, not someone looking for trouble. I had to be sure."

"Of what?"

"You. I had to be sure there was nothing between you. What would you have done? Why is she asking for him? Something's still there? So it was good to know—there was nothing. Nobody goes to bed with anybody. That's all in the past. So I could breathe again. You meet Peter, that's good, he likes that. And you have a new life in Dresden. So. A good arrangement. But all the time she's sick and she's waiting to tell me. I don't know why, maybe she thinks it's better I don't know." He looked up. "But she told you."

Martin said nothing.

Kurt looked over to the bed. "She's supposed to have more time."

"Maybe she will," Martin said, suddenly anxious to leave. "We should let her sleep. I'll get Peter home."

"Thank you for this. So it seems we help each other again."

Martin looked at him, disconcerted, through the looking glass again.

They took a taxi to Weberwiese, Peter quiet, brooding. Upstairs, he played host, showing Martin where things were.

"You'll be in here. Kurt uses it for an office sometimes, but it's really a bedroom. "

An extra room in East Berlin, another of Kurt's privileges, like having someone follow your wife. A professional job, a report at the end. Before they'd taken the walk on the Jungfernsee, or did even that seem innocent at a distance? Nobody goes to bed with anybody. So I can breathe again. Martin looked around the room. A single bed, built-in desk and shelves, like a hotel room, an open briefcase, left behind in the rush to the hospital, papers scattered on the desk.

"Just move them if you need room," Peter said, coming in with towels. "He works here." He put the towels on the bed. "There's an extra toothbrush under the sink. The studio car comes at six thirty. I can let myself out if you want to sleep," he said and then stopped, a motor stalling.

"You okay?" Martin said.

Peter nodded, still stalled.

"You don't have to go to the studio if you'd rather—"

"No, they need me tomorrow. They can't shoot around me." His voice flat, a monotone. He looked up. "But if anything happens—"

"Nothing's going to happen."

"How do you know?"

Martin looked over at him, their eyes locked, tell me the truth.

"I don't know," Martin said.

Peter nodded, a thank-you for not pretending. "Is she going to die?"

"I don't know," Martin said again. "But I don't think so. Not yet."

"But if she does—"

"What?"

"Do I live with Tante Helene? Stay here with Kurt?" Now a tremor in his voice.

"I hope you'll live with me."

"You'd want that?"

Martin nodded.

"Kurt would want me to stay here."

"We don't have to worry about this yet."

"She's sick. You know that. She's been sick for a long time."

"But she might get better. A new doctor. Better medicine."

"She's at the Charité. Where could she get better medicine?"

Martin hesitated, Peter's eyes on him, a matter of life and death. "In the West. It's possible."

"The West? You'd take her to the West?" Alarmed now.

"They sometimes give permission, no? For medical reasons." Improvising. "At least, a consultation, another opinion. It wouldn't take long. We could all go."

"No. They make the child stay behind. So the parents return. You hear of such cases. And sometimes they don't come back. And the children—"

Martin dropped to his knees, eye level, and took Peter by the shoulders. "I would never leave you. Never. If we don't go together, we don't go. Okay?"

Peter gave a little nod, still uncertain, then, a move so sudden that it almost knocked Martin off balance, he flung his arms around Martin's neck. A rush of blood, unexpected, Peter hugging tighter. "Okay?" Martin whispered again. "We go together. All of us."

Peter pulled back, pragmatic again. "Kurt too? He can arrange it."

"No, just us. I'll arrange it."

"But it's what he does."

"I know. But not this time. He wouldn't like it. So we have to keep it to ourselves. Our secret. Can you–?"

As Peter nodded, Martin looked away, the elation of a minute ago now a stab of dismay. Peter one of them now too, another secret, complicit. But how else to do it?

"When?" Peter said.

"I don't know. Your mother has to get better–she can't go anywhere like this. And I have to get permission." Keeping the story going. "Now, how about bed? You have an early car."

"Martin?" Peter said, hesitant. "You mean it? If anything happens–"

"You're with me."

"You might have to share with Kurt," Peter said, working this out.

"Let's cross that bridge when we come to it." On the other side of the wall. "I'm your father."

"You want to know something? We walk the same way. You know, we're supposed to notice things. Actors. How people move, expressions they make. I look in the mirror and I can see a resemblance, that's natural. But walking? We walk the same way."

Martin stood there, not sure what to say, the words like another hug. "Get some sleep," he said quietly. "Peter? She's going to be okay. She's going to get better." A good-night hand stroking his forehead.

Afterward he sat on the living room couch, sipping a brandy, looking at the walls, the books, the framed family pictures, the life she'd agreed to leave. Impossible now, unless she got well enough to travel. The plan wouldn't work otherwise. Assuming it would work at all. Not something you did on the spur of the moment—you had to know when. He took another sip. Something always went wrong with a plan—a betrayal, a last-minute hitch—but he hadn't expected this. It might be weeks before she could go, Hans working on his story all the while, the police talking to waiters, the woman from Schiffbauerdamm looking at pictures. Maybe this one, the way he's standing. And Nugent, hurrying State to make a deal, no time to wait, something bound to leak. The machine in gear, no stopping it, unless you stopped it for good. If she got better, they'd have to be ready.

He got up and went to his room, looking at Kurt's papers on the desk, what he'd asked Sabine to do. He started to gather them into a pile, some kind of order, then stopped. Something Kurt would notice. Instead he leafed through. Legal papers, his day-to-day business, letters asking for help to reunite families. Invoices. Salary reviews for his staff. Office paper. Martin leaned over and picked up the briefcase. Papers in manila envelopes. A list of prisoners for an exchange, what Kurt would have finalized in his West Berlin meeting. But no listing for young Hitzig, who'd met a different fate. Something like a knife. Inventory sheets, presumably duplicates of Hindemith's. Accounting forms, some of the line items in initials, a kind of code. But Martin could read numbers. He knew numbers. He sifted through the pages, putting together the story, what he already knew: the East Germans were selling prisoners and the West Germans were using the Church charities to launder money to buy them. Forty thousand deutschemarks a head, sometimes more. Traded for citrus fruit and machinery. The story he knew, but now in black-and-white, laid out in rows of clear numbers. The story Hans Rieger didn't know. So much paper. Kurt was right, easier to transfer cash. But maybe not as easy to launder.

Martin looked through the forms again, trying to memorize this time, something he could do, how he'd managed at Los Alamos, where any copying would have been suspect. The government ministries that distributed the goods, the lawyer contacts in the West. Could anything be secret if so many people knew? But this was East Germany. Everything was secret.

———

In the morning, he had the studio car take them to the Charité first.

"We can make up the time. I know you want to see her."

She was awake, but barely, her mouth fixed in the weak smile of the gravely ill.

"You'll be late," she said to Peter, holding his hand. "I'm all right."

"Martin says we can make it."

"Oh, Martin."

"He stayed with me."

"Did he? Good." She looked behind Peter, where Martin was standing. "Good."

"What does the doctor say?" Peter said.

"More tests," she said vaguely, waving this away.

"Are they giving you something for the pain?" Martin asked.

"Yes, I'm all right. Don't worry," she said, her voice faint. "It's good to see you together. My men."

203

Martin turned to see if Kurt had heard, a reflex, but he was at the door with the doctor.

"Go," she was saying to Peter. "I'll see you later. Don't worry. Be Erich—that smile he has, all right?"

Peter leaned over and kissed her forehead.

"That was nice. I feel better already."

He kissed her again. "For the tests."

When he was at the door, she looked over at Martin, the first moment they'd had.

"I'm sorry. Have I ruined everything? All your plans?"

"No, no, there's time. We'll wait for you. You'll be better soon."

"You think so? Watch Kurt's face, that tells you something."

"We'll be fine, I promise. It's all going to work."

She looked at him, studying his eyes, then smiled a little, resigned. "Well, then it will." She looked away, toward the window. "What a mess we've made of everything. I was thinking this morning, how different everything would have been if I hadn't gone to Georg's party. Different for you."

Martin, sensing Kurt coming up behind, took Sabine's hand, patting it. "Less thinking, more sleeping."

"Peter's waiting," Kurt said. "Thank you again for this."

Martin shrugged this off. "You've got enough to do here. I'll take care of Hindemith."

"Don't let him poke around," Kurt reminded him. "He likes to do that."

"Feel better," Martin said, a final pat on her hand.

———

Hindemith was waiting outside the Ostbanhof, his bright white collar and clerical suit like a piece of theater in the drab crowd.

"Where's Kurt?"

"His wife is sick."

"Nothing serious, I hope."

"They're doing some tests. So I'm standing in. I have the inventory lists. It shouldn't take long. Any trouble crossing?"

"No, the collar's like a visa," he said, touching it. "They look and pass me through. Where did you get the car? And a driver." He nodded toward the front. "He's reliable? I mean, this business—"

"Better than reliable—he doesn't care. It's a DFF car. Kurt says he's all right."

"Don't be naïve," Hindemith said, his voice lower. "They all listen." He raised his voice. "I thought it was a Russian car when you pulled up. I thought, here it is, the Russians have come for me. Where does he drive for the DFF?"

"The studios in Adlershof, back and forth."

Hindemith leaned forward, loud now for the driver. "Have you met von Schnitzler? Karl-Eduard? They say everyone here watches him on *The Black Channel*."

"No," the driver said simply.

"*The Black Channel*," Hindemith said, sitting back. "Have you seen it? Lies, from beginning to end." He shook his head. "What a place. It didn't used to be like this." What Ruth had said, for different reasons.

"You're from here?"

"Leipzig. Have you been? You should go. In the Thomaskirche you can still see the organ Bach played. Something new every Sunday. Imagine. A very different Germany."

"Well, this is the one we have now."

Hindemith nodded and fingered the envelope with the lists. "*Kopfgeld.*"

"You don't approve?"

"It's not for me to approve or disapprove. It's a humanitarian business, we have to do it. Get these poor people out. What I don't approve of is what made them prisoners in the first place. I don't mean the spies, the real ones." He stopped for a minute, embarrassed. "But the others? What's their crime? Years of their lives in these places. You hear the stories. What's money to that? So we pay. For Kurt it's something else, I think. He could be trading Zeiss lenses, not prisoners, it's all the same to him. But he's honest. Always accurate." He tapped the envelope. "Of course he has his own people to deal with. We send a shipment to Rostock, something always disappears from there to here, a little off the truck. But he always gives us full credit for the order. Like here," he said, indicating the warehouse. "I'm only responsible for the count here. Where it goes after that is his business. If he honors the list. And he does. In his own way," he said, playing with it, "he's an honorable man."

Old Max let them in and took them to Kurt's section. Stacks of pallets, marked for the Ministry of Health.

"After that, who knows?" Hindemith said. "I'm one short. You?"

"It's over here," Max said.

Hindemith made a checkmark on his inventory list.

"Next to the wine, I see," he said. "Medical supplies for the people, wine for their masters."

Max shrugged, noncommittal.

"No label."

"The old one was changed. Maybe he's waiting for new instructions, so I keep it over here."

Martin nodded an okay. "So it's all here. Nothing off the truck," he said to Hindemith.

"What's this?" Hindemith said, ignoring him.

"Not yours," Max said, a watchdog. "SED. Office supplies."

"More paper," Hindemith said. "Just what they need. Yes, the count is correct. Do you want to open the boxes, make sure you're getting what you asked for?"

"I don't think we need to do that. If you can't trust the Church, who can you trust?"

Hindemith looked at him, but let it go.

"All right. I'll need a signature. Goods received. You'll sign for Kurt?" He held out a clipboard. "Here, under mine."

Martin took the pen, oddly tentative. Really part of it now. *Kopfgeld.* Head money. He signed.

"Thank you. So. I'll see you at the exchange, perhaps?"

"Not unless Kurt needs me."

"The loyal friend. Who keeps his hands clean. Well." He turned to Max. "There's a toilet here?"

"At the end. Follow the row."

"A minute only," Hindemith said, moving off, Max watching him.

"What?" Martin said.

"A priest in this business. I don't understand it."

Martin said nothing, leaning against the set-aside pallet to wait.

"Ask Herr Thiele where he wants this sent. The Ministry of Health, like the others?"

"I'll ask," Martin said, looking more closely at the box, shipping tags removed. "Where was it going? I mean, why the change?"

"Warehouse 7," Max said simply, then looked at him, suddenly suspicious. Something Martin should have known.

"Warehouse 7?" Martin said, as if he hadn't heard correctly.

Max nodded. "Herr Spitzer. So we had to—" He stopped, cautious. "Tell him to let me know where to send it."

CHAPTER 8

He met Andrei at Konnopke's, the wurst stand at the Eberswalder U-bahn station.

"Grab a table. The bauernwurst?"

"You're paying?" Martin said. "A first."

He cleared one of the stand-up tables. Around him people were eating, heads down, conversation covered by the trains overhead and the tram stop across the street. Andrei handed over a paper plate with a cut-up wurst and a splotch of mustard.

"Best in the city," he said.

"Another special meeting?" Martin said.

"Our friend is coming to town. You'll want to see him."

"Any particular reason?"

"He's not going to Geneva. They turned down the visa request. So he's going to need a shoulder to cry on."

"What?" Martin said, louder, his stomach falling. Stefan had to go, the only part of the deal that really interested Nugent. "Why?" Lowering his voice, the next table going back to their wursts.

"The East Germans don't trust him."

"That's crazy. I told you—"

"I know. I had your report. And I believe you. But no one can guarantee he'd come back, not with his wife gone. And he's been fighting with people. He wants them to work on a reactor and they want to work on what they want to work on."

"Weapons."

Andrei nodded. "Their own program. They think he'll use the conference as a soapbox. And they don't want to hear a discouraging word. Not from him, not from anybody."

"That's crazy," Martin said again.

"Welcome to East Germany. They think he's a loose cannon. And I don't know if you've noticed, but there's not much loose here. It bothers them. So, no Geneva."

Don't panic. Nothing in your face.

"They're making a mistake. He wants to be here."

"Well, it's theirs to make. We're not going to fight them on this. It's not worth it. Anyway, you'll want to have dinner and make all the right tut-tut noises. He's at the Berolina, so that's easy. We don't want any letters going back to Dubna. Remind him how wonderful it will be to work together."

"I thought they wanted an international presence. The East Germans. A place at the table."

"They do. But they don't like to be contradicted. Schell's been stamping his foot at the wrong people. Look at Ulbricht's face. He strike you as someone with a lot of give? They're part of the Hotel Lux crowd. That's where the Party put them, this hotel in Moscow, when they were on the run from Hitler. During the terror, so they're just sitting there, wondering if they'll be picked off too. Imagine what that's like. You've got to hang on to something, so they're more Party than the Party. Somebody questions it, he threatens everything. So nobody does. Not somebody running around Geneva saying things are on the wrong track." He took a bite of wurst. "He'll get over it. But right now he's probably a little—touchy. So, your move." He opened his hand. "See if you can calm him down. And let me know if you can't."

"Christ."

Andrei looked up. "It's not the end of the world."

Be calm. Pick up the pieces and reshuffle.

"Why bother having me do this if nobody's going to listen to what I say?"

"You're not working for them, you're working for us. We listen. But this time, we give them their heads."

"Why? What's our objective?"

"I wish I knew," Andrei said, looking away, into the street. "It's not like before, is it? Harwell, valuable stuff. Now what. Give the Americans the finger to see if they'll give it back to us. Wave a prick. So what's our objective? To keep going." He looked over. "But that's not your worry. Just keep Schell on the rails."

"He's going to be disappointed."

"Then cheer him up. You're not going to finish that?" he said, picking at a piece with his fork. "What's wrong? This is nothing. We've been through worse."

"I like him."

"But that doesn't matter, does it? Only the job."

Sensing something off. Move away from it.

"I know. I just wasn't expecting to play babysitter. Sabine's sick, in the hospital."

"It's serious?"

"They're running tests. So it's been on my mind. I'll see Stefan." He looked over at Andrei. "And how do we feel about his sending a speech for someone else to read? He'll want to."

"Nobody would like that. Not us, not the Germans."

"I'm not saying they read what he's written. But what if they read what we've written? Under his name."

Andrei stared at him for a second. "Sometimes I forget what it's like to work with you. Always a step ahead."

"Just an idea. In the end, somebody will leak and we'll have to deny it. So is it worth it? Me, I'd let him go to Geneva with a speech everybody can live with. Cut the mike off if he doesn't follow it. Technical difficulties."

Andrei smiled. "Your good friend."

"Either way, he'd be a presence at the conference. The Soviet Union believes in the exchange of scientific ideas. Now all you've got is a big hole. People wondering."

Andrei was quiet for a minute. "It's an argument."

"But you're not going to make it."

"I don't make arguments. I just do the job." He looked up. "See how the wind blows with him. What we should expect. You should go to Rossendorf."

"They're finding me a place to live."

"The sooner the better. He needs a friend. And you? Everything's all right?"

"I'm worried about Sabine."

"Is there anything we can do for you?"

"As a matter of fact—"

"Just say. A doctor?"

"No, nothing like that. She's at the Charité, so that's all right. It's not about her. I need a gun."

"What?" Andrei said, surprised.

"As soon as you can. Have someone put it in my room. We don't want to pass it on the street."

"There aren't so many guns in this country. No need."

"You'd be surprised. Will you do it? I don't ask much."

"And why do you need this? Put a gun to Schell's head?"

"I've run into some people in the criminal world you say doesn't exist here. Tough customers. One took a potshot at me. You remember. I'd feel a lot safer if I had some protection."

"I told you what happened to him, the kid. He's gone."

"He wasn't the only one."

"Your assignment is Schell."

"But I stumbled into something else and I need a gun, just in case. You won't be sorry. It'll give you a whole new opening to the black market."

"We don't care about the black market. Let the Germans take care of it."

"Except they're in it. And so is Kurt. I'm going to give you some leverage to use. You've always wanted that, to own him. He'd be yours. You could run him."

Andrei waited a minute, staring at him. "And why would you want to do this? He made the arrangement for you."

"It's difficult to share a wife."

"So you'd do this?"

"He'd be happier with you. More useful anyway."

"You surprise me."

"Why? I learned it from you. Why not use it for something I want?" He looked over. "I can give him to you. Just leave the gun in my room."

———

Stefan had already made dinner plans, so they agreed to meet afterward for a drink instead. This left Martin alone in the hotel dining room, one of several solitary diners, an open book next to his plate. The restaurant was the kind Western journalists made fun of, gristly food served by resentful waiters, another Soviet legacy, and ordinarily Martin would have watched the people, wondering who they were, but tonight he concentrated on the book, a prop to let his mind run through the plan, imagining it play out, like working equations in his head. Keep it simple. The more steps there were the greater the chances of something going wrong. If someone betrayed you, he could only betray the piece he knew. But who would? He thought of the Last Supper, Jesus looking around the table. Lord, is it I?

He looked up now in the dining room to see Hans Rieger come in with a heavy-set man in a suit. He nodded to Martin but didn't stop, the man presumably higher in Hans's pecking order, maybe one of his sources. Would he betray me? In a heartbeat. But so would Kurt, even Peter, not knowing. The trick was to work around the weak links, the betrayal just an obstacle then, like traffic to a getaway car.

Sabine had looked better, or at least no worse, when he stopped by the hospital earlier, more alert, some color in her cheeks.

"They think she can go home soon," Kurt said, looking worn.

"You understand, the underlying condition is the same," the doctor said. "There's nothing we can do about that. Except keep her comfortable."

"Radiation?" Martin said. "You hear—"

"She's had those treatments. This has been with her for some time. You take a step forward, and then two back. I'm sorry. There are some new chemical treatments, experimental only, but we don't have access to that yet. Only in the West." He looked around. "If you believe the research papers. But these complications with the heart, it's a little better now, she's responding well to the medicine. Of course, she'll have to be careful. Nothing strenuous."

"But she's not confined to bed?" Kurt said.

"No, a normal life. Just be careful. Each time this happens, the heart's weaker."

"Ticking, like a bomb," Kurt said to himself.

"If you like," the doctor said, indulgent. "So bed rest, quiet."

But then Tante Helene arrived with a bouquet of flowers, and the room erupted in a flurry of activity—summoning nurses for a vase, plumping the pillow behind Sabine's head, swooping Peter to her for a hug. Sabine smiled a little.

"How did you hear?"

"I hear everything, you know that. Here," she said, taking Sabine's hand. "Let me feel. Ouf. Better in no time. Don't you think, Peter?" Bringing him into the circle.

Martin watched from the door, a film clip playing out. The trusted friend. But could she be trusted? One way to make the plan better. Useful. But where were her loyalties? To Sabine, to the studio she'd moved east for, the DDR who was its gatekeeper? But if she only knew a small piece? Still, there were no small pieces. In the end you had to choose. You had to trust someone.

Kurt saw the doctor out and came over, following Martin's gaze to Sabine's bedside.

"And we're supposed to be keeping her quiet," he said.

"It's another kind of medicine," Martin said. "You must be tired."

"It's not so bad. I fall asleep in the chair. So, it went well with Hindemith?"

Martin nodded. "Everything there. We both signed off on it."

"Good. Now it's only the list. I'll go to the West after we get her home. It shouldn't take long."

"Max wants to know where to send Spitzer's pallet." His voice flat, nothing out of the ordinary.

"I'll talk to Koch," Kurt said, offhand, Martin just part of it. "Come, help me with Helene," he said, nodding to her, busy now arranging Sabine's night table. "Look, she's dressing the set. A sickroom."

Now, in the dining room, he thought of her hovering over the bed. It wasn't much to ask. She could always deny knowing, an innocent party, taken in. And if she wouldn't, they could work around that. Useful, but not crucial. Stefan was crucial. But now he wasn't going to Geneva, an easy place to defect. Crossing the border with Martin was something else. How to do this? If you scared him off, everything collapsed.

Stefan's hair was wilder than usual, sticking out in tufts, as if he'd forgotten to comb it. His face was red from drink, but unhappy, distracted. They found a corner table in the lobby bar, just under one of the speakers filling the room with piped-in music, loud enough to cover their voices.

"I shouldn't," he said, when Martin ordered brandies. "So much wine already."

"Just one. Pleasant dinner?"

"Pleasant? No. A job interview. And I didn't get the job."

"What are you talking about?" Wondering if he'd really had too much to drink.

"Mender. You know, at the university. There's an open chair in theoretical physics. And who better? So I thought. A vanity. The Ministry won't allow it. They have so many others qualified for this," he said, sarcastic. "Mender was embarrassed to have to say it. But he said it. So, him too. Anyway," he said, picking up the just-delivered snifter, "I won't be teaching. My own work, as it happens. But somebody else knows it better. *Prost.*"

Martin raised his glass. "Why do you want to teach? On top of—"

"Instead of. I'm leaving Rossendorf. They're not going to use my brain anymore. It's not theirs."

"Leaving? They know this?"

"Not yet. Only you. I wanted you to know, before it's too late. Don't take the job there. I won't be there, if that means something to you. It stops. Using my brain. They're worse than the Russians. At least the Russians felt threatened. Maybe they were. But the Germans? What do they want this work for? Why not build the reactors, stop using lignite. But no, weapons. What for?"

"To please the Russians," Martin said quietly. "Isn't that why they do everything?"

Stefan looked down. "And to what end? The Russians don't care about them. A united, neutral Germany? Under their control? They'd do it in a minute, let Ulbricht and the others hang. But of course this won't be offered, so Ulbricht keeps his job." He smiled to himself. "But I'm not keeping mine. Would you like to go to Geneva? There's a spot now. Well, maybe not you. They can't send a spy."

"You're not going?" Martin said, his voice steady.

"Visa denied. I don't blame them. Think what I might say, in such a situation. The whole world listening."

"Reapply. Give them a script they approve. It makes them look good if you go. The world will be listening. You just have to get there."

"And be their mouthpiece? No. No more."

"The speech they approve—it's not necessarily the speech you'll give."

Stefan looked up. "Lie to them? And then what?"

"Then you're in Geneva. How much do you want to give the speech?"

"I'd have to stay in Geneva."

"Yes. Or Germany. You're automatically a citizen there."

"Of West Germany." He looked over at Martin. "You've given this some thought."

"You want to leave Rossendorf. Where else will you go?"

Stefan leaned back, taking out a pipe and filling it. "You know they have people who encourage you to leave the Republic so they can trap you."

"You think I'm one of them?"

Stefan stared for a second, drawing on his pipe. "No. But how do you come to know all this?"

Martin hesitated. Draw the moment out.

"I'm not going back to Rossendorf either."

Stefan said nothing.

"You said to me last time, where is home now? For either of us. Not Russia. Not England. Not here. What are we leaving? You're German. You're already welcome there."

Stefan looked at him. "You've been approached?"

"No. I'm not German. Nobody really wants me—except the East Germans, ironically enough. But I don't want them. So."

"It's dangerous to do this."

"It doesn't have to be."

"You're serious?"

"They're not going to use my brain either."

"Even to talk about it. What if they ask me, what did you talk about?"

"Tell them. Maybe they'll trust you again and give you a visa."

"No, it's too late for that. They'll never trust me. And do you think I would do such a thing?"

Martin shrugged. "People do things."

Stefan tapped his pipe into the ashtray. "And how will you do this?"

"I can't tell you that. This way you could say you don't know."

"Something foolish? A tunnel under the wall. You don't hear about that so much anymore. They catch them."

Martin smiled. "I don't have to do that. I still have an American passport."

"So you just—leave?"

"Not exactly. I'm not going alone."

Stefan raised his eyebrows. "You're taking Sabine?"

"And Peter. I want my family. I'll never have them here. Kurt will."

"But it's dangerous. To risk a child—"

Martin nodded. "But I think I can do it."

"Because you don't want to work at Rossendorf? Your conscience would make you do this?"

Martin looked at him. "Yours would."

"Yes, maybe, but I don't have—"

"There's something else. You might as well have it all. Sabine's sick."

"Sick?"

"She's going to die. But I think I can buy her some time in the West. I want my wife back. So, yes, it's worth it to me. If she dies here, I'll never get Peter. Not in an East German court. With Kurt fighting me. And they'll never let him leave. They can't. He's Erich Schmidt. So I have to do something else."

Stefan thought for a minute. "Maybe you shouldn't tell me this."

"You have to trust somebody. I trust you. And—well, I know it's been on your mind. If you got to Geneva. Have you talked to anyone?" He held up his hand. "Never mind, don't tell me. It's better."

"No, no one. I'm not so organized as you. And what's the point? They'll never let me go. I know that." He waited. "Unless there's another way."

"You'd consider it?"

"A way that involves a man's family—it would have to be careful. Safe."

"Nothing's safe. You have to know that."

"Let me ask you something. What happens—if something goes wrong?"

"You'd go to prison. An East German prison. Not a joke."

"Not a Russian prison, though. Not the worst. And then your friend Kurt arranges an exchange. Both of us, on Glienicke Bridge."

"Kurt would never exchange us. Not us. We'd rot. You know that."

"And maybe I'm in the way."

"No. But you have to be sure."

"To make such arrangements—you'd have to have help."

Martin said nothing.

"You know, they're no better, the other side."

Martin nodded. "I can't do it alone. Neither can you. You want somebody waiting for you."

"And then work for them?"

"That's up to you. If they offer."

"And have they—offered you?"

"No."

"I've never done such work."

"I don't think they're recruiting. Me? I was used up years ago. You're a little late in the day to start. Just having us come over gives them bragging rights. And they like needling the East Germans. That's how it's played these days."

"A chess game," Stefan said, then sat back. "What a world you live in."

"Not anymore." He looked up. "But you're right. I need help to get out. If you did this, you'd be a part of that. A defector. The

Russians would denounce you and the East Germans would hound you. If you don't want that, apply for another visa. We never talked, just old times. It depends how much you want to go to Geneva."

"You have a taste for this," Stefan said, looking at him. "No wonder you—"

"I have a family to get out, that's all. It won't make much difference to anybody if we do get out, but it will if you do. So. But you decide. If you do nothing, you're safe. I understand that. I'd feel that way myself if it wasn't for Sabine. I need to get her help. Safe doesn't matter."

Stefan was quiet for a minute, staring into his glass. "You know, they say when you get older, you get more cautious. Something to do with falling, maybe, breaking the hip."

"We're not that old."

"No. But for me it's the opposite. I was safe all my life. I said yes to them. Arzamas. Dubna. Rossendorf. Always yes. To give them more power, enough to blow us all up, me too. So how safe am I now? A gun to my head and who supplied the bullet? Just do what they want, Liesl used to say, we have to do it. To stay safe." He looked down. "And now she's gone and who's safe? So maybe it's time—to say no. I want to say no to them. It's too late for apologies. I did what I did. So did you. But it's not too late to say no." He looked up at Martin, almost a smile. "So let's say no to them. But tell your new friends—I'm not like that. I won't work for them. Now I say no to everybody."

"I'll tell them. You don't have to worry."

"No, just if I can trust you with this. But I remember how you were with exams—always prepared. So, what do I do?"

"Nothing. Have your passport ready, that's all. A few days. Just be prepared to leave when I call. Right then."

"For Berlin?"

"Yes, for Berlin."

"And then what? You'll have papers?"

"I'll have papers." Not quite a lie. "For now, this is all you have to know. That way—"

"That way what?"

"If anything goes wrong with this piece of it, I'll know it was you."

Stefan held his gaze for a minute, then looked away. "My old friend. I wonder what I would have said. At Göttingen. If someone had told me that one day we would be sitting here like this. Saying such things to each other. What would I have said?"

"We didn't make the world."

Stefan looked back at him. "We said yes."

Martin felt the presence behind him before Stefan looked up.

"Well, it's as I say, you see everybody at the Berolina. Professor Schell, again a pleasure. You remember? Hans Rieger."

"Of course. The interview. You know Dr. Keller?"

"Yes, we've had dinner." The night at the Ganymed now part of an intimacy. "How is Sabine?" Concerned, one of the family.

"Better, thanks."

"Good, I'm glad to hear it. It's a day for good news. You know who that is?" Nodding to the burly man. "Inspector Kalisch."

"Police inspector?" Stefan said.

Rieger smiled. "Yes. One of the good ones. Like in the old days at the Alex, the bloodhound."

"Like you," Martin said, a compliment.

"Well, not so much as before. Not like Kalisch. A break in the case already."

"Oh?" Martin said, waiting.

"The witness. She's identified one of the men."

"What?" Martin said, thrown. "How?"

"In a lineup," Rieger said simply. Pointing to a stranger in a line. Encouraged by Kalisch? Scared? "They're talking to him now. To give up the other."

"Talking to him," Martin said, a knot in his chest. The interrogation rooms at Hohenschönhausen.

"They have their methods. Of course, not so pleasant. But if they get results—" His voice smooth, unconcerned.

"Who is it?" Martin said.

"Well, that's the interesting part. A man who worked for Spitzer, not somebody at the restaurant. So, no more questions. Kalisch thinks he followed him and they fought outside. You know, in that business—these things happen."

"She's sure?" Trying to keep his voice even, just curious.

"Kalisch thinks so. We'll see what he has to say. His interrogation."

At Hohenschönhausen, where it was easier to confess. He felt a sour taste in his mouth, bile rising. An unsolved case was one thing. This was something else, blood on his hands. A man now past saving. Unless someone said no. But you couldn't save everybody. Not now. Protect yourself first. Still, there was blood.

"So it's good news, yes?" Rieger was saying. "A very efficient job. You have to give him credit, Kalisch."

"And now you have your story."

"Well, the story. If it was Springer, yes, good placement, above the fold. But here— So, I'll let you finish your drink. I just thought you would like to hear. A relief to have an end to this. You know, I will never forget—that you and Kurt would vouch for me. It's a debt," he said, earnest, putting his hand on Martin's arm.

"Of course," Martin said. "I wonder if they'll find the other man."

"Well, Kalisch is very good at getting them to talk." Proud of it somehow. Another innocent man hauled in, questioned, punished, an end to it, the books balanced, East German justice. They had to get out. Martin looked down at the hand still on his sleeve. White, no visible stain.

Later, in his room, he found the gun from Andrei in the night table drawer. He ran his hand over the cool metal, checking the cartridge. Another Service magic trick. He wondered who had done it—a maid? A gun and a change of sheets, courtesy of the Berolina. A passkey somewhere. Easy to slip in while he was out. Or asleep. He took the desk chair and wedged it under the door handle. Just as Digby had promised, one prison for another.

———

Kurt couldn't postpone his meeting in West Berlin any longer, so Martin took Sabine home, settling her onto the couch with pillows, water by her side.

"I'm not an invalid."

"Just be lazy for a few days. Get your strength back."

"So I can make a run for it. When we get to the wall."

"Nobody's running anywhere."

"Where are we doing this? Friedrichstrasse?"

"Not at the station. The other end, the international crossing. In a car."

"Checkpoint Charlie. Where the Americans cross."

"We're American. You have your old passport?"

"It's expired. I told you."

He shook his head. "It doesn't matter. You just want something in your hand. If we play it right, they won't even look."

"They will on this side."

"A German passport, yes. An American—"

"And if you're wrong?"

"I won't be. But if I am, we'll do it another way."

"You think there are second chances with this?"

"Where's the passport?"

"The second drawer on the left."

He went over and started rummaging through the drawer.

"In the back. Peter's ID papers too." She paused, biting her lip. "You know, he has a good life here."

"No one has a good life here. It's a police state," he said, preoccupied, more dismissive than he intended. "Here we go." He flipped open the passport and stopped for a second, looking at the picture. Sabine as she had been when they were just married, hair cut short, her eyes alive even in a passport photo. "No expiration stamp. You really have to look at dates to see it's lapsed. Just like mine."

"Wonderful. Two expired passports."

"With any luck, we won't have to use them."

"You're excited about this."

"I just don't want anything to go wrong. There's a lot at stake."

"The way you used to—" She stopped, moving away from it. "So organized. When does this happen?" she said, drifting a little, the indifference of the ill.

"That depends on Kurt."

"On Kurt?"

"When he makes the next exchange. It's better if he's out of town, don't you think?"

———

He waited across from Gerhard's office until Ruth came out, catching up to her in front of St. Hedwig's.

"Time for a coffee?"

"What's the occasion?"

"Thanks and good-bye for a while."

"You're going somewhere?"

"Dresden. To start work."

"Shall we sit by the Dom? I've already had coffee. You surprise me."

"Why?"

"I thought you'd stay in Berlin."

"It's not far. I can't stay at the Berolina forever. A guest of the state."

They found a bench at the edge of the Lustgarten.

"So everybody works in the workers' state?" she said.

"It's time. Stefan's been patient, but it's time. They're finding me a place."

"And the boy?"

"Weekends. It's an easy train."

She took this in, not saying anything, then turned to him. "How did it go with our friends?"

"So-so. Nobody's doing me any favors. About the passport. I think they want to make it more trouble than it's worth."

"It's worth the trouble, whatever it is. Maybe they'd like something in return."

"Would they?"

"You could be useful to them. It's hard to put someone in the East. You're already here."

"I'm out of the business." He took a second. "Did they ask you to ask? Or is this your idea?"

She smiled a little. "A good man is hard to find. I'd get a gold star."

"And if the Service found out, I'd be dead. I don't want a passport that much."

"It's not like that anymore. Little jobs. Information."

Martin looked at her. "There are no little jobs. Not when you're working both sides."

She looked away, uncomfortable.

"If that's the price, I'd rather be East German. I'm not that patriotic."

"Don't be so sure. Once you give it up, the passport, you have no legal rights here."

"What rights do I have now?"

"More than you think. For one thing, you could leave. They'd make it hard, but they'd do it. They don't want to pick a fight with Uncle Sam over one passport. They'd honor it."

"But I'm not leaving. My life is here now."

"Then why did you want the contact?" she said sharply.

Martin shrugged. "I thought I'd keep my options open. Like Brecht. But they made it clear that I could be facing jail time if I went back. That changes things a little. Dresden starts looking better."

"Don't give it up. They'll renew it. They have to." She looked down. "It's who you are. That's something to hang on to. If things here—" She stopped.

"What?"

"Don't go the way you like." She took another second. "You surprise me."

"Why, this time?"

"A passport renewal—that's all you wanted? I thought you had more on your mind."

Martin turned to her, matter-of-fact. "I did."

She looked at him, waiting.

"Peter," he said. "He's the child of two American citizens. So what's his status now? What could it be?"

"And did they make trouble about him too?"

"No, they'd love to get their hands on him. Erich Schmidt. But they're not going to. I just wanted to know for later. Maybe he'll be Brecht."

She thought about this for a minute, then nodded, another quick smile. "I wonder if anybody thinks about that, if it came out. Erich Schmidt, an American. When do you go to Dresden?"

"The next few days. As soon as the flat's ready. But I didn't want to go without saying—"

She waved this away. "It's what I do, take messages to people." She looked at him. "Little jobs. I do them favors, they do me favors."

"And now me. Thank you."

"I have to run." She got up. "Don't give up the passport," she said, then started walking east. Maybe to Alexanderplatz again and the U-bahn out to Magdalenenstrasse. Make the report while it was all still fresh. Martin Keller was going to Dresden, eager to start work with Stefan Schell, make a life here. The Stasi had nothing to worry about.

Nugent used the Adlon side entrance, just as before. A busier day on Wilhelmstrasse, people on bicycles, workers swarming over a building site, shouts and clanging noises. He reached into his breast pocket and took out an envelope. Martin glanced at it quickly, just long enough to see the passports, and slipped it into his own pocket.

"They still need photos. I assume you know how to do it. Service training."

Martin nodded. "Careful with the glue. Thank you. And the rest of it?"

"Agreed. You're more popular than I thought. They're looking forward to talking to you."

"So, immunity?"

"That depends on what you have to say."

"Then there's no guarantee."

"What the fuck? You don't sign a contract for something like this. They said yes. You don't trust it, that's up to you."

"Would you?"

"On my mother," he said, sarcastic.

"Wonderful woman that she must be."

Nugent stared at him. "You're a piece of work, you know that?"

Martin held up his hand. "You're right, we don't have time for this. Now that the clock's ticking."

"How do you mean?"

"How many at the Agency know about this? Messages to State. Little conferences here. It would have to be. Which means it's just a matter of time before they know on this side. Maybe they already do."

"We don't have a leak. Not at the station."

"Don't bet your mother on that one. It's Berlin. It's safer to assume something will leak. So."

"You mean you're coming over right away?"

"I have to fix these first," Martin said, patting his pocket. "But now we don't have a lot of time."

"I still don't see how you're going to do this."

"You're going to help."

Nugent stopped. "I told you that wasn't part of the deal. We don't exfiltrate."

"You're in this too. Something goes wrong, the East Germans will say you bungled it. They'll like embarrassing the Agency even better than catching me. So we don't want them to catch me. We've got a shared interest in this."

Nugent looked at him. "A piece of work and a prick. We can't send people into East Berlin. It's a rule."

"Understood. We get ourselves out."

"With your brand-new passports." A sudden thought. "And the professor?"

"He's going to the Atoms for Peace Conference in Geneva. He's expecting to see you there. Let's hope you're nicer to him."

"Which leaves you. And the family. Not the easiest group to move. How are you going to do it?"

"As I said, with your help." He held up his hand. "You don't send a single man into East Berlin. But you get all the credit. They'll always think you ran the operation. I wouldn't be surprised, they give you a promotion."

"Really."

"And no leaks. Nobody knows enough of it, not even you. You're protected if I don't make it. Sound all right?"

Nugent waited for a minute, eyes on Martin.

"I'm taking the risk," Martin said. "Not you."

"That part I like."

"But I need you to arrange something."

"What?"

"A lunch."

———

He walked back to Unter den Linden, glancing at his watch. Still time to catch Kurt. A bus had just pulled away from the corner stop. A long wait for the next, standing just outside the Russian Embassy. He kept going, swallowed up in a crowd of office workers streaming through the gates. Then, suddenly, Andrei was beside him.

"What are you doing here?" he said. "You have a contact number."

"I wasn't looking for you. I was at the Adlon."

"It's not safe here. They watch the embassy. Let's cross, at least," he said, steering Martin to the other side of the street. "So, the Adlon. A rendezvous?" Teasing, but asking.

"*Neues Deutschland*. They'd like another piece. They pick up the tab, so why not the Adlon?"

"Maybe you'll let me see this one before it runs."

"Is that a request?"

"A curiosity. For your protection. You know what journalists are like. They have you saying things you don't mean to say."

"The last one was all right, wasn't it?"

"A precaution only. Your friend has made them nervous about the scientific community, so they read with extra care these days.

So. As long as you're here, how is he? Dinner went well? I assume yes or you would have alerted me. That's why—seeing you here—"

"He's all right. Disappointed. I still think they're making a mistake."

"We've discussed this. It doesn't matter what we think. How disappointed?"

Martin began to shrug and stopped, suddenly aware of the envelope in his pocket. Impossible to explain the passports, not to the Service. He felt the weight of them against his chest, as if they were growing, something Andrei would see in a moment, too big to hide.

"Disappointed. Not being with his colleagues. He feels sidelined."

"And now he's angry? So who knows—"

"Come on, Andrei, he's harmless."

"So harmless that he sent a letter to his friends in Dubna, urging them to stop work."

"And did they?"

"The letter was intercepted."

"He thinks you're tapping his phone," Martin said. "I told him he was imagining things."

"Is it any wonder? World peace is one thing. Fine. Stopping work at Dubna is something else. Treason, in fact."

Martin looked over at him. Just a matter of time now. Once the word was used, it was only a question of working out the details. Another clock ticking.

"He's not like that. His head's in the clouds, that's all."

"And maybe in a noose if he's not careful."

"He's not careful, that's the problem. But he's not disloyal. I'm going to Dresden soon. I'll stay close to him. No more letters."

"And you can control that? You didn't even know about this

one." He was quiet for a minute. "Martin, we've worked together for many years. I want to be sure you understand the assignment. You're not his protector. You don't make apologies for him. You listen, that's all. Then someone else decides what to do."

Martin looked at him. "Take me off the case, then. You've already decided. Or somebody has. What do you need me for?"

"Evidence."

Martin stared at him. Already preparing a trial.

"It's not possible to change now. You're close to him. And how would it look, for you? A sentimentalist. In the Service. There's no room for that." He put his hand on Martin's shoulder, the envelope just inches away, bulging. "I know you. You're a pragmatist. Like me. What needs to be done. The rest—" He opened his hand, letting the rest drift away.

Martin turned toward the street. Show nothing. "Who do I see in Dresden? Is that set up?"

"No change. You see me. Here. I don't have so many men. Besides, we already understand each other. It's more efficient."

"Here? When?"

"On the weekends, when you come."

"To see Peter."

"A few minutes only."

Martin turned to him. "I don't want to be at his trial. Promise me that."

"Of course. We don't want you publicly compromised. With your new colleagues."

Martin looked at him, seeing the future stretching out behind him, years of it, one betrayal at a time.

"I have to turn off here, get back. You're walking?"

Martin nodded.

"Did you get the—" Not saying the word. "In your room."

"Yes, thank you."

"Have you shot anybody yet?"

"You think I'm overreacting."

"I see you're not carrying it," he said, glancing toward Martin's jacket pocket, the passports heavy again against his chest.

"To the Adlon? No."

"Why not the Adlon? It's as dangerous as anywhere."

"A different class of crook."

Andrei smiled. "Just don't use it unless you have to. It's hard to explain a gunshot wound. You can't make it go away. Stick to the Adlon crooks." He started to leave, then stopped. "A piece of advice?"

"Always."

"Kurt is useful to many people. He's been useful to us. Unless we can really own him, it's better to leave him as he is. Poke a hornet's nest, you get stung."

"An old proverb?"

"Folk wisdom."

"Don't worry. You'll really own him."

But not me, he thought, walking away. The Service's man at Rossendorf, listening to everybody. First Stefan, then the others. The rest of his life. Say no. They wouldn't come after him. He wasn't important enough, not even as an example. And the Agency would protect him. But Andrei. Called back to Moscow, perhaps. A serious lapse of judgment. He felt the envelope in his pocket move. What needs to be done.

Kurt was still in his office, surrounded by piles of paperwork.

"You take time off, it's so hard to catch up. Of course it was Sabine—you take the time. But then afterwards— And now the exchange."

"When?"

"Tomorrow."

"Do you want me to go?"

"No. Hindemith can handle it. I sent him the list. Not so many this time. He can do it. The guards know him. But thank you." He sat back. "It's a social visit?"

"I thought I'd walk you home." Motioning up with his eyes to the ceiling, the invisible microphones.

Kurt smiled. "We can talk freely. I have so much—"

"I'm going to Dresden soon. We may not get another chance— to catch up." Now staring, an unmistakable signal.

"Well, a short break. I'll come out with you. Wait till you see what they're putting up in Alexanderplatz."

They crossed over to the Marienkirche and headed toward the station.

"What is it?" Kurt said.

"I thought we'd better talk. You've heard the witness identified someone?"

"Yes, a break for the police. And Hans. I thought at first it was one of God's little jokes, that it should be Hans, but he got lucky."

"The other guy didn't. Whoever he is."

"Somebody in that world, Hans said. A prison record. Just what you'd expect."

"But what are we going to do?"

"Do? Be grateful."

"He could die for this."

"But I won't," Kurt said easily. He stopped. "And neither will you. So they have the wrong man. What do we do, turn ourselves in?"

"We can't let this happen. You fix things."

"What do you suggest?"

"People make mistakes. Have the witness take another look. This time with her glasses. Give the guy an alibi. Tell the police it couldn't have been him because—I don't know. You'll think of something."

"Let me explain how this is," Kurt said, his voice deliberate. "The police have solved the case. It's finished. Now they can close the book and move on."

"But he'll hang."

"If not for this, something else. At least this way, he's useful."

Martin stared at him, taking this in. Who he really was.

"What?" Kurt said, catching the look. "There's nothing I can do. Why are you asking me this?"

"I guess to see what you'd say."

"What else can I say? I can't tell the police what to do."

"You had Karl Hitzig moved."

Kurt looked up. "Who told you that?"

A slip. Martin shrugged. "Hans said it was the gossip. Did you?"

"As usual, the nose where it doesn't belong. He was in Hohen-schönhausen. That's not police."

"Stasi."

"A different thing entirely." He stopped for a second, looking up. "Almost finished," he said, nodding to the TV tower. "You'll be able to see the whole city from up there." He turned to Martin. "Why do you trouble yourself with this? It means we're safe."

"Safe. We're not safe. How long before Hans puts two and two together? He's the one who figured out Invalidenstrasse, that

Hitzig was shooting at you. And that he worked for Spitzer. He doesn't know how the exchanges work, but when he does—"

"What will he know?"

"That Spitzer was on the take. Not from you—you just had to turn a blind eye while something slipped off the truck."

"And why would I allow that? If I knew."

"Because you were told to. By Koch, would be my guess. And as long as the West Germans were paying in commodities, you didn't have a choice. He fenced the stuff on the black market and paid your boss his share. So you had the bright idea to make the exchanges a cash-only deal. Your boss could still skim off the top—it's a government account—but it cuts out Spitzer altogether. No goods, no market. And he didn't want to be cut out."

"And if it's true?"

"If I can connect the dots, so can Hans."

Kurt looked at him. "But you're part of it. He isn't. There's nothing for him to know— Correction, no way to prove it. And no way to prove what happened to Spitzer. One witness and she's unreliable. There are no dots to connect. You're worried about nothing. We're safe." He took a breath. "Sabine said you always had a cool head, when you were doing the work. In Los Alamos. Some incident, I forget what now, when you had the paper in your hand, the one you were stealing, and Bethe—was it?—walked in and you talked your way out of it. So where's that famous cool head now?"

"We can't let someone hang for this. If they think he's capable of doing it, then so is every two-bit crook Spitzer tried to strong-arm. Let them go after him, crook X. You'd still be safe. The witness is worthless now. So there's no one—"

Kurt looked up. "Except you."

Martin said nothing.

"Of course, it's not in your interest to say anything."

"No."

"I can see this has upset you. And we want the cool head now. So let me see what's possible. I warn you, if the police already—well, let's see how things are. Maybe it was Hans after all," he said, playing with it. He looked up. "It's lucky he doesn't know what you know—or what you guess. It's complicated, the exchanges."

"No, it's just numbers."

"To a mathematician. Spitzer never saw it. He liked goods, something he could feel. A primitive imagination. As you guessed."

"There's one thing I still don't know."

"One?"

"Why did you have Hitzig killed? After he was moved."

"I didn't," Kurt said simply.

"You didn't."

"Do you think I would do that?"

"Who, then?"

"Who. In that prison? Not such a rare occurrence."

"He was no threat to you."

"You forget. He tried to shoot me. But you're right, he was no threat. I'm not a thief. I don't involve myself in that business. Just a fee to make the arrangements." He looked over. "You don't involve yourself either. Some of these people, not so civilized."

"He'd know about Koch. Embarrassing if that came out."

"But it won't. Not from Hitzig, not from you. Do you understand? It's not a guessing game. You don't know, you don't guess. You go to Rossendorf. And there's an end to it." Eyes hard. He took a step back, a kind of truce signal. "So. Let me see about the police, yes? You're okay?" He tapped his temple. "Cool heads. Come, over by the world clock. You won't believe how big."

He pointed to the façade of a department store, now displaying a giant poster for *Die Familie Schmidt*, sitting at home, Peter standing in front, looming over Alexanderplatz.

"Well, well," Martin said.

"It's good, yes? Imagine how many people see it every day."

But the crowd seemed mostly oblivious, women in print dresses and cheap shoes, men in blue coveralls, all heading for the station, gray faces in the bare concrete plaza, the Schmidts' world a pipe dream.

"What does Peter say?"

"It just went up. I'll show him tomorrow." He turned. "You know, Martin, it's important we stay together. On Spitzer, all this business. It's not easy to share a son. When you came I thought, how is this going to be possible, but I think we can do it. We have interests now, we look out for each other. You at Rossendorf, I think that's easier too. An arrangement to share. And then Sabine is happy, yes?"

Martin looked at the poster, a shiver running through him, ice along his spine, hearing what Kurt was really saying. He's my son. We'll pretend to share him. And when Sabine dies, that arrangement dies too. You'll never get him. We have interests, the only witnesses who know. Hitzig was no threat to me, but you are. And standing there in a crowd of head kerchiefs and lunch pails, a socialist poster come to dreary life, he knew they would never share anything, that Kurt was already thinking about the arrangements he'd need to make. Two people can keep a secret, if one of them is dead.

———

Back at the Berolina he borrowed a typewriter from a reluctant front desk and spent the rest of the day putting the exchange operation on paper, the general outline, the delivery procedures, the cash values. He had taken some notes in Kurt's home office, but mostly he relied on memory, the same mental camera gift he'd used at Los Alamos. Deutschemarks this time, not formulas. Forty thousand per prisoner, more if he was valuable. Paid off in equipment and fertilizer and oranges, with the usual inventory shrinkage, enough for Spitzer and Koch to share, not enough to draw attention. Unless you were looking. Reverend Hindemith and his clipboard, checking off names. Laundering money to rescue souls. Everything about the exchanges, except the haunted look on the prisoners' faces when they got off the bus.

The report ran only a few pages, closely typed, not enough to bulk out the envelope. He marked it "Notes for Lecture" and slipped it into his pocket, then called Stefan.

"When are you coming?"

"Soon. Just typing up a few loose ends." Vague enough for whoever was listening. "Maybe tomorrow."

"Ah."

"If I can. I'll call when I know. Can you pick me up?"

"Of course. Just tell me what train. I'm looking forward."

What they would have said if it were true, Martin on his way to Rossendorf at last.

He picked up the typewriter and left the room, heading for the elevators. Only one more piece.

"We have to make a charge," the desk clerk said. "For the use of the machine."

"Fine," Martin said, waving his hand to put it on the bill.

"A cash charge. It's not authorized."

Martin looked at him, about to argue, then pulled out his wallet. Another thing to leave behind, the sullenness of daily life. He felt eager, expectant, someone with a ticket in his hand.

Hans Rieger was in his usual chair, smoking a cigar.

"Herr Keller."

"I was hoping I'd find you."

"Oh yes?"

"Do you have a few minutes? Maybe outside?" He looked around the lobby, as if he could feel people listening.

"*Naturlich,*" Rieger said, getting up, interested now.

They went out onto the empty plaza, half-lit by the Kino International marquee.

"I'd like to ask a very great favor."

"Herr Keller—"

"Martin. But if anything I say makes you uncomfortable, just stop me and that's it. We never had this conversation."

Rieger leaned forward.

"It's just—you're the only one who could do it. Whom I trust."

"Yes?"

"I'm going to the West tomorrow." He held up his hand. "Nothing illegal. I have an American passport. But I think people might try to make it difficult."

"You're leaving?"

"Yes. If this troubles you, I understand—"

"But what do you want me to do?"

"Contact your old friends at Springer—I think you can do this, you wouldn't cut all ties—and have somebody meet me on the other side. It's easier for me if someone's waiting, the guards can't turn me away if they're being watched. An American citizen. Tell them to bring a camera too. Just in case. Nobody wants an incident. If they meet me, I'll give them an exclusive for *Die Welt*—the spy who came back. I don't expect them to do it for free."

"Herr Keller, what you're asking—"

"I know. A certain amount of risk. But not to you, I think. You know how these things are done."

"But why do you want to leave? An honored guest."

"Doesn't everybody? Don't you?"

Rieger looked away, embarrassed. "Of course not. The Republic is the future."

"Let's hope not. So. Will you do it?"

"Herr Keller, I'm grateful for your help, in that other matter, but you have to understand my position here—"

"I don't expect you to do it for free. I have—a proposition."

Rieger looked at him.

"You're too good for the papers here—you know you ought to be back at Springer. I saw how you covered the shooting. At my exchange. No one else understood it. It was you who tracked down Hitzig and then—gone. End of story." He paused. "I know who killed him. Or had him killed. It's the kind of story you could use to buy your way back to Springer. I know, I know," he said, holding up his hand again, "but that was then and this is now. Not just a crime story. A corruption scandal that goes to the top. Not Ulbricht, but close. A Springer dream. The Republic corrupt, ministers on the take. The story can run for days. And it's yours, details and all, if you want it. If you want to go back."

Rieger's eyes, wide and unblinking, stayed fixed on Martin, trying to take this in.

"And you have such a story? How?"

"You started it. I never thought about the shooting, the ambulance, until you brought it up. But then I wanted to know. At first

I thought he'd been shooting at me. But Hitzig was working for Spitzer—you found out—the black market, nothing to do with me."

"No, he was shooting at Herr Thiele. So, why? Unless he was involved too. You would expose him? Your friend?"

Martin shook his head. "He had nothing to do with this. He just got caught in the middle of a turf war and managed to duck. The rest of them can trust him, so they use him, that's all."

"But Spitzer? Who killed him?"

"I don't know. Whoever won the turf war, I guess. Or somebody working for him. I doubt we'll ever know. Unless you find out—that's your beat. But he's not the story here. The black market's been around forever. Not nice, but not news. But the government working with them? Springer will have a field day. They like any chance to embarrass the Republic and now they've got them with their hands in the cookie jar. It's the kind of scandal Springer would kill for—even welcome back the prodigal son, all sins forgiven. Isn't that what you want?"

"You think it's so easy. Springer. He built an office building so high he could see over the wall. So he's always looking down on us. He hates the Republic."

"Well, this is one way to make a lot of trouble for it."

Hans looked down, thinking. "May I see it, what you have?"

Martin tapped his head. "It's up here. I couldn't take the chance of putting any of it on paper. But it's there."

"Why give it to me?"

"You're the journalist, not me. I can give you facts and figures, but you put it the way Springer likes it. You were the one who started it, with the ambulance, so I figured you had a claim. And there's the favor tomorrow. It's a fair trade." He paused. "And to tell you the truth, I don't want Kurt to know. He's innocent, but some of the people around him aren't, so it's not going to be an easy time for him when this breaks. I don't want my fingerprints all over it. Let him be mad at you." A small smile.

"Yes, mad."

"Once I'm over, I'll put something on paper and get it to you. You take it from there. Should I tell the Springer people you have something for them?"

Watching Rieger's face now, visibly calculating, the eyes narrowing, sniffing the bait.

"How do I know you will do this? You'll be gone."

"Strictly speaking, you don't. You have to show a little trust. But why would I tell you all this if I wasn't serious?"

Another minute calculating, sorting options.

"When?" he said finally, hooked.

"Lunchtime."

"At the International Crossing? Checkpoint Charlie?"

"No, back to Invalidenstrasse. It's usually empty. Easier to get a good picture of me walking out."

CHAPTER 9

Sabine had a rough night, coughing, restless, so Kurt took Peter to the studio.

"I'm sorry," she said to Martin. "Today of all days."

"It's all right. You can't help being sick. That's why we're going."

"That's right. I'm the story."

They were sitting on a bench in the little park in Weberwiese, looking toward the apartment building.

"I took a few pictures. I know you said take nothing, but it's not much. For ten years of your life."

"Nothing from before?"

"Yes, a few. You're there. There's one from The Hill, when we took that hike in Bandelier, remember? It reminded me—how I used to wait for you to come home. The other wives complained. They wanted to do something. But I didn't mind. Making dinner, hours making dinner, and then you'd come through the door— Well. And here we are again."

"Sabine—"

"I know, we don't love each other anymore. Not like that. Now it's—what? You're the other person in the story. My fate, something like that." A minute. "What if it goes wrong?"

"It won't."

"You don't know that, you're just saying it so I won't worry. But, you know, I'm not. It's like when you're waiting backstage to go on. At first it's nerves, but then you're calm. No backing out. And then you're onstage, in it." She looked toward the apartment tower. "It's a good building. I'll miss it. What do you think we'll have in the West?"

"I don't know. Here, you better have these," he said, handing her two passports. "Peter's too. In your purse. In case we get separated."

"Separated? Why would we get separated?"

"We won't. Just in case."

She opened one of the passports, fingering Peter's picture. "So, an American boy now. And that's it? We just show these at Friedrichstrasse and walk through?"

"No, you'd still need an exit visa there. These are for when we get to the other side. We'll need them then."

"For what?"

"The hospital, for one thing. The military hospital doesn't treat Germans. An American citizen is something else."

"But then how do we cross? You haven't told me anything."

"It's safer."

"We're going to cross with no papers," she said.

"We don't need papers. Kurt is going to take us through. He has a special visa."

"Why would he do this?"

Martin hesitated. But it was too soon. Follow the plan.

"He'll do it for you."

Sabine looked away. "And that's your idea? It's wrong, what we're doing."

"Why? You need a better hospital. He loves you." He took a breath. "I'd do it."

She blinked, blinded for a second by a patch of sun poking between the clouds.

"You twist everything. How can we use him this way?"

"Because we have to."

"He won't forgive you for this. Especially this," she said, touching the passports. "To make us American. He believes in the Republic."

"Does he?"

"In the idea of it. Even with all the rest, he still believes in the idea." She stopped, looking down, fingering the passports again. "What did you do to get these? What did you promise?"

He took a minute. "I'll tell you. But not now. If anything goes wrong, you don't know anything. I forced you, you and Peter. I was crazy with jealousy. You didn't think I could do it. How could anybody cross, just like that? You have to be able to say that. You didn't know anything."

She stared at him. "But nothing's going to go wrong."

"Better put those away. There's the car. Let me talk to him alone—it'll be easier."

Sabine nodded, then started to cough, covering her mouth with a handkerchief.

"*Mutti*," Peter said, getting out of the car. "You're okay?"

Sabine nodded. "It's that cough again, that's all. How was the studio?"

"You're sitting outside?"

"The sun's good for me."

"We're taking her to the doctor," Martin said, then went over to the car. "We'll need you a little longer," he said to the driver. "You don't mind?"

"We can use my car," Kurt said.

"No, everybody knows your car. I need a Russian car."

"What?" Kurt said.

"Give us a minute," Martin said to the driver, moving Kurt away from the car.

"What is it?"

"Don't react. Just listen. We're taking Sabine to another hospital. In the West."

"What—?"

"Don't react. Peter too. We can't just leave him here. We don't know how long it will take. If there's a treatment."

"Are you crazy? You can't just—"

"No, but you can. You go back and forth. The guards know you by sight." He looked over. "You can talk us across."

"With no papers."

"We don't need papers. We're being exchanged. You arranged it. I didn't have papers when I came through."

"And who are you being exchanged for? Where are they?"

"They're coming later. Nobody's going to ask you. They know you. If we're with you, we're being exchanged. No questions."

"And after this miracle, the wall opens, then what?"

"We see a doctor."

"But this isn't a visit. You're not coming back. Is that correct?" Martin nodded.

"And what do I do?"

"I don't care. You mean, what do you say when people find out? Tell them I forced you. At gunpoint. I will too, if you don't do this." He touched his jacket pocket.

"A gun." Surprised at this detail. "Where would you get a gun?"

"Friends."

Kurt said nothing for a second, thinking.

"And Sabine? She knows this? It's not just a visit? Or do you have a gun to her head too?"

"She knows," Martin said simply.

Kurt stared at him. "You must be out of your mind to think I would do this. You want to kidnap my family and you want me to help? What did you think I would say? What did you tell Sabine? Did you promise her some miracle cure? There is no cure."

"No. But I'm not going to sit here and watch her die if there's something more we can do. I'm not going to see my son when you decide I can. They're my family and we're leaving. And yes, you're going to help."

"Never."

"Never. You haven't heard the rest of my offer. Isn't this what you do? Make deals? You'll want to make this one."

Kurt looked at him, waiting.

"This is an outline of the prisoner exchange program," Martin said, flashing the end of the envelope in his breast pocket. "The prices, the cast of characters, the skimming for Koch, the links to Spitzer."

Kurt looked up.

"Not all of them. I wouldn't do that to you."

"Or to yourself."

Martin shrugged. "I'll be gone. If Hans Rieger keeps sniffing around, he might trip over something, but he won't get it from me."

"Am I supposed to thank you for that?"

"What he will get is a scandal story that could buy his way back to Springer. He knows some of it, but he doesn't know all of it. You could stop him before he gets anywhere. I won't think how. Get us to the West and this is yours. I don't care what you do with it. Otherwise, it goes to Hans and you've got trouble that even you won't be able to talk your way out of."

Kurt said nothing, staring.

"And by the way, there's a copy. Anything happens to me and it'll get to Hans. It's all arranged. We get through, I hand you this. And I'll stop the copy. You have my word."

"Your word."

"And I'll have yours. That you'll get us through the crossing. Kind of a protection racket. We both have too much to lose not to do it."

"What else?"

"Nothing else. You might want to play happy family for Peter's sake. A doctor's visit and a look around, that's all. We can explain things later."

"You think that's going to be so easy. He has an affection for me."

"Let's keep it that way, then. Let's not tell him what you do—or have him read it in the papers."

"And if I say no?"

"You won't. Then I'd have to give Hans the rest of the story and you'll hang. Nobody wants that. Not you."

Another silence, everything suspended. "You think you know what you're doing, but you don't. You're new here. You don't know how things work."

"We need to start," Martin said, an end to it.

"You would hang us both?"

"If I have to. Or just you. Or nobody. You pick."

"And where does this famous exchange take place? Checkpoint Charlie? Are the Americans waiting for you?"

"No, they don't know you there. Invalidenstrasse. Go out the way I came in. No ambulance this time."

"You'll get us all killed. *Republikflucht*, they have orders to shoot."

"But this time I can shoot back."

———

Kurt sat in the back with Peter and Sabine, barely looking at her, as if even a glance would set something off, his eyes like kindling.

"But I thought the Charité was the best hospital," Peter said when the trip was explained to him.

"It is," Kurt said, "but it's not the only one. It's always good to get another opinion."

"Can we go to KaDeWe?"

"If there's time. We'll see," Kurt said, playing along, his fatherly voice.

Martin looked out the window, the Stalinist blocks of Karl-Marx-Allee rushing by. Really going now. The Berolina, his Bodo Jahn suit still hanging in the closet. He turned to face them in the back.

"Have you seen yourself in Alexanderplatz?" he said to Peter, who shook his head.

"Someone at school told me."

"Otto, can you pull up by the World Clock?"

They stopped short of the pedestrian square, the poster looking down on them.

"And who's front and center?" Kurt said.

"Think how angry Dieter will be," Peter said, giggling a little.

"You look so handsome," Sabine said quietly, her body folded in on itself in the corner.

But Peter was somewhere else, brooding. "Are they going to give you tests?" he said to Sabine.

"Probably."

"Then you'll have to stay?"

"I don't know. We'll see."

"But how is it permitted?" Peter said to Kurt. "To leave without papers?"

"I can cross back and forth. You know that. For my work."

"Exchanging spies. But we're not spies."

"It's a favor. So we can be with your mother. If she has to stay overnight. Otto can bring you back. With Martin." Pitched to the front, a complication for later, needling Martin.

"How late will that be?" Otto said, the first time he'd spoken, someone just there, a silent listener, maybe a paid one.

"This afternoon," Martin said. "We'll get you back in time. Kurt can get another car if he stays over." A volley back.

"It's an early call tomorrow," Peter said. "We have to reshoot some scenes. Gruber was there, from the Ministry. He said they were too Western. A fight with Lehmann, in front of everybody. Usually they go into his office."

Martin glanced over at Otto, listening.

"Why too Western?" Kurt said.

"Materialist," Peter said. "Erich wants a radio. You know, for the pocket. They're hard to get. Gruber said I should only want what's available. So, new scenes. It happens more and more now."

Sabine started coughing again, hunched over, shoulders shaking. Peter put his arm around her, patting her back, quieting a child. She smiled at him, catching her breath. "You're the best doctor," she said.

"Let's hope the new one has an idea what to do," Kurt said. "Where is the hospital? In Dahlem? The American sector?"

Martin nodded. "Clayallee." He turned to Otto. "You know where that is?" Playing it out.

"I can direct you," Kurt said. Both of them now, a tennis match with an invisible ball.

They were sweeping past the old Schinkel buildings on Unter den Linden and now turned into Friedrichstrasse, heading toward the station, the first traffic they'd encountered. The usual gray crowds, the shuffling line of people waiting to cross. One stop on the S-bahn, if you got through passport control. People from the West with packages. Bits of paper and trash swirling in the gusts of air from the moving trains overhead. Then the Spree, the water pewter, like the overcast sky, and the big theaters up ahead.

"I used to live near here," Sabine said to Peter. "When I first met your father. Albrechtstrasse."

"Oh yes?" Peter said, interested. "How did you meet?"

"At a party," Sabine said, her voice distant.

"When he was a student. At Göttingen." A story he'd heard before. "And what did you think?"

"What did I think?"

"You know, the first reaction. Beate says it's hard to do, in a scene, to show it in your face, your first reaction. She always rehearses first, so we get it right. So what did you think?"

Sabine smiled to herself and then, oddly, began to laugh, quietly, hearing some joke that had been whispered in her ear.

Kurt turned to her, surprised, then prickly. "It was funny?"

"No. Not funny. It's just—" She faced Peter. "What did I think? I thought, He's American. He can get me out of Berlin."

"That's what you thought?" Peter said.

"Well, other things too. I thought he was nice. Polite."

Martin looked back, seeing her on the stairs in Albrechtstrasse, pressed against the wall. The other person in the story.

"And did he—get you out?"

"Yes, later. A train from Zoo Station. There was no East and West in those days."

"And now it's you who can do it," Peter said to Kurt.

"But not as far as America. Only to Dahlem."

"What did you think when you saw Kurt?" Peter said, a game now.

She looked at Kurt. "I thought he was someone who would take care of us. And he did."

"And nice too?"

"Yes, very nice." Another look to Kurt. "Understanding. Sometimes people have to do things—"

Kurt looked away.

"Turn here," Martin said to Otto.

They made a left on Reinhardstrasse.

"We're going to the Charité?" Sabine said. "I thought—"

"Pull up by the curb here." Martin turned to Kurt. "Switch places with me. You should be in front where they can see you," he said, getting out of the car.

He opened the back door. Kurt looked out, hesitating, not the way he'd planned it, then got out of the car. Martin pressed the lock down and closed the door.

"We'll take it from here. You can get a taxi at the station."

"But I have to be there. They're expecting—"

"You. That was my guess too. They'll be expecting us at Invalidenstrasse. The whole reception committee. In fact, I'm counting on it."

"Counting on it."

"Someone always betrays you. I thought this time I'd pick the one. Hans isn't a very good reporter—he's just a snitch. He knows he's never going back to Springer. So why not earn some brownie points with Normanenstrasse? Even better, be useful to you. He's always wanted to work with you." He looked over. "He has no idea you're going to kill him. When the time is right."

Kurt said nothing.

"So. They're waiting at Invalidenstrasse. By the time you get there to tell them what's happened, we'll be long gone. Unless you call from the station. If there's a phone working. But by then we'll be through Checkpoint Charlie. I'd thank you for your help, but you didn't mean to help, did you?"

Kurt took a step toward him, not quite a lunge, and Martin put his hand in his gun pocket, thrusting it forward. "Don't. I'd do it. I really would."

"You'll never get out. They know you're making an attempt. Do you think they'd let Peter go?"

"They'll have to catch us first." He motioned toward the station. "Better find a phone."

And then, before Kurt could move again, he slid back into the front seat and slammed the door.

"Get going," Martin said, locking the door.

"Herr Keller—"

"Do it." He pointed the gun pocket. "Now." A pounding on the door, Kurt yelling.

"But Herr Thiele—"

"Now."

The car started to move, Kurt running after them.

"To Luisenstrasse, then take a right."

"To the checkpoint? Without Herr Thiele?"

"We're not going through. We're just going to take a look."

Kurt farther behind now, slowing. They passed the Deutsches Theater. There'd be a phone there. Minutes would make a difference.

"Faster. Right to the end." The Charité buildings flashed by.

He turned to face the backseat, Sabine folded into the corner again, Peter's eyes wide, anxious.

"It's okay."

"Do you really have a gun?"

Martin nodded.

"Why are you fighting with Kurt?"

"He doesn't want us to go. He was leading us into a trap."

"They'd arrest us?"

"But they're not going to. We're not going to cross at Invalidenstrasse."

"Checkpoint Charlie."

Martin shook his head. "I just wanted him to think we were. So they'd chase us there."

"Where, then?"

"Nowhere. We're not going to cross. We'd never get through." He turned to Otto. "You won't get in trouble. Tell them I had a gun on you."

"We're not going to the West?"

"You're not. You'll be fine. Okay, here we go. At the intersection, make a right."

"Away from the checkpoint?"

"I just want to be sure they're there. Nice and easy, so they don't spot you."

A glance to the left, toward the bridge. Guards at the barrier, alert, a cluster of unmarked cars, men outside, smoking. Someone who looked like Hans. Or maybe just the same raincoat. But more people than there had been at his exchange.

"Still waiting. Kurt hasn't got through yet. Okay, a little faster. It worked."

"What worked?" Peter said.

"They'll have to check all the crossings now. And we won't be at any of them. Anybody behind?"

Peter turned to look out the back window, involved now. "I don't think so." He turned back. "But if we're not going to cross, what are we doing?"

"We're waiting, until it's safer. Then we'll cross."

Peter thought about this for a second. "Without Kurt."

"He doesn't want to go."

"That's not why you were fighting. He knows you still love *Mutti*."

Martin looked at him, at a loss. The only way it made sense to him.

"Oh, Peter," Sabine said, her voice tired.

"But you wouldn't shoot him."

"No."

"I didn't think so." Another pause. "What about the hospital? She needs to go there."

"She will."

"In Dahlem?"

Otto sitting up, listening.

"A good one. You'll see," Martin said, evading.

"You know what I would do? I'd wait awhile and then go back to Invalidenstrasse. It's the one place they'll never look now."

"But we'd still have to get past the guards. And we can't take Otto into West Berlin without Kurt. He'd get in trouble."

"So will we."

"Not if we get across. You have something he doesn't have. Sabine, show him."

She opened her purse and took out the passports.

"This is me?" Peter said, opening it, running his hand over the picture. "I'm an American now? They won't like that on the show." More amused than alarmed, playing with it.

They were on the fringes of Prenzlauer Berg, near Schönhauser Allee and the wurst stand where he'd met Andrei.

"Now where?" Otto said.

"Pankow."

"Why are we going there?" Peter said.

"Another place they won't think to look. Farther east."

Martin sat back for a minute. A black Zil in Pankow, where Party officials lived, too familiar to be noticed. He imagined the scene at Invalidenstrasse, men climbing back into cars, pulling away. New cars arriving at Checkpoint Charlie. Then all the crossings. Chausseestrasse, down to Oberbaumbrücke, out to Schönefeld, everywhere, any crossing a possibility. Martin smiled to himself. They'd look everywhere except where he was.

They went north toward Oranienburg, then headed west, circling the city, following the jagged path of the wall. The French Sector, then Falkensee, heading south.

"I know," Peter said, trying to work out the route. "You want to go across at Glienicke. The spy bridge."

"No. We're not going to West Berlin. That's what they're expecting."

"But the hospital—"

"We'll go another way."

Peter frowned, an impossibility, but let it go, looking out the window. Potsdam.

"Herr Keller," Otto said. "How much longer? They'll look for me at Adlershof."

"Not long. Don't worry, you won't be blamed for anything."

"But it's my responsibility, to make sure Peter gets home."

"As far as anybody knows, that's just where he is."

"But Herr Thiele—"

"Has other things to think about. Alerting everybody, so they look for us at the crossings."

"They know Peter's face."

"Another hour, no more."

"But what are you going to do? Disguise him?"

"No. Me."

Tante Helene was waiting for them in Babelsberg, shooing them in and closing the door behind them.

"It's in there," she said to Martin, cocking her head toward the bedroom. "Try it on, see if we need to take it in."

"What's going on?" Sabine said.

"Here's some tea," Helene said, brisk. "You look— Here, sit. And how's my little star?"

"We're taking *Mutti* west."

Helene put a finger to her lips, looking up. "Isn't it terrible? I don't hear a thing these days. It's all wasted on me." She went over to the window. "The driver's waiting?"

"He has to get Peter back, then he's finished for the day. We can't stay long."

"No, of course," she said, motioning Martin to the bedroom. "I saw you in Alexanderplatz," she said to Peter. "How does it feel to be so famous? Here's your tea."

"Oh, Helene," Sabine said, embracing her, a good-bye.

Helene patted her. "I know," she said and then, a louder voice, "More sugar. I don't know how you can drink it so sweet." All of them onstage, playing to an audience that wasn't there.

Martin came out of the bedroom wearing a Russian officer's uniform.

"Martin—" Peter said, eyes wide.

"I think it's all right, the jacket. Maybe a little big?"

"Don't worry, you'll grow into it," Helene said. "Men do."

"Thank you. So. A new jacket for Rossendorf. And the right price. Are you sure I can't—"

Helene waved her hand, as if someone were watching, not just listening. "Such waste at the studio. They don't want it anymore. Otherwise, it would have an inventory number. I can't even remember who wore it. A crime film, I think. Anyway, not a scientist. Won't they be surprised at Rossendorf. So stylish."

"Thank you," Martin said, looking directly at her.

"Good luck with the new job. And you," she said, turning to Sabine and embracing her again. "Take care of yourself." Holding her close. "And you," she said to Peter, another hug.

Martin leaned down to her ear. "What's the rank? Do you know?"

She shrugged. "Colonel? I don't know." She took the hat and put it on his head. "Lots of gold," she said, fingering the front embroidery. "Maybe a general. Good luck." Then, to Sabine, almost a whisper, "Write when you can. Letters still get through."

"I didn't know," Sabine said, opening her hand to take in Martin and the uniform.

Helene nodded. "It's better." She touched her fingers to her mouth, then put them on Sabine's cheek, a kiss. "Now hurry."

In the car, Otto just stared at him, speechless.

"It's why I needed you. A Russian officer wouldn't drive himself."

"Drive himself where?"

Martin made a go signal toward the windshield. "Potsdam. One more stop and you're done."

They drove through the town center, then past the Neue

Garten, Sabine looking out, where they'd walked along the water. Past the Cecilienhof.

"Why are you Russian?" Peter said.

"I remembered Helene had the uniform. And I had to disappear. The last time anyone saw us was on the way to Invalidenstrasse. After that—pouf." He spread his fingers. "We could be anywhere. Where we're going, they're used to Russians visiting. The guards won't think anything of it. Even later. Everybody will be looking for us, not a Russian family." He turned to Otto. "It means you disappeared too. There was half a chance you were Stasi, but I took it and you stayed outside in Babelsberg. So all you have to do now is explain to the studio. Kurt and I had a fight and I ordered you to drive us back. You dropped us at—how about Alexanderplatz? Nobody notices anything there. Peter was with us, so that was all right. But it made you late back to the studio."

"The Stasi will ask too."

"No one saw you drive us anywhere after we left Kurt. So you can tell them whatever you want. I'd go with Alexanderplatz. It would make sense for us to go there. You can get to most of the crossings from there. Just take the U-bahn."

Now Neu Fahrland, the streets leading down to the lakeside villas. Am Lehnitzsee. Peter spotted it first, the American flag in front of the house, a giant pole in the circular driveway, tall as a beacon.

"What is this place?"

"Military Liaison Mission. A holdover from the Occupation. US territory once we're past the gates."

"Herr Keller, I can't—it's forbidden."

"You're just dropping us. Not staying. Tell the guard you're driving Colonel—I don't know, Rostov. We're expected for lunch. They can check inside if there's any problem."

"The guards are German?"

"We're in East Germany. You never left it. No heroics, please. Stay invisible."

Otto stopped at the gates.

"Colonel Rostov for lunch. From Karlshorst. He's expected."

The guard nodded, then bent down to peer in. Just another minute more. A Ford in the driveway. Martin stared ahead, military posture.

"Who's in back?"

"His family. Also expected."

"He looks familiar, the boy."

Martin froze, not breathing. Suddenly a streak of Russian, Peter's voice but lower, a Russian boy. The guard looked away from the car, waving to the gate attendant. An American soldier appeared on the steps of the house. The gates swung open. Through. The crunch of gravel on the tires.

"What did you say?"

"That we were already late and you'd throw one of your fits if he made us later. They're afraid of the Russians."

"How do you know Russian?"

"School. Everyone learns Russian. But not on the show. Only in real life."

Martin's car door was opened.

"Welcome. I'm Lieutenant Furman, the OIC." And then, to Martin's blank expression, "Officer in charge."

Martin got out and shook hands, then bent down again to talk through the window. "You can go," he said to Otto. "Thank you." He lowered his voice. "You were never here. You'll be all right."

Otto turned to Peter, who was getting out. "Good luck. I'll miss our drives."

Peter put his hand on Otto's arm and nodded, then started

up the steps with Sabine. Martin followed with Furman, a formal party. The Russians had arrived for lunch.

Inside, Ed Nugent was waiting. "Better hurry and change out of that," he said. "We don't want to hang around. No one's happy about this, using the Mission this way. The Russians find out, we won't hear the end of it."

"Here's your suit," Sabine said, handing Martin a bag with his clothes.

"Oh, excuse me, Mrs. Keller," Nugent said, dipping his head. "Ed Nugent."

"Mrs. Thiele," Sabine said.

"Of course. Thiele," he said, not expecting this. "And you must be Peter. Ready for the ride?"

"Ride?"

"I haven't explained yet," Martin said. "Why don't you fill them in while I change? In here?"

"Your dad tell you what the Mission is?"

"US territory."

"Well, in the diplomatic sense. After the war, each of the Allies had a military liaison in the other occupied zones. Keep an eye on things, coordinate. Of course this made a lot more sense when we all *were* allies. Now it's just a way to see things the Russians don't want us to see. We have free access anywhere in their zone except the PRAs—Permanent Restricted Areas—which naturally are what we really want to see. Army bases, ordnance depots, things like that. Off-limits. But we get pretty close, and sometimes we get lost *in* a PRA, which makes the Russians nuts."

"Why don't they just stop you? Close this down?"

"Because they're doing the same thing to us, out of Frankfurt, and they don't want to give that up. So what they do is tail us when we leave the grounds here, see where we go. And then we lose them and you've got an American car running around East Germany and there's nothing they can do about it. And that's where you come in."

"How do you lose them?"

"Faster cars. Streets around here, it's hopeless, so they tail us for a while, but then we hit the autobahn and off we go. Next stop, anywhere in the DDR. Unless they spot us or we have to get gas somewhere. People notice the plates. The way around that is we have special tanks. The Ford can hold thirty-five gallons. Go anywhere on that."

"And that's what we're going to do? Drive to the border in one of those cars."

"That's your dad's idea."

"But isn't it dangerous?" Sabine said.

"Oh, the East Germans like to play cops and robbers, but you don't see many guns. The Russians don't want any incidents. Well, that's better," he said to Martin, now back in his suit. Nugent looked at his watch. "We'd better get moving. The garage is this way. Anybody need to use the facilities before we start? You don't want to make stops once you're on the road."

"But the guards just saw us come in," Peter said, intrigued by the logistics.

"And as far as they're concerned, you're still here having lunch. They change in an hour and the new ones won't know anything. Just keep your head down when you leave. They're used to seeing soldiers in the Mission cars, that's all, not a pack of civilians in the back. We don't use the cars for this. Hell of a stink if the Russians caught us."

"And worse for us," Sabine said.

Nugent nodded. "It was your husband's idea."

They followed Nugent through the kitchen and into the garage, dim with the outside doors closed. At the car, Sabine held back for a second.

"You're working for them," she whispered to Martin. "Are you crazy? If we get caught now, it's espionage, not *Republikflucht*. Espionage."

"I'm not working for them. We're trading favors."

"And what's yours? As if that makes any difference if we're caught."

"Let's not get caught, then." He took her arm. "I'm not working for them. Anybody."

"Then how do you know about this place?"

"Ruth Jacobs mentioned it. She knows everything about Berlin."

"And tells it to the Stasi. Why else would they put up with Gerhard?"

"A loyal wife," he said, looking at her. "Watch your head."

He crawled in behind her. The driver turned to them.

"I'm Lieutenant Courtney and this is Staff Sergeant Aiello. You'll have to keep down for a few minutes, until we lose them. I'll let you know. We've done this plenty of times, so don't worry. It's just a little game we play—they chase us and we get away. Hey, Erich," he said, recognizing Peter. "It's you, right? The one on the show?"

"You've seen it?"

"Sure. Now I get it. Why all the hush-hush. They're not going to like you taking a walk." He moved his head, another angle, taking in Martin. "You can see the resemblance."

"Everyone says that," Peter said, pleased. "That we look alike."

"Okay, here we go." The garage suddenly flooded with light as the doors rolled up. "Heads down. Won't be long."

They passed out of the driveway and into the street, Courtney and Aiello chatting, a typical mission. Around the corner, threading their way toward a major street.

"There they are," Courtney said, "right on schedule. Old Herman and the other one, if that's his name. We should have a drink with them some night, find out."

Aiello grunted.

"Are they still there?" Peter said, head down, in a scene.

"Yeah. We take it nice and easy till we hit the autobahn. Turn a few corners just to give them something to do. Ben, you remember to bring the map?"

Aiello patted his pocket.

"It's a new part of the Zone for us," Courtney said to the back.

"What is?" Peter said.

"Dresden."

"Dresden? That's not on the border."

"First stop," Courtney said. "Express after that."

"Martin—"

"We're picking someone up."

"To come with us? How can he fit?" Peter said, practical.

"We'll squeeze in. It's not far."

After a few turns, they hit a straight, broad street, picking up speed, a smooth ride, then a sudden spurt, foot on the pedal, and the car shot forward onto the highway.

"Hold on," Courtney said, as if they were on horses.

"Still there?" Peter said.

"Uh-huh. They can do seventy easy, so we'll go with them a little while yet. Everybody comfy?" The car moving faster now, keeping up with the light traffic whizzing around them.

"Who's coming with us?" Peter said.

"A friend. You'll see."

"Does *Mutti* know him?"

"Yes. An old friend."

"Okay," Courtney said, "don't bump your heads."

The car suddenly shook, gears catching, and shot ahead, pitching their bodies forward.

"Take it easy," Aiello said. "You don't want to get stopped."

Even faster. "There's the first curve. They still with us?"

"Yeah."

"Another mile and we're behind the hill. They don't catch up, they'll lose us."

"They're doing all right."

"Second hill. Where's the goddam exit? I thought it was right here."

"There," Aiello said, lifting a finger.

They kept right, sweeping down off the highway, through an underpass to the other side, and slowed down to an intersection, partly hidden from the road.

"There they go. See us?"

"No, they still think we're up ahead somewhere on the highway."

"You can sit up now," Courtney said. "Everybody okay? Little cowboys and Indians—the old double back. And they never pick up on it. They just keep going till they run out of steam. All right, let's head back. They think we're on our way to Rostock."

They settled themselves in the back for the drive, Sabine nestled again in the corner.

"Martin?" Peter said.

"What?"

"Otto. When he said good-bye. We're not coming back, are we? We're leaving."

"Yes."

"But you didn't tell me."

"It was safer for you."

"They don't tell me things on the show either. They talk as if I'm not there. Too young to hear." He took a breath. "Why are we going?"

"I think it will be a better life for you. For all of us."

"In America?"

"Maybe. Maybe Germany. That might be easier."

"But we're already in Germany."

"No, we're in Russia." He turned to Peter. "They want me to do things and I won't be able to say no. If I stay. So—"

"What things?"

Martin hesitated. "Build bombs."

"To use against the Americans."

"Anybody. And I don't want to do it. It's crazy."

"But you helped them before."

Martin stopped, the logic tightening around him. "That's right. I did. I can't change that. But I'm not going to help anymore. And I'm not going to give them you. I want you to have choices, not this." He motioned out the window.

"And you agreed?" Peter said to Sabine.

"I want Martin to take care of you."

"You take care of me."

"Yes, yes, but it's better to have both."

"And if we're caught? What happens then?"

"To you? Nothing," Sabine said.

"Because I'm Erich Schmidt?"

"Because you're a child. Tante Helene would—"

"No. That's not what happens. They told us in school. *Republikflucht*. If you're caught. The children are taken from the parents. As a punishment. They put us in homes. Orphans."

"That won't happen to you," Sabine said, her voice unsteady, thrown by this.

"You guys all right back there?" Courtney said.

"Fine."

"Good. We got a ways to go, so get comfy. Put your feet up. Read a magazine and then you're in Baltimore."

Peter looked at Martin.

"An American song. About a train."

Sabine had been quiet, but now turned to Martin. "It's Stefan, in Dresden?"

Martin nodded.

"So now we're risking him too?"

"He wants to go."

"But you arranged it."

"Like Kurt," Peter said.

CHAPTER 10

The drive took longer than it should have because Courtney left the autobahn a few times to take secondary roads, checking the rearview mirror to see if anyone followed. They skirted a PRA to avoid any Russian military vehicles. It was the landscape Martin remembered from the train, flat and wet and dotted with garden allotments, a factory chimney in the distance belching lignite smoke.

Outside Dresden, traffic picked up, a swarm of East German cars, but then the roads were free again, winding up the hills to the suburbs. Stefan had a substantial Jugendstil house near the edge of a village, perched for views on a steep grade.

"There's a driveway on the side," Martin said. "We don't want to be on the street. Somebody sees the plates—"

Stefan was in a professor's formal suit and tie, everything neat except for his tufts of hair.

"Come in, come in. Sabine, how nice. Let me get you some tea. And look at you, so tall. I think our first time meeting, yes?" He shook Peter's hand, then turned to Martin. "Any trouble? I've been watching the street. Nothing, I think. But then you start imagining and everything looks suspicious. I've been nervous all day. Maybe a little bit of a coward."

Sabine put her hand on his upper arm. "You're sure?"

"Sure. You're only sure when it's over. Anyway, too late now. If you think about doing it, it's the same as doing it. That's the way things are now. If you just think about doing it. Forgive me. My manners. Stefan Schell." This to Courtney and Aiello, who introduced themselves. "Tea?" he said, going over to a bubbling samovar, a souvenir of the years in Russia. Otherwise, the room was German burgher, dark wood and Meissen knickknacks and doilies. "I made sandwiches so we could have something before we go."

Sabine was looking at the photographs on the piano. "There's Liesl. So young."

"And me with hair."

"Don't you want to take it?"

Stefan shook his head. "I have others. We're supposed to leave things as they are. Or the housekeeper will—"

"So now she thinks you just disappeared? They'll know soon enough."

"Even hours would make a difference." He patted her shoulder. "You're like me, nervous, that's all. But think. When we're there. So have some tea. It's over soon. It's clever, how Martin arranged it. Kurt thinks you're still in Berlin trying to leave, so he stays there and we go—" He stopped. "Anyway, not Berlin. Let's just hope no one sees the car here. They want to wait until dark to leave, but I think it's safer to be on the roads. Nobody looks for us there. Well, let me see if the Americans need anything. We want to keep them happy, no?"

Sabine went over to the window, moving the lace curtain to peek out. The driveway had a high retaining wall on one side and a line of trees on the other, as good a hiding place as any, off the street. You'd have to come into the driveway itself to see a car there. But why not someone walking a dog? Why not anyone?

"Looks like Peter has found some new friends," Martin said.

Sabine followed his look, Peter with the American soldiers. "He's a boy. It's an adventure to him."

"You all right?"

"I wish it was over. Why are they doing it?" she said, still looking at the soldiers. "If anything happens, it's—"

"It won't. We're going to be okay. Otherwise, they wouldn't do it. Not even for us."

"Us. Stefan, you mean."

"All of us. We're all valuable to them."

"For propaganda."

Martin shrugged. "You defect, you send a message."

"Defect," she said, as if the word were new to her. "And you think Kurt will let this happen?"

"Kurt doesn't know where we are."

"And we don't know where he is. Maybe he thinks like you. Where would they go? Not the obvious. Somewhere else."

"It takes a lot of people to cover the Berlin checkpoints. He has to assume we're going to try there. Otto dropped us. We don't have a car. A train? Maybe. But trains don't go right to the border. They'll check the obvious stations, but then what? You don't take a taxi to West Germany. We have to be in Berlin."

Sabine thought about this for a minute. "So how do we do it, then? The Americans can't take us over the border."

"We walk in. With the rest of the group. We're being exchanged."

She turned away from the window, eyes fixed on him. "We're going to Herleshausen?"

"It's the one place he'd never suspect. His turf. We'd want to

273

stay as far away from him as possible. But he won't be there. He'll be in Berlin looking for us. He's letting Hindemith handle this one. And his deputy."

"His deputy."

"Me. I've acted for him before. So I'll be him tonight. He's still going to get us out. He just won't know he's doing it."

She was still for a minute.

"He'll hate you for this."

"But it'll work," he said, asking her, a team again.

She nodded. "It's like one of your math proofs. The logic."

"Yes? You were always the one who planned things."

"Before I thought, why this charade with the uniform? Then I saw the guards were Germans, not Americans. To keep other Germans away. Like a border crossing. We had to get past them."

Martin nodded. "And they're used to seeing Russians. With their wives. And nobody's going to question the Russians." He looked over. "What else? Anything?"

"I don't know. I can't think."

He put his hand on her arm. "We've been in worse spots. And you never blinked."

"That's before I had a child. It's easy when it's just you to worry about." She moved her arm. "So now I'm a nervous old woman. We're going soon? I'd better use the 'facilities.' As your friends call them."

"Sabine," he said, his voice lower. "It's for all of us. A new start."

She nodded.

"Have you eaten something?" Stefan said, playing host. "They want to leave."

"Who can eat?" Sabine said.

"I know, I know. But it takes your mind off things too."

"I'll be right back. It's upstairs?"

"First on the left."

"You folks almost ready?" Courtney said. "That's a nice boy you've got there," he said to Sabine. "Mind if he rides shotgun?"

"Shotgun?"

"Up front, with us. You'll be like sardines back there."

It took another half hour to get everybody out of the house, Stefan putting things away and checking the locks, as if they were just going out for the evening.

"Leave a light on in the study, so they'll think you're home."

"Who?"

"Anybody who looks."

It was dark enough to need headlights but not yet night. No one followed them down the hill. Outside Dresden they caught the highway to Chemnitz. From there it would be a straight shot to the border. Not long now. Still no one behind.

"I can't find it on the map," Aiello said. "Chemnitz."

"They changed the name," Peter said. "Now it's Karl-Marx-Stadt."

Where they were probably starting to load prisoners onto the bus, checking them off, the Republic's side of the deal.

The heavy air had turned into a light drizzle, the slap of the windshield wipers the only sound in the car, a kind of metronome.

"It'll make us harder to see," Peter said.

"Well, that works two ways," Courtney said. "What I like is when we can find a place in the woods. Just sit there and count the trucks, or whatever we're watching. We see them, but they don't see us."

"Camouflage," Peter said.

"I guess. How we doing back there?"

"The lap of luxury," Stefan said, turning a little in his seat to face Martin. "I brought the passport, but I still don't see—"

"Not to cross. ID later."

"We're American again," Sabine said from her corner. "I never thought—"

"If we're stopped," Courtney said, "be sure to show them that. We're not supposed to be running a bus service, but if you're US citizens it makes a little problem for them. Arrest you and they start something."

"Did they ever arrest you?" Peter said.

"Sure. A bunch of times. We call it getting clobbered. We have a right to be anywhere except the PRAs, but you stop somewhere for a beer or spend the night and right away some snitch calls the cops and bam, suspicion of espionage. Which they know won't stick, just make some trouble for us. Then HQ calls and they let us go, sorry about that, how'd you like the jail? The usual drill. But this would be a little different. We're not supposed to carry passengers, strictly military, so I hope you've got some story ready if we do get stopped."

Martin said nothing.

"Is it always a snitch?" Peter said. "The way they find you?"

"Sometimes the car, the special plates with the flag. But mostly. Whole country's full of them. Always ready to help out."

"That's not very nice to say."

"No," Courtney said, embarrassed. "No offense. They probably think they're doing the right thing. Enemy of the state. Lock him up. It's just hard to appreciate when you're the one being locked up."

Peter turned to the back. "Are we enemies of the state now?"

For a second, no one said anything. "Not you," Martin said finally. "You didn't have a choice."

"But you would be?"

Another second. "Yes."

Peter turned to face front again, the spray of the windshield wipers.

"You're not to worry," Sabine said.

"That's right," Courtney said. "We'll get you out okay."

"Not too soon for me," Stefan said. "Look at this." He held up his hand. "An actual tremor. Thank god Liesl isn't here. It would kill her. The whole time in Russia she was afraid."

"You aren't happy here?" Sabine said.

"Happy," Stefan said, surprised, a foreign word.

"It wasn't always the way it is now," Sabine said, half to herself. "So much hope."

"Yes it was," Stefan said. "Worse. At least Stalin's dead. You can't imagine, when he was alive— Now the Russians want to forget him. But not Ulbricht. That's all he knows, that world. So we have to live in it."

"But they give you everything," Sabine said. "A good position. Anything you want."

"And what do I want? To leave. Even like this. You think I should be grateful? For all my privileges. As long as I do what they want. Keep the Stalinist state alive." He stopped, catching himself. "I know," he said, his tone kinder, "it was different in those days. The Communist future. But now look at us, like criminals. A getaway car." He turned to Martin. "Thank you for this. Whatever happens, people will hear. That we tried to do it. That's already something."

"They'll never trust you in the West," Sabine said, still moody. "Any of us. You're in Russia all those years, a loyal Communist. And yet you want to leave. They'll think the Service sent you. A perfect double."

Stefan looked at her, at a loss. "That's how you think? Pretty Sabine. So full of— And this is how you think? Like them."

"Yes, like them," she said softly. "Who else?" She looked at Martin. "It's who we are."

"Not anymore," Martin said. "Not even if we wanted to be."

"What do you mean?"

"Stefan's right. No matter what happens, they'll know we tried to get out. A betrayal."

"Yes," Sabine said, leaning back farther into her corner.

Now it was dark, the car a shadow on the road, license plate invisible unless you were right behind. Everyone had relaxed a little, slumped against the seat, lulled by the swish of the wipers.

"Do you like it in Germany?" Peter said to Courtney.

"When they're not chasing me, but somebody always is," Courtney said, a wink. Then, seeing Peter take this seriously, "It's okay. I like the Germans. They're straight with you."

"Do you think so?" Stefan said.

"Why do they chase you?" Peter said.

"Well, mostly they don't. I exaggerated a little. Usually when we're spotted, people think we must have some reason for being in the Zone and they don't bother you. There's three hundred and fifty thousand Soviet troops. So an American soldier must be on official duty or out of his mind to be here."

"Guess which," Aiello said, jerking a thumb toward Courtney.

"So we're safe," Peter said, still watching the road in front. "Who chases you? When they do. The Soviets?"

"The Soviets, the Vopos, the East German military, everybody. We're popular guys."

"How do you know who it is?"

"The vehicles. Soviets are almost always in a UAZ, kind of military jeep, the Vopos in a Trabant. You get to recognize them by their cars."

"Here's your chance," Aiello said, sitting up, eyes on the rearview mirror. "Professor, would you move a little to your left? I think we've got company."

Everyone now alert.

"You sure?"

"Same headlights for a few miles now. Slow down, see if he does too."

Courtney dropped back a little, letting a car pass. The headlights stayed behind.

"Is it a UAZ?" Peter said. "The Soviets?"

"No. I don't know who it is. Let's see if he stays with us." Accelerating.

"It's not the Vopos either," Aiello said. "Maybe just somebody got curious about the plates."

"Oh, god," Stefan said in the back.

"Peter, put your head down," Sabine said, putting her hand on the seat back, a substitute for clutching him.

"He's all right," Courtney said. "If they really meant any trouble, they'd try to run us off the road. Pull over. They're just keeping up."

"If they know who we are, it's already trouble," Stefan said. "If they follow us."

"How could they know?" Martin said.

How could they? People only knew a piece, and nobody knew about Stefan. He went over things again, a piece of chalk on a mental blackboard. Hans betraying him, as Martin had known he would, Kurt fixed on the wrong crossing. Ruth reporting to the Stasi that he was moving to Rossendorf. The phone tap waiting for him to call Stefan with a train time. Any of these could be taken away and the rest still play out. Otto? The Alexanderplatz story worked for him too. And if he'd been turned, he'd only lead them to a dead end in Potsdam. But a proof was never perfect. Some unexpected number. Unless the one had nothing to do with the other. A policeman following an American flag plate, just to see where it was going. Think it through again.

"There was no one at the house," Stefan said. "I'm sure of it. I watched. And Frau Nadel had the day off."

"Is it the Stasi?" Martin said.

"I don't think so," Courtney said. "Why would it be? They don't bother with the Military Mission."

"But now you've got passengers."

"Okay, let's see how much they love us. Watch your head, kid."

The car picked up speed, shooting over to the passing lane and swerving back, putting another car between them and their tail.

Peter swiveled around to face the rear window. "Still there. Can you go faster?"

"Put your head down," Sabine said. "Stop this. You'll get us all killed."

"He's a good driver, *Mutti*."

Even faster now.

"Like glue," Courtney said. "Well, now we know. He's either following the Mission or he's following you, but he sure as hell is following somebody."

"How could he be following us?" Stefan said. "Nobody knows where we are. How?" he said to Martin.

"I don't know. The question is, does he know where we're going?" Talking to himself. "And if he does, why not just go there and wait. So maybe he doesn't. Can you lose him?" he said to Courtney.

"Watch."

Another jolt of power, moving to pass, really speeding now.

"You'll get us killed," Sabine said again, her words broken by a cough. "Pull over and see if he stops."

"And then what?" Martin said. He turned to Stefan. "You didn't say anything. To anybody."

"Of course not. Who would I talk to?"

"No farewells at the office."

"No," he said, annoyed.

"Okay, I'm just thinking, that's all."

"And meanwhile he's driving like a maniac," Sabine said. "We'll be killed and then what's the point?"

"We'll be killed if we stop too."

"They won't do that."

"They'll kill me. Kurt will fix it. He can do that. He's done it." Sabine stared at him, not expecting this.

Martin turned to Courtney. "They still with us?"

"Just barely. But we're coming to town. I can't keep this up."

"Let's see if you can lose him there."

"On city streets? That's not asking much," he said, sarcastic.

"Sorry. I just—"

"I get it. All right, we'll give it a try. Welcome to Chemnitz." They had left the highway, stopped by their first red light.

Peter had raised his head, looking at Martin. "Would Kurt really kill you? Why?"

Martin looked away. "It's a figure of speech. He'd be upset."

A few more blocks, the weak streetlights poking through the drizzle. Chemnitz was dreary even on a bright day. Now it seemed almost sinister, dingy Soviet apartment buildings and empty concrete plazas fuzzy with mist.

Courtney made a right, then another, an arbitrary square to make sure the other car was tailing. A random path through some side streets, a market square, then the main road heading back to the highway, the other car behind. A red light, impossible to run through the cross traffic, a rumbling tram.

"Well, now we know they're not police," Courtney said. "They'd get out and pull us over. So who are they?"

"They don't want us to stop?" Peter said.

"They haven't yet. So it's not a clobber. They don't want to arrest us. They want to see where we're going."

"We have to lose them, then," Martin said.

"Roger."

The signal turned green and they shot ahead, the city lights falling behind them. The outskirts now, darker, warehouses lit by security lamps, repair shops, and empty lots with weeds. Suddenly Courtney killed the lights and swung hard into a dark parking lot. A factory building with one bulb over the entrance door. They waited, not saying anything. The other car swept past, forking right.

"That's the way to the border. They know," Courtney said.

"Or they're guessing," Martin said. "Now what?"

"We let them lose us."

"You did it," Peter said.

"Not yet. Let's see if they come back."

Waiting, watching the minutes on the dashboard clock.

"My god," Stefan said, just a sound.

"Okay, I guess not," Courtney said, starting the car again. "Keep your eyes open."

The highway was darker, no lights overhead, just discs of red taillights, like bicycle reflectors, and blinding headlamps on the oncoming side. More trucks, splashing the windshield with back spray.

"At least the rain is stopping," Courtney said.

More driving, everyone tense, something still out there in the dark. Aiello was checking the map with a pocket flashlight.

"Half an hour. Maybe less."

"Better kill the light."

"Hello," Aiello said, looking up into the mirror.

"You sure?"

"Positive. Just pulled out of that lay-by."

"Which means "

"What?" Martin said.

"They're professionals. They figured out what we did. Anyone else would have gone back. They just pulled off and waited. So who are they?"

"Professionals?" Sabine said.

"They know how to handle a pursuit. Not army. Okay, let's play."

He swung out again, passing a truck, picking up speed.

"You want to take a back road?" Aiello said.

Courtney shook his head. "Night like this, we'd never get there. Can't see your hand in front of your face. Let's see what they have under the hood." He put his foot down on the gas pedal, a surge they could feel in the backseat.

"You sure about this?" Martin said.

Courtney didn't answer, concentrating, pulling around another truck.

"They're right with us," Aiello said, looking. "That's no Trabant."

Martin looked over at Stefan, his face white, eyes closed. Who should have been getting off a plane to give a speech in Geneva, not being chased through Saxony. Too dangerous to be let out, an enemy of the state.

A curve, jostling them against each other. Not part of the plan. It had gone wrong somehow, some snapped link. Hans? Otto? But neither knew. Nobody did.

Courtney turned off the windshield wipers, the sudden silence jarring, like the wind stopping. Aiello went back to the mirror, visibility better without the rain.

"Civilian car. Dresden plates. But he sure as hell isn't driving like a civilian."

"Dresden," Martin said to Stefan. "Someone must have been watching you. Maybe all along."

"But I didn't see—"

"None of us did. It's not your fault. But if they're part of a surveillance operation on you, then they don't know where we're going. You didn't know that."

"I still don't. The border, that's all. Which crossing, you never said."

"Uh-oh," Aiello said, a flash of light from behind. "They want us to pull over."

"We can't," Martin said.

"You don't want them to ram us. They've been known to do that. Dodgems."

"Try some more gas."

"You're the boss," Courtney said, pulling ahead.

The first shot startled them, loud as an explosion, the sharp ping of metal being hit.

"Jesus," Aiello said, ducking.

"They're aiming at the car, not us," Courtney said. "They still want us to pull over."

Another ping of metal, maybe coming from the license plate, the target decoy in an arcade game. Courtney went faster. Sabine gasped, grabbing at Peter's arm.

"And if they miss?" Stefan said.

"Just keep down," Martin said. "If they're shooting at us, they're not kidding. You have any more juice?"

"Hold on."

"Why would they do this?" Sabine said.

"We're enemies of the state," Peter said, his voice steady, pretending not to be afraid.

"They could just follow," she said to the air.

"What are you doing?" Courtney said to Aiello, who had taken out a gun. "You want to start World War III?"

"One shot's one thing. They're not warning us anymore. If I can take a tire out—"

"We don't know who we're shooting at."

"We know they're shooting at us."

He rolled down the window, cold air rushing in.

"When I say, pull into the passing lane so I can get a shot at the car."

"You that good?"

"Marksmanship merit badge."

Another shot from behind, this time hitting Aiello's outside mirror, shattering it.

"Jesus," he said again, pulling his hand back, away from any flying shards. "Okay, keep her steady. When I say."

He turned, laying his arm on the car window frame, a line of sight, holding the gun steady, eyes squinting.

"Now."

The car pulled left into the passing lane, moving Aiello's sight line to the center of the car behind. One shot, two, deafening in the car, both aimed at the radiator grill. The car behind swerved, surprised, than ran out of control as the hit registered, tearing into the motor. The driver pulled to the left, compensating, but now the car spun wildly to the right, veering toward the edge of the highway, then over it, a screech of brakes, then bouncing into a gully, shuddering to a stop, wisps of steam rising out of the front.

"He's getting out. They're all right," Aiello said, still turned around.

"Hot shot," Courtney said, indulgent. "You crazy? In East fucking Germany?"

"So we don't want any casualties. We just want them to go away."

"Dresden plates," Martin said, thinking.

"You're a good shot," Peter said, but his voice was deflated, no longer in an adventure.

No one said anything for a few minutes, letting the air settle. Guns had been fired. No second thoughts now, everything irrevocable. Martin had the queasy feeling that the car was going by itself, set in motion and now out of his control, racing to some unknown future. He had planned everything but the end.

"I wonder how they'll explain me," Peter said. "On the show. Where did I go? Will I have to give interviews? In the West? Like Matty did." His grown-up voice, preparing.

"Maybe one or two," Martin said, only half a lie. "Then we'll have a normal life. That's why we're going."

"To be together," Peter said, making sure. "And take care of *Mutti*."

"I have to do the interviews," Stefan said. "For once maybe they'll print what I say."

"Almost there," Courtney said. "You folks have what you need? We won't be able to hang around if we want to get back to Potsdam tonight."

The crossing was as Martin remembered it, a sleepy stretch of road outside the town, a guardhouse with a stove, a barrier pole, already up, guards with guns on either side, a mirror image. He thought of Invalidenstrasse, the same solemn face-off over a piece of road, a pretend war with real bullets. The prison bus was already there, Reverend Hindemith checking names on a clipboard as the prisoners got off, the same wary, expectant look, a quiet shuffling to the other side, where the West German bus was waiting, flanked tonight by two cars with men in hats leaning against them. The Schell party would go by car. Martin peered across into the pool of light. Nugent and someone who looked like him. They flicked their cigarettes away when they saw the Mission car and came closer to the west side of the border, stopping short, as if the no-man's-land between the sets of guards had an invisible electric fence.

"You made it," Nugent said as Martin got out of the car.

"We had company," Courtney said.

"Oh? Who?"

"Didn't have time to ask. We lost them. Everything okay here? We need to get going."

"Thank you," Stefan said. "Look." He nodded to the border. "Just a few steps and everything's different."

"Nice riding with you," Courtney said to Peter, shaking his hand. "Good luck."

"You're a good driver," Peter said.

Courtney smiled. "Just reckless. Good-bye," he said to Sabine. "Hope you feel better."

"Oh, she will. Once we're in the West. A new doctor."

Sabine looked at Peter, a wince of dismay, but said nothing.

Hindemith had come over to the car. "What's going on?" he said to Martin.

"Didn't Kurt call you? A few more for the exchange."

"That's not possible. So late. There's already a list."

"You won't have to pay for them. A bonus from the Republic."

"How many?" he said, but distracted, watching the Mission car pull away. "Who are the Americans? What are they doing here? It's not allowed."

"They gave us a lift, that's all. And they're legal. I'll explain later. Right now we should get your new prisoners across. The names are Schell and Thiele," he said, waving his hand to take in Sabine and Peter. "And Keller."

Hindemith stared at him. "You can't be serious. And Herr Thiele?"

"He'll come later. Strictly speaking, you don't need the names.

287

We're being met, so we won't take up any seats on the bus. No cost to the program."

"But part of the exchange group," Hindemith said, piecing things together. "So the border guards—"

"Won't need to go to any trouble checking. Shall we start with Professor Schell?"

"Stefan Schell?"

Stefan nodded, almost a bow.

"And when I'm asked about this? I'm responsible. You'll endanger the whole program."

"I came with instructions from Kurt. He's in charge of the prisoner side. You're getting everyone you paid for—and a few extra. It's not going to endanger anything. You know how much this is worth to the East Germans. They're not going to give up their *Kopfgeld*. And you can help save a few more souls."

"You put the Church in an awkward position."

"The Church is already there." He paused. "Orders from Kurt. Shall we start? Stefan, join the line there."

Stefan looked at the East German guards, then at Hindemith, who hesitated but finally nodded.

"Now us," Martin said, following, making sure Stefan joined the prisoner line before turning back to Hindemith. "No one will blame you."

"Do you realize what you're doing?"

Stefan was passing the East German guards, heading toward Nugent, everything quiet, the air hushed, so the sound of car wheels seemed even louder, freezing everyone in place. The car swerved around the bus and stopped. For a second, Martin expected policemen to jump out, an arrest squad, but only the back door opened, a single head, close-cropped hair.

"So, we're in time," Andrei said. "What happened to your escort?"

Martin took a minute shuffling the words into place, as if he were translating. "They're Service?" he said finally.

Andrei nodded. "In Dresden. Evidently not so expert at following. Other skills. You disappoint me, Martin. You were supposed to watch the good professor, not get him in trouble. Now what do we do?"

"Watch me?" Stefan said faintly.

"A friendly eye," Andrei said. "And now it's—treason. If we want to call it that."

"You can call it whatever you want," Stefan said.

"Well, don't be too hasty. It's your life. And you," he said, turning to Hindemith. "A man of the cloth. You think that will protect you?"

"I am not East German. I'm here only to assist Herr Thiele. Talk to him."

Andrei nodded. "Kurt," he said, raising his voice.

Another car door, Kurt stepping out. Andrei looked at Martin, his eyes amused.

"You underrate us," he said. "Playing your little games. We already own him. Why do you think he made the swap for you?"

"How did you know we were here? Nobody knew."

"It's always the same with you. A real instinct for the work. Clever. Everything just so. But sometimes not the best judge of character."

Martin looked at him, back at the blackboard in his head. Write the proof out. Eliminate. The Mission car free all day, no tails. Andrei arriving in a rush, the last moment. Eliminate. And then, a tightening in his chest, he came to the end of the proof, his chalk hand still raised in the air. He turned to Sabine.

"You called him from the house. From Stefan's. Nobody knew until then. Nobody. And then I told you. Sabine—"

She looked away. "What was I supposed to do? Have my child taken away? If we're caught. And look—I was right, we are caught."

"By you." Falling, the ground opening. "Did you ever want me to come? Was it only the Service? Their idea?"

"We always bring our people home," Andrei said. "You know that. It's our promise to them. No matter how long it takes."

"But once Stefan was here and you thought I could be useful, it took no time at all."

"It took time," Kurt said.

"And you went along with it," Martin said to Sabine.

"I wanted you here. I thought you were the same. I didn't know you had changed. Everything we worked for, all those years, and you want to walk away."

"Is this everything we worked for?" Martin said, opening his hand to the border.

"It's the beginning."

"My god, Sabine, you're dying and you still can't see it?"

"She's not dying," Peter said, his round eyes taking in all of them.

"No," she said, putting her hand on his shoulder. "Just sick. We'll go to the Charité again. Kurt can get me that room I like."

Kurt stared at her. "Are you crazy? Do you think we're going back to Weberwiese? After this? If I don't denounce you, I'll never work again. It's finished."

"Kurt," she said, stunned, the space around her hushed, like another no-man's-land, full of mines.

For a second no one spoke, then Peter took her hand. "Never mind, *Mutti*. He never noticed you were sick. Martin will take us across."

"Nobody's going anywhere. Least of all you, Professor," Andrei said, louder. "Not another step."

"I'm in the West now. Are you going to shoot me?"

Andrei took a gun out of his pocket. "If I have to. Now stop."

"I'm in the West."

"And who's to say which side of the border you were on when the shooting started? The guards have seen it before. Shot while trying to escape. It's not the first time this has happened."

The guards, unprepared for this, raised their guns, looking to Kurt for instructions. The line of prisoners had stopped moving.

"Just keep coming," Nugent said to Stefan, his voice low. "Nice and easy."

Stefan stopped, looking from one side to the other, trapped in the border's overhead light. He was there, a matter of steps, guns drawn around him but locked in another standoff, watching him in slow motion, a hair-trigger silence. Nugent almost in reach, the shadowy countryside beyond a kind of safety zone. And then he panicked, running toward the West German bus, into the protection of the dark, and a series of explosions ripped through the quiet, Andrei firing, Nugent firing back, the guards firing in confusion, everyone ducking, the chaos Martin remembered at Invalidenstrasse, everything happening at once. He heard a grunt behind him, the sound of a body falling to the ground. Andrei, who shook with a kind of convulsion, then went still. He raced over and grabbed Peter, forcing him down, shielding him. Another round of shots, which seemed to go nowhere, random bullets fired into the fields, as if there had been a real prison break, not a cowering group of exchange prisoners, huddling together out of the line of fire, guards on both sides shooting, not at each other, into the general confusion, the invisible border still in place, neither side crossing it. Then, suddenly, a silence, suspended in the air, as if someone had turned off a radio.

Martin was just getting up to look for Sabine when the bullet caught him, slamming into his shoulder, making him stagger, his body flung back. His eyes locked on Kurt, holding the gun. A flash of pain. Not like this. Some other ending, not this. He looked down behind him and shooed Peter away, "Quick, over there," then turned back to Kurt. "Do you want the boy to see?"

Kurt hesitated, just long enough for Martin to pull out his gun. Another jolt of pain in his shoulder.

"Now we can kill each other. Is that what you want?"

"Don't shoot," Peter said, out of sight.

"Nobody's shooting," Kurt said into the air, still looking at Martin. "It was an accident."

"I never told anyone," Martin said. "I kept the bargain."

"What's that to me? You will one day."

Martin stared at him. The moment that was always going to happen. "Put the gun away."

"Now? Why would I do that?"

"Self-protection. I can't miss at this range. And I wouldn't. Even if you shot first." He looked at him for another second, then broke eye contact, as if it had been decided. "Stefan!" he shouted. "You all right?"

"Yes, yes. With the Americans." A disembodied voice from the other side. The prisoners began to get up.

"Stay there, then." He turned to Kurt. "Tell the guards to stop. They'll listen to you. And have them call an ambulance. Andrei's shot."

Kurt kept looking at him, gun in hand, then bent down and felt Andrei's neck. "No need. He's dead."

"Dead?" Martin said, something not real. Andrei.

"Martin! Martin!" A wail. "She's hurt."

He jerked his head away from Kurt. She was lying on the ground, Peter kneeling beside her. Another glance at Kurt, holding the gun. And suddenly he didn't care. He ran over to her. She was clutching Peter's hand, eyes open, blood welling up on her chest, her blouse soaked with it.

"She's bleeding," Peter said, frightened, his body shaking.

"Call an ambulance," Martin yelled to the guards, then looked back at Kurt. Another moment, two guns still out, then Kurt nodded and repeated the order.

"Listen to me," Sabine said to Peter, her voice just louder than a whisper. "Go now. With Martin."

"You're hurt."

"It doesn't matter. I'll come later."

"Later," Peter said, vague.

"You won't have another chance. You have to go now. Before it's too late. Do you understand? Now."

Peter stared at her, eyes darting. "You're bleeding."

"I know. Go with the pastor. Do this for me, yes?"

"But you're hurt—"

Sabine tried to smile. "It saves the pain later. I won't have to go through that." She looked over at Martin. "With your chemicals."

"*Mutti*—"

"In my purse," she said, her face clenching. "Your passport. You're going to need it."

Hindemith was walking toward them.

"Give me a kiss now, yes? Careful of the blood. You don't want to get it on your clothes. You have to look nice. On the cheek."

Peter leaned over, his lips grazing the side of her face.

"Oh, that's nice. I'll remember that. Now go, while you still can. You too," she said to Martin.

"Sabine," he said, looking down at her, taking the other hand, feeling the rest of her slipping away. The other person in the story.

"I know. You don't have to say. I'm sorry for this."

"No. Hold on. There's an ambulance coming."

She shook her head a little. "It doesn't matter. I can feel it. It's the first time I'm sure of anything."

"*Mutti—*"

"Go to the pastor. I want to say something to Martin. You'll cross with the others, yes?" Her mouth turned up, an attempt to smile. "My two men."

Peter got up, uncertain, taking a few steps toward Hindemith.

"So now look what I've done," Sabine said. "Your plan. And who ruined it?" She licked her lips, mouth dry. "Promise me. You'll stay with Peter."

"Yes."

"It's why you came. Not for the Service. That was their idea. That's always their idea. So now—" Her face tightened. "Now you have your family."

"Without you."

Another faint smile. "I want you to pretend we still love each other. So he thinks that."

"Pretend."

"Yes. He wants it to be that way."

"We did."

"Yes," she said, her eyes on him. "And then we made such a mess. I made such a mess."

"No."

"I thought it was right. Everything we did. It would make a better world."

"It is better."

"But not here." She looked toward the guards, then over toward the West. "Maybe not there either."

"Maybe not."

She turned back to him. "Don't poison him against me. Because I believed those things."

"No. Now just hold on. We'll get you to the hospital."

"I don't want to hold on," she said, still clutching his hand. "It's time. If I know you're both across. Imagine, in one of Kurt's deals. So now he's exchanging his family. Go. I want to see you do it."

"I can't leave you like this."

"No," she said. "That's your nature. So."

She closed her eyes, resting, and Martin felt her slip away again, pulling away now, her head still there but the rest of her going back into herself, a film loop running backward, so that he was watching her lying here in the road, then in the hospital the night Peter was born, smiling, then on the bed in the prefab house in Los Alamos, wrapped in a Navajo blanket, then on the couch at Georg's party, feet curled up beneath her, smoking and looking at him. And then the loop ran out and she was gone. He stared at her for another minute, his ears ringing, her hand different, heavier.

"Is she dead?" Peter said, his voice steady, self-possessed, more disturbing somehow than tears.

"Yes." An echo, as if someone else had said it.

"Come." Peter held out his hand.

"No one's going anywhere," Kurt said, holding up the gun again.

Peter took another step, standing in front of Martin. "*Mutti*'s dead. You don't have to denounce her now," he said, isolating the word, precise, a line reading. "So it's enough."

"Get out of the way. Do you think this is something on television?" Kurt said.

"No," Peter said, but so calmly that Martin realized that's just what it was, that Peter had become Erich Schmidt, taking a stand. "Martin," he said, holding out his hand again.

"It's not possible. How do I explain it if you don't come back?" Kurt said.

Martin looked at him, disconcerted. His real concern, not Sabine lying on the ground. "You can say anything you like," Martin said. "Andrei's dead and the Dresden people are somewhere in a ditch, so you're the only story the Service has. They have to believe you. This? A border incident that got out of hand. Luckily none of the prisoners was hurt. But your wife—" He stopped. "So you're a sympathetic figure. You can do the rest. Now we're going to join the exchange line. If you shoot me again, you've got a child and a minister both witnesses to murder. That would be a lot harder to explain. Reverend?"

Hindemith stared at him, paralyzed.

"Come," Peter said again, leading Martin by the hand, in charge.

"You can't—" Kurt started, then stopped as Hindemith held up his hand.

"Put the gun down. We have innocent people here."

"Prisoners," Kurt said, then to Martin, "You think you can just walk away? I'll get him back."

Martin turned to Kurt. "You can try."

"The Republic will fight for him."

"No they won't. They'll get another Erich Schmidt. Maybe they'll get another Kurt Thiele too. Maybe not. I don't care. We're done."

"You think so?"

Instead of answering, he walked with Peter toward the shuffling line, the guards watching, not sure what to do.

"Hindemith," Kurt said. "Don't let them through."

Hindemith looked at him for a minute, then down at his clipboard. "They're on the list," he said finally, then nodded to the guards.

Past the first guard, then the second, Hindemith with them, a shepherd. When they reached the open space that was the border, Nugent came forward from the other side.

"Welcome to West Germany. Better get in the car. Before somebody else gets trigger-happy." He looked down at Peter. "I'm sorry. About your mother." He hesitated. "Did you see where the bullets came from?"

Peter shook his head. "Everywhere. She was just—in the way."

Stefan came out of the shadows. "Come. You can ride with me."

"Can't I stay with you?" Peter said to Martin, his voice no longer controlled, out of character, a boy again, even his body smaller.

Martin couched down, taking him by the shoulders. "Of course. We'll go together. Like she wanted."

"I don't know anyone here. On this side."

"You know me."

"Will Kurt try to kill you again?"

"No."

"How do you know? He said he'd come for me."

"He won't. I'm going to fix it. Okay?"

Peter nodded then leaned forward, putting his arms around Martin's neck, holding him. Martin pressed back, dizzy, clinging to him.

"You know *Mutti* was very sick, don't you?"

"Yes," Peter said in his ear.

"So this was going to happen."

Peter pulled back. "But now there's no pain."

"Not anymore. So," he said, steadying his voice. "Get in the car. I'll be right there. They won't go without me."

"Can I ride in front?"

"That's up to him," Martin said, tilting his head toward Nugent.

"Sure. Leo," he said, handing Peter off to the other Nugent.

"How long were you reporting on me?" Stefan said. "From the first?"

"It wasn't like that."

"How else could it be?"

"I never said anything that—"

Stefan held up his hand. "Never mind. I should have known. Nobody leaves the Service. What were you doing all those years? Listening. Stealing secrets. So why not from me?"

"Because I didn't."

"In Russia, it was like another country, their own state. After a while it's in the blood, you can't be anything else."

"Not anymore. Now I have new friends." He nodded to Nugent. "And you're here. We're all here. So that's the end. Except one thing. I'll be right back." He looked up at Stefan. "Service rule. You do what you have to do."

"Where are you going?" Nugent said, alarmed. "Don't go near the border. It doesn't mean shit to them."

"Don't worry," Martin said, passing some straggling prisoners heading for the bus. He stepped into the outer circle of light and called to Hindemith.

"Stay back," Hindemith said. "Do you want more trouble? I'll come to you." He walked across the pool of light. "That's the last of them," he said, looking at the back of the line. "How's the boy?"

"It'll take a while. Seeing her like that."

"And you? The arm?"

"I'm still standing." But he could feel himself becoming more unsteady, slightly dizzy from the pain. He took a second, looking to the guardhouse. "Where's Kurt?"

"On the phone."

"Reinforcements?"

"No, making arrangements for his wife. What do you want? There isn't much time."

"Can I ask you something? Why don't you get out? How do you live with this?"

"How can you not want to help these people," he said, pointing to the bus.

"By buying them out."

"Yes, buying them. Should they wait for the country to change? The world? While they rot in prison. What's the morality of that?"

"When it comes out, people will blame you. They'll think you're like him. Another Kurt."

"What matters is what God thinks. Now what is it? We don't have time to worry about my soul."

Martin took an envelope out of his pocket. The Rieger letter with an extra sheet, what happened to Spitzer. "Would you do me one more favor and mail this? In the East. If it comes from the West, they'll open it."

Hindemith took the envelope and looked at it. "What is it? Who's Ruth Jacobs?"

"Someone I know in Berlin. It's a story she's working on. She needed more details. Before Hans Rieger gets his hands on it."

"What story?"

"Wait and read it in the newspaper. I don't know how she's going to cover it. Maybe get her self-respect back. Maybe not. We'll see."

"Self-respect. It's trouble?"

"Not for you. Just drop it in the box. Our secret."

Hindemith looked at him, about to ask more, then put the envelope in his pocket.

"Thank you. For everything. There's Kurt," Martin said, looking toward the guardhouse. Beyond it headlights were coming down the road, bright, ambulance lights.

"Take the boy to America," Hindemith said softly, in a rush, as if they could be overheard. "It won't be safe in Germany. Kurt will try to get him back. You don't know him."

Kurt walked over to Sabine's body, still lying on the road, covered now by some guard's overcoat. He looked down. Thinking what? How they met? The story he'd need to tell now. How Martin betrayed them.

"No," Martin said. "But he doesn't know me either. I was with the Service. They teach you how to protect yourself." He began to turn. "Thanks again for the letter."

"What did you mean before, her self-respect?"

"She'll have a choice to make. She can file the story in the West and become non grata here. She'd have to leave—this would give her the push. Or she can give it to the Stasi and get in deeper. Either way, though, it's the end of Kurt."

Hindemith raised his eyebrows and without thinking touched his jacket pocket.

"Don't worry, they won't give up the exchanges. You might be out of a job. They're going to do it with cash, so you won't have to count oranges anymore. But the people will get out."

Kurt was now on the Eastern side of the border light.

"You're still here?"

"No, here. In the West."

"You think this means anything?" Kurt said, indicating the empty space.

"Not to you. You can cross anywhere." He looked to his side. "At least no wall here. Not like Invalidenstrasse."

"You got what you came for," Kurt said.

"Not everything," Martin said, looking toward the ambulance.

"But you won't keep him. It's too bad. You could have had a good life here."

"Do you?"

Kurt looked up, not sure how to take this. "I should have killed you when I had the chance."

"Yes, you should have. Now it's too late."

"You're sure of that?"

Martin glanced over at Hindemith, meeting his eye. "Sure," he said.

Kurt looked at him, puzzled again, something off.

"I'll let you know where to send the ashes. Peter will want them."

Another surprise, something he hadn't thought about.

"Where is the border, exactly?" Martin said. "Here?" He pointed to the middle of the circle. "Here?"

"Relax," Nugent said, coming from behind. "You're over it. Ready?"

"Ha, your new control?" Kurt said, sarcastic.

And in the light, his shadow behind him, Nugent did feel like another Andrei, the same outline, the same presence.

"That's right," Martin said. "The new Service." Then, feeling Nugent's hand on his shoulder, he nodded again to Hindemith, a thank-you, and turned to go, Nugent's hand still on him, his property now.

The bus began to pull away, heading for Giessen's makeshift cots and questionnaires. He thought of Invalidenstrasse, before the shooting started, that first minute of perfect freedom, out of prison. Now he felt he was going back, one prison for another, the last exchange.

"We're going to hear from the East Germans about this one," Nugent said. "They got two wounded."

"And Sabine."

Nugent nodded. "I'm sorry." A second. "Still, it worked. You're all here. Slick."

The way Andrei used to talk, Martin clever at his blackboard.

"We'll get your arm fixed up and then we can talk. I've been looking forward to it."

Weeks of it, months of it, so they'd know what the Service knew. And the Service would know that they knew. Back and forth, over the invisible border, until Martin was empty, out of chalk. But you did what you had to do. He'd always thought it would be hard to kill someone. But it was as easy as handing over an envelope. He watched the bus headlights sweep across the stubby field, then catch Nugent's car, the small head in front, waiting, and took a breath.

AUTHOR'S NOTE

The Berlin Exchange is fiction, but the trading of political prisoners that forms the background of the story really took place. I have taken some liberties with the chronology. Here the program is in full operation in 1963, the year the swaps actually began. The standard price set was DM 40,000 (then $10,000) per prisoner, adjusted for length of sentence, value of the prisoner's occupation, etc., the amount payable in kind or (later) hard currency. From relatively modest beginnings in 1963, the swaps grew into an important revenue stream for the DDR. Estimates vary, but one account claims that between 1964 and 1989, when the wall came down, the DDR released more than 33,000 political prisoners and more than 215,000 citizens to reunite families for some DM 3.4 billion ($850 million). Whatever the actual figures, there is no doubt that the swaps made a contribution to the DDR's economic viability. The ethical questions this raised for both sides are still subjects of debate.

To readers familiar with the period, Kurt Thiele's career will suggest that of Wolfgang Vogel, an East German lawyer who specialized in such East–West exchanges (most famously, Gary Powers for Rudolf Abel), but his is a very different character and not intended to be a commentary on Vogel's. The real Klaus Fuchs did indeed work at the nuclear research center at Rossendorf (where he was deputy director), but the Klaus Fuchs here lived only in my imagination. Similarly, the US Military Liaison Mission did in fact work out of the Villa Sigismund in Potsdam and frequently outran their East German pursuers. Their exploits are the stuff of Cold War legend, or at least reminiscence, but so far as I know never extended to jeopardizing their legal mandate by helping people escape East Germany. Finally, *Die Familie Schmidt* never existed, though the TV studios at Adlershof are still there. Had it done so, it would now offer a unique time capsule look at a stranger-than-fiction society, but since it didn't, we are left with fiction.

INTRODUCTION

B erlin, 1963. American physicist Martin Keller, jailed for ten years in an English prison for being a Soviet spy, is suddenly offered his freedom and a new life in East Germany. The price is reasonable: a Cold War prisoner exchange—Martin for two American students who tried to help a friend escape over the Berlin Wall and an old MI6 operative. An irresistible offer. But has he merely traded one prison for another? His freedom has been arranged by his ex-wife's new husband, Kurt, a man who works all sides of every conflict, and his old spymasters still see him as a valuable chess piece. But to what end?

Steeped in atmospheric tension and dizzying layers of secrecy, *The Berlin Exchange* follows Martin as he finds himself more and more deeply involved in Kurt's morally ambiguous dealings and political entanglements until finally he has to navigate a treacherous path that could put not just his own life at risk but also that of his ex-wife, Sabine, and their young son, Peter, all the while trying to find answers. Did he do the right thing during the war? How do you live day to day in a surveillance state? And, most urgently, what did all the sets of eyes watching his every move want from him?

TOPICS AND QUESTIONS
FOR DISCUSSION

1. In chapter 3, Martin meets up with his old handler in Russian intelligence, Andrei, who asks him to begin spying for them again; we learn Martin passed atomic secrets from the United States to Russia. How did this affect your view of Martin? How has his position changed since going to prison?

2. The eyes of the Stasi are always watching. Discuss scenes where you noticed characters being careful about what they said, even when the Stasi weren't mentioned. What did they seem most nervous about discussing and what did that say about the values of East Germany?

3. In chapter 3, Martin is shocked to learn that political prisoners are ransomed for money to fuel the Eastern economy. When he asks Kurt if that's legal, Kurt responds, "Legal is what the state says is legal." How is the line between legality and morality blurred?

4. Kurt frequently brings Martin along with him when he works, allowing Martin to see the illicit dealings that make his new

life in East Berlin possible. Why does Kurt want Martin to see what he does, especially given the recurring mantra, "There is no crime in the DDR"? What does it reveal about Kurt's character?

5. A journalist, Hans Rieger, constantly dogs Martin about a violent incident that occurred during his exchange, in an effort to answer the same questions Martin has about it. In chapter 4, Kurt insists again that "nobody wants such a story," yet goes out of his way to throw Hans off the trail. What does this signal about the importance of Hans's story? Who do you think could be interested after all?

6. In chapter 4, Martin is at a meet and greet with other physicists working on nuclear energy for East Berlin when he begins talking with Klaus Fuchs, an eminent German physicist and former atomic spy, who feels safe in East Berlin. When Martin questions him, he answers, "No FBI, no more army intelligence, with their questions, trying to trap you. All those years, not knowing if– But now it's safe. You can breathe." How is his perspective different from Martin's?

7. In chapter 5, Martin is with Peter for a photoshoot for an East German television show, *Die Familie Schmidt*, and Peter mentions that Kurt only allows photographs of the new plazas, free of damage from the war, otherwise "everybody thinks East Berlin is all like that." How does Kurt's vision of East Berlin compare with the one you had at the beginning of the novel?

8. In chapter 5, Andrei asks Martin to find out his old colleague Stefan's intentions for the atomic peace conference in Geneva.

What is he concerned Stefan will do or say? Why would Stefan leaving East Berlin be bad not only for East Berlin but also for Russia?

9. In chapter 5, Stefan reveals that he will call for an end to the arms race at the conference in Geneva. Then he asks Martin, "What do you say to [your son], when he asks someday? Why you do this work? How do you answer him? . . . How would I explain myself? For making these bombs. What explanation could there be? . . . All of us have to answer for it." How does this affect Martin going forward? Do you think he would have made different decisions if Stefan had not made it so personal?

10. Martin's actions during the war landed him in English prison and would have gotten him executed in America; he feels incredible guilt for helping create weapons that would kill hundreds of thousands of people. Stefan's decision to call for peace goes against the Cold War objectives of East Germany and Russia. Discuss the role that individuals can play in global events and the idea of personal accountability. How are these themes important today?

11. The moment Martin decides not to betray Stefan changes everything. What would you have done? Could you put your life and the safety of your family at risk to make sure the truth was spoken? If Martin knew at the time how it would turn out, do you think he would have made the same decision?

12. On page 220, as Martin convinces Stefan to make a run for the border, Stefan reminds him, "You know, they're no better, the

other side," referring to the United States. Both Martin and Stefan have felt the sting of Western justice, both disagreed with its values, yet they both ultimately decided to return and leave East Germany and its tarnished dream of a Communist state behind. What makes them believe in a better life on the other side of the wall? What do you make of their quest for a better future?

13. In chapter 8, Stefan accuses Martin of having a taste for espionage, something Sabine and Andrei also echo as Martin's plan unfurls. Martin denies it each time. Do you believe him? Would his enjoyment of solving the puzzle to save his family invalidate the morality of his actions? Discuss the complexity of mixed motivations in high-stakes circumstances.

ENHANCE YOUR BOOK CLUB

1. Reread the author's note and, as a group, follow up on one of the real-life figures that inspired the characters in *The Berlin Exchange*. How are their lives different from those of the book's characters?

2. An omnipresent concern of East Germany was the optics of its citizens leaving for the West. Research firsthand accounts of life in East Germany. What aligns with the story and what is different? What is the role of propaganda in building a nation? What are some examples of modern propaganda?

3. Watch the documentary *Behind the Wall* (2011), the film *The Debt* (2010), or the film *The Lives of Others* (2006) and discuss as a group.